THE OPENING DOOR

Persons this *Mystery* is about—

EVE FLAVELL,
whose shining chestnut hair waves back from a face that would delight a sculptor, left home to run a book shop. She has never been close to her father, and the sight of her aunt Charlotte rubs her the wrong way.

CHRISTOPHER McKEE,
the head of Manhattan's Homicide Squad, has a long, brilliant record. For all his good manners, he's an astute and clever man, able to reach beneath the surface of things.

CHARLOTTE FOY,
Eve's aunt, a good woman who thrusts her correctness down your throat, brought up Eve, Natalie and Gerald. The only thing she and Eve have in common is a love for Natalie.

NATALIE FLAVELL,
Eve's half-sister, 21, and rich, is smart-looking in a long and narrow way. Eve adores her volatile sister and her aunt Charlotte fusses about her health, though she isn't frail.

LT. BRUCE CUNNINGHAM,
Natalie's fiance is in New York on convalescent leave. He has humor and gentleness in his firm mouth, and intelligent eyes in a well-modeled face. Women take to him instinctively. Although he is now engaged to Natalie, he and Eve were once absorbed in each other.

HUGH FLAVELL,
Eve's and Natalie's father, was formerly an economics professor, but is now busy being father of a rich daughter. He has a neat, stubborn mouth in a serene face and only a threat to his own comfort moves him deeply.

JIM HOLLAND,
a family friend, is engaged to Eve. He is big, solid, dependable and clever, and won't demand the impossible. He is a production engineer, and limps slightly.

GERALD FLAVELL,
Eve's tall, impeccably turned out brother, is too attractive. Things have always been made easy for him, and he has learned to live expensively.

(Continued on next page)

THE OPENING DOOR

Persons this *Mystery* is about—cont.

ALICIA FLAVELL,
Gerald's handsome wife, is older than he, and has a greedy mouth and ball-bearing eyes. Everything about her is calculated and arranged.

SUSAN DE SANGE,
tall, in her middle forties, exuding richness and vigor, has known the Flavells for twenty years. Alicia disapproves of Hugh's devotion to Susan.

DOCTOR HENDRICKS,
stout, gray-haired, with a pontifical presence, has attended the Flavells for years.

SPENCER GORHAM,
Natalie's Boston lawyer, is a small, spare man with a dry manner and twinkling eyes.

CAPTAIN PIERSON,
a member of New York's Police force, is very vigilant.

KENT,
is McKee's birdlike male stenographer.

PHILIP GRAHAM,
in his forties and plump, insists that Bruce stay with him while on leave.

JOE BUCHANAN,
an artist, lives with Phil Graham.

JOHN FRANCIS DWYER,
New York's dynamic District Attorney, has a short and chunky figure.

SERGEANT CUTTS,
one of the best ballistics experts in the world, can't be hurried.

ANTHONY BURCHALL,
New York's most eminent criminal lawyer, is retained by Natalie.

EDGAR BENTLY,
Susan De Sange's cousin by marriage, is a shrewd fellow who lives by his wits.

FERNANDEZ,
New York's Chief Medical Examiner, is a slim, dark, elegant man with bright hazel eyes.

THE OPENING DOOR

What this *Mystery* is about—

• • • A red STICKINESS, partly coagulated, on the hand of a child of five . . . A BROWN STAIN carried to a hall carpet from a pool of blood under a dead woman in a park . . . a three-cornered FRAGMENT torn from a photograph . . . A GOLF BAG carried up fire escapes and over roofs in December . . . A MORPHINE COCKTAIL which shows murder can be anybody's game . . . A pair of practically new OXFORDS reposing in the brook . . . A CHEST containing a handful of yellow CLOTH and pink STONES which Charlotte took from the bank the day before she died . . . A DIRTY PINK BEAD for which Susan searched her house inch by inch . . . An open CISTERN in a third-floor tank room beside which lies one white SLIPPER . . . A TINY SHRED of GREEN STUFF, invisible to the naked eye.

Wouldn't You Like to Know—

• What *was* so terribly wrong with Charlotte, and the rest of the family, too, for that matter?

• Why Eve carried a golf bag over roofs in December?

• How the man on the other side of the marble angel caused Eve to look death in the face the second time in 48 hours?

(Continued on next page)

THE OPENING DOOR

What this *Mystery* is about—cont.

- About that exceedingly clever business concerning the bullet?

- How a speck of pink china found miles from the scene helps solve an almost perfect crime?

———————

YOU will learn the answers—as Eve did, at what a cost!—in this clever piece of cunningly planned death in which a murderer dishes out a bullet for one, a bludgeon for one, and poison for two, and very nearly, within a hair's breadth, defies detection.

AN *INSPECTOR McKEE* DETECTIVE STORY

THE OPENING DOOR

By HELEN REILLY

Author of "Mourned on Sunday,"
"Murder on Angler's Island,"
"The Dead Can Tell," etc.

All of the characters and incidents in this
novel are entirely imaginary.

WILDSIDE PRESS

THE OPENING DOOR

List of *Exciting* Chapters—

The Opening Door

Chapter One

LIKE A WARNING BELL

THE MURDER DIDN'T TAKE PLACE until after 7 p.m. on the
night of December 2nd. At twenty minutes past four on
the afternoon of that day, Eve Flavell reached the house
that had once been her home on Henderson Square. She
looked at her watch as she went around the corner. It had
turned cold in mid-morning and fog had come sweeping
in from the sea. The Square was full of it. The tops of
the trees in the private park about which the Square was
built stood up out of the fog faintly golden or black-
branched against grayness; the leaves still clung tena-
ciously to the oaks and beeches. Lighted windows had begun to surround the Square on all four sides like colored
lanterns hemming in a lovely wood.

Most of the children in the park had gone home. Those
that were still there behind the high iron fence and the
concealing shrubbery weren't making any noise. A spar-
row chattered and a taxi honked. The wind was bleak.
Eve Flavell shivered and flattened her shoulders under the
raspberry tweed of her coat. Almost there now, she
thought. How long was it since the last time—two months,
three? She couldn't remember.

She paused opposite the house she had come to visit,
the house in which she had lived for a good many years.
It was her half-sister Natalie's. The family had come here
from the country when Nat was five, so that she could go
to Miss Grant's kindergarten on Henderson Place, where
her mother, long since dead, had gone as a child. It was
a beautiful house, of warm red brick with blue shutters
and a white fan-light door. It had a groomed, cared-for,

a washed and brushed and combed look, was prosperous, graceful, benign. It stood on the west side of the Square between two less ornamental neighbors and the anonymous and soaring bulk of an apartment hotel.

Eve stared at the brass knocker glimmering through the dusk. In a moment she would cross the street, mount the steps and use the knocker. It would rap with a brisk thud, the door would open and that would be the end—of one part of her existence, at least, a part for which she had fought hard and that she hated to relinquish. She put out a narrow arched foot in a red calf sandal, drew it back and remained on the curb, asking herself for the twentieth time in the space of an hour whether it wouldn't have been just as well to phone. The news would be the same over the wire as if she delivered it in person. She told herself angrily that she was being a fool. What difference did it make how the thing was done as long as it was finally accomplished? Sooner or later she would have to meet them all face to face, and there were generally people to tea and it would be easier in a crowd. Or would it? The matter was taken suddenly out of her hands.

"Eve, *hello*."

A woman was calling to her from inside the park. Eve turned. It was Alicia, her brother Gerald's wife. She was coming down the path between bushes beaded with moisture. Alicia walked stiltedly on high heels, her hips swaying. Eve wondered how long she had been there, whether she had been watching her own imbecile indecision. Alicia's eyes were bright and inquisitive as she opened the tall iron gate, let it fall to behind her with a clang and joined Eve on the pavement. She began to talk in her soft, clear, mannered voice when she was ten feet away.

"Eve, dear, this is wonderful. It's *ages* since we've met, centuries, practically. Why didn't you come to my Thanksgiving party? I was sorry I was out when you called or I wouldn't have taken any excuse. Work's all very well but you can run it into the ground. What a perfectly stunning hat, my dear—but then you always look marvelous."

Eve knew she looked nothing of the kind. You couldn't fight your way through a mental knothole for forty-eight hours and come out on the other side unscathed. She was unpleasantly conscious of her pallor, her burning lids, although she had done what she could with pancake lipstick and rouge.

Alicia was examining her with large brown eyes that appeared to operate on ball bearings. They were slightly protuberant and exceedingly acute. Eve was afraid of them. She asked hurriedly after her brother, her five-year-old nephew. "How is Gerald, Alicia? How's Bunny?"

Gerald and Bunny were fine, simply fine. Gerald was worried about business. The investment market was shot. But definitely. And nurses—Alicia threw up her hands—they were practically impossible to get. She'd had three in as many weeks; she'd just been in the park checking up on the latest gem, a woman with no teeth and a jaw that ought to be tied up in a rag. She said with a thin ribbon of bitterness under her vivacity, "It's funny, isn't it, Natalie's grown richer and richer and we're getting poorer and poorer? Well, that's the way it goes."

Her meaningless laugh grated against Eve's ears. The silver fox jacket Alicia had on was a present from Natalie and probably the hand-sewn shoes and the alligator bag. Eve said flatly, "Natalie can't help it if her money's invested in a factory that turns out what's in demand, can she?"

Alicia gave a cry. She looked resentful, hurt. "Of course not, don't be *silly*, Eve. That's not what I meant at all. You *do* manage to twist things. Are you coming or going?"

"I'm on my way in."

The two women crossed the street together and mounted

the steps. Eve thought, *It's coming closer*. Alicia kept on talking. "Aunt Charlotte's back, you know. Her stay on the farm doesn't seem to have done her the slightest bit of good. She looks worse than when she went up to Vermont in July. She looks frightful, really. Wait until you see her."

Eve said quietly, "I have seen her. She stopped in at the shop the day before yesterday."

Alicia showed her surprise. "Then you've made it up. Oh, my dear, I'm *so* pleased. Feuding's silly." Her tone was cordial, her eyes were probing. "She isn't looking well, is she? I was horrified when I first saw her. Of course she isn't getting any younger. . . . So you're friends again."

Eve and Charlotte Foy, the aunt who had brought up the three of them—her brother and Natalie and herself—could never be friends. They were as far apart as the poles, had absolutely nothing in common, except a vast mutual distaste and their mutual love for Natalie. Her aunt had disliked and distrusted Eve since she was a child. It was to prove Charlotte wrong, to keep her from hurting Natalie, that Eve was there. She wasn't going to tell Alicia that. She said aloud, smiling lightly, "We were never anything but friends, underneath. It was simply that we didn't understand each other. But one grows older and wiser—we'll hope."

The door was opening. Eve tried to relax tight muscles and followed her sister-in-law over the threshold. The staircase rose gracefully at the right and swung up across the rear wall. A great clump of rust-colored chrysanthemums bloomed on the Pembroke table beneath an old mirror that reflected the exquisite lines of the red chalk drawing Cheverin had done of Natalie's mother as a bride. The clock ticked on the landing; it was around Eve again, untouched, unchangeable, the atmosphere from which she had fled, orderly and gracious and serene and, to her, at least, completely poisonous. It pressed up against her stiflingly. Almost, then, she made a movement of retreat. It was too late. The maid closed the front door behind them, shutting out the fog and the cold December air. As she did so, Eve's young half-sister, Natalie, came through an archway on the left.

Natalie wasn't pretty but she was ineffably smart. She was tall for a girl, five feet six, with a narrow, fine-featured face set in a frame of hair the color of unbeaten flax. It was cut in a long bob that swept her shoulders. Her eyes, big and brown and shining under a convex forehead, gave her the air of a serious child. Everything about her was long and narrow, her straight nose, her wide delicate-lipped mouth, her arms and legs and hands and feet. Blue veins showed in her slender wrists below the bracelet sleeves of a brown wool dirndl with a swinging skirt. She wasn't really frail, but Charlotte had fussed over her health from babyhood. In Eve's opinion, if her young half-sister had been flung out into the Maine woods with a rusty tin cup to forage for herself, she would soon have put on the weight her bones called for. Her expression was aloof and a little haughty. It changed to one of quick pleasure when she saw Eve.

"Darling—I didn't know you were coming," she exclaimed. "I expected Alicia but not you. I'm so glad. . . . How did you manage to get away? Never mind—you're here now anyhow. Come on in to the fire." She linked an arm through Eve's with one of her quick impetuous movements. "There are some people, but they'll go soon and we can talk. I was going to call you. I was thinking we might all go up to the country for a week-end when Bruce gets back. He's in Washington, you know."

Bruce Cunningham, to whom Natalie was engaged, was a lieutenant in the Air Force. Wounded in an engagement in the Pacific he had been invalided home.

Eve said she couldn't stay long. She noticed with a

flicker of uneasiness that Natalie looked tired, that she was thinner, more vibrant, that her laugh was too brittle, her voice too gay. Her very white skin, skin that went naturally with her fair hair, had a faintly sallow tinge, and the spatter of freckles across the bridge of her straight nose was in evidence—always a sign that she wasn't her usual self. When she was little, when she was growing up, it was the first thing that people—nurses, governesses and tutors, Charlotte—always said: *You're freckles are showing, Nat.*

Alicia said it now. She was extremely observant. "Freckles, Nat, darling. . . . What's the matter? Have you been overdoing it with your countless social aid things? You'll wear yourself out. You shouldn't—"

Natalie said with a touch of impatience—she could be imperious when she wanted to—"I'm all right. I wish you wouldn't, Alicia. I mean—don't say anything in front of Charlotte, for heaven's sake. She worries so—and she's not well."

The three women entered the big sunken living-room, to the left of the hall and down a shallow flight of steps. The sea-green draperies at the windows were drawn. Lamplight drew gleams from the fine pieces of old furniture rubbed to a mirrorlike smoothness, shone tranquilly on low bookcases, gaily colored satin chairs, and the few good pictures punctuating the ivory wall. Natalie had done the room over in April, on her twenty-first birthday. It was a decided improvement. Men and women stood or sat about in groups, talking in the muted well-bred way in which the Flavell parties were always conducted. Alicia darted off to join friends, and Eve nodded to several people she knew distantly and followed Natalie to the fire.

Sofas flanked the white mantel under which flames leaped cheerfully. Eve's father Hugh Flavel and her aunt, Charlotte Foy, were on one of the sofas; Charlotte sat upright behind the tea things, her capable hands busy.

Hugh lounged beside her, tall and thin, with his slight scholar's stoop, his eyes palely blue behind pince-nez, his receding hair brushed smoothly back from the high forehead of his handsome aquiline face. His serenity, his *savoir-faire*, his air of being able to command any situation under the sun were contradicted and betrayed by a small neat mouth under a clipped mustache that pouted in repose and was stubborn.

He looked younger and more alive than Eve could recall. Charlotte, on the contrary, looked older and stonier, yet there was very little difference between their ages; Hugh was fifty-one and Charlotte fifty-four.

"Dad, Charlotte—look who's here," Natalie said gaily. "She came of her own accord, I swear it."

If Eve's unsolicited presence in the house from which she had voluntarily and drastically separated herself a long while ago caused either her father or her aunt any surprise, there was no evidence of it except, perhaps, in an overlong glance from Charlotte.

Hugh said, "Ah, Eve, my dear. How are you? You're looking well." There was courtesy but no pleasure in his greeting. Eve didn't expect it. Her father and she had never been close, and after some of the things she had said in her young violence, four years earlier, they probably never would be. Hugh was not a forgiving person. She could hardly blame him. Charlotte produced words as though she were measuring spoonfuls of sugar. She now said in her measured tones, "Nice to see you here, Eve. Sit down. Tea? No? You'll probably want a drink."

Eve had wanted tea. She settled herself in the corner of the opposite sofa and smiled at her aunt. "A drink, please, Charlotte—but I do wish you'd get over the horrid habit of being right. You know me too well—and all my sins."

The moment the remark was out she regretted it. Charlotte flushed and drew in her breath, and Hugh's brows rose humorously. Natalie, who had turned aside to beckon to one of the maids, looked distressed. Eve knew she was being a fool, but for the life of her she couldn't help it. The very sight of Charlotte rubbed her the wrong way. It always had. She was so correct, so wrapped in rectitude; if only she wouldn't thrust it down your throat, Eve thought, and reminded herself that she hadn't come to quarrel; she had come for another and very definite purpose. Once it was accomplished she could go and not return.

Nevertheless, sitting there in the familiar room, a sudden childish lump rose in her throat and for a moment she found herself wishing that she had had a more normal youth, that her mother had lived, that her father hadn't married again, into money, even that her stepmother hadn't died—in which case Charlotte would never have appeared on the scene. She and Eve's own mother had been sisters, but the love Charlotte had for Gerald, Eve's brother, had skipped Eve and had fastened on Natalie, Hugh's daughter by his second wife.

Stop being maudlin, you're accumulating a genuine complex, she told herself. Charlotte was a good woman, as honest as the day, just, never deliberately unkind and about as imaginative as a flagpole. It wasn't her fault. It was the way she was made. Her position as the keeper of the keys, the manager of the household she ran on velvet had added to a bump of authority already too well developed. It was a pity she had never married. She was still good-looking, her black dress was smart, her iron-gray hair becomingly arranged. She turned to speak to a guest, and a start went through Eve. Alicia and Nat were right. There *was* something wrong with Charlotte, something terribly wrong. Firelight flared. In its momentary brilliance she looked frightful. Her skin was a bad color and she obviously wasn't well, but it wasn't only that. There was a queer fixity to her, as though within the ramparts of her substantial body her spirit had crumpled and was dead, or dying.

Eve felt it then for the first time but not for the last time while she was in the room, the house, on that December afternoon: a sense of strangeness, of something wrong, twisted, that had no connection with her own private problem. The tension was in her father and Natalie as well as in her aunt. She tried to track it to its source and failed. But it was there, oh, very distinctly, in Hugh's absent pleasantries to his guests, in the tightness of his mouth, in the restless straying of his shapely hands. It was in Natalie, behind surface brightness, in her dutiful circling around the room, her fair head shining above brown wool.

Eve frowned. Natalie was volatile and flew off the handle easily, but their father wasn't like that. The only thing that moved him deeply was a threat to his own comfort. Eve reflected, watching her young half-sister, that Charlotte had done her best to spoil her, but there was one quality in Natalie Charlotte hadn't been able to touch, and that was her generosity. The purse strings of the fortune left to Natalie by her mother were never drawn. She was always wide open, foolishly so sometimes, to an appeal for help. She had given a pension to Pussy, their old nurse, for life; she had sent the furnace man's son through college; she was god-mother to a half dozen local relief organizations, and Alicia was always running to her with "cases," not to speak of Gerald's demands or the demands of her long list of friends and acquaintances.

Eve tossed her cigarette into the flames. If she was watching the others, Charlotte was watching her. Eve's spine stiffened. She turned toward the hearth, sipped a highball and answered Hugh's polite questions. The shop was doing very well, much better than she had expected.

Her father didn't flinch. His small keen eyes were cold, but his manner remained bland, as if what she did were no longer of any importance. Yet he had objected furi-

ously to her going into business, had wanted her to remain on and to marry, well, under the aegis of Natalie's
wealth and position, which would have added to the Flavell prestige. The book shop he might have been able to
swallow, books were cultural and not undignified, but
when she had added stockings and gloves he had thrown
up his hands: "A female haberdasher, after four years of
college—my dear girl. What an achievement! You must
be proud of yourself."

That was on the day she had refused to live an hour
longer in Natalie's house, on Natalie's money. She had
been very young and very stupid and crude in the way
she went about it, accusing the others by indirection—
her father and Charlotte, her brother Gerald and Alicia
—of doing just that. No wonder they had resented her
attitude. They had said she was pig-headed and ungrate-
ful and eaten up by jealousy. This last at least was untrue.
She was very fond of her young half-sister, but Natalie's
wealth, her friends, her amusements, pursuits, and out-
look were not Eve's and never could be.

She had made the break as complete as possible. It had
been difficult at times but on the whole exhilarating. The
only one she had had any real trouble with was Natalie.
With a large income at her disposal she couldn't understand why Eve wouldn't use her charge accounts or have
her apartment furnished, and at first, anyhow, she had
been hurt and unhappy at the division between them.
But if their daily association had been curtailed their
affection for each other was as strong as ever.

Eve looked at Natalie's bent head, pale against a fall of
green brocade, where she stood at a desk writing a check
for some charity or other for a stout woman in elegant
beige and sables, and warmth stirred in her around a core
of central deadness. She had been right. She had done the
only thing there was to do.

The room was beginning to empty. Departing guests

kept coming up to say good-bye to Hugh and Charlotte. Eve smoked and waited, holding taut nerves in check. It wouldn't be long now. "How's the book coming, Father?" she asked during a lull.

Hugh was writing a book on Economic Victorianism. He had been engaged on it for a long while. The first volume, published nine years earlier, had been well received. The notices, all good, were pasted neatly in a scrapbook that occupied a lectern of its own in his study.

Her father nodded without removing the cigarette from his lips. His aloof gaze said, *Don't try to come over me with that. You haven't the slightest interest in my work, or in me. You never had.*

Eve flushed and persevered. "There must be a tremendous amount of research to do."

"There is." He was, definitely, thinking of other things.

The conversation withered. Charlotte made no effort to keep it alive. Her labors at the tea table over, she had taken up her knitting. Her silence was disagreeable, menacing. It gave her the air of a judge—which was what she always had been to Eve, condemning her unheard, in advance, of the gravest crimes. But when she got up and went to speak to someone, it was no relief. Eve had always hated to be alone with her father. She never knew what to say to him. Now, in his absorption in whatever engrossed his thoughts, he was doubly formidable.

Fortunately Alicia dropped into Charlotte's vacant place. Hugh was fond of the daughter-in-law whose social background was excellent, who was decorative, whom he considered a good wife and mother and who knew how to flatter him. Talk flowed between them easily.

"You're not looking too well, Dad." Alicia put her dark, madonna-smooth head on one side. "Your eyes, yes, I think it's your eyes—they have no light in them. Have you been doing what Doctor Hendricks ordered?"

Hugh relaxed insensibly. "I can't be bothered with all

that nonsense."

"Oh, but you must. Exercise—have you been taking your walks?"

"That I do do. Five times around the Square after breakfast, five times after dinner."

"And something to eat before you go to bed?"

"I generally have a banana and a glass of milk."

"It's about the only fruit you care for."

Alicia was in good form. Natalie threw Eve an amused glance over the shoulder of a man she was talking to and made a face, and they smiled imperceptibly at each other. Natalie had grown, Eve decided. She wasn't a child any more. She was out of Charlotte's leading strings. Freedom, marriage, a new deal, were going to be splendid for her. She would lose her flashing restlessness and flower like a plant in the sun. Presently Charlotte came back. "How many for dinner?" she wanted to know, lighting a cigarette. Eve shook her head. "Not me, either," Alicia said. "I'd love it, but we're dining with the Beauferts. Gerald's calling for me at— There he is now."

Eve thought, with an inner flicker of irony, *I'm going to have a full house,* and watched her brother advance toward the fire, tall and erect and graceful in a well-cut gray suit. Gerald was always impeccably turned out. His bills used to cause riots when he was at college. He was much too attractive for his own good, she thought. Things had always been made too easy for him. He had their father's face but their mother's eyes—gray, thick-lashed, appealing, smoky eyes. There were new sets of lines at the corners of them, little crow's-feet of strain. As Alicia had said, he was probably worried about business. He had an expensive establishment to keep up— but it was the way he wanted to live.

Gerald greeted Hugh and Charlotte affectionately, pecked at Alicia's cheek, showed surprise at seeing Eve— and pleasure. "The return of the prodigal, a nice prodigal. That hat's good on you, my lass. What brings you to the old manse? Business folded?"

It was her cue, Eve thought. But she wanted to wait for Natalie, who was saying good-bye to a man and a girl near the archway. "The shop? Thanks, no, it's flourishing, Gerald," Eve said aloud.

Natalie joined them then, and Hugh and Gerald both got up. Her father hadn't risen for her, Eve reflected. He wouldn't. That was part of the unstudied discourtesy with which he had always treated her. Natalie did look tired. Her thin cheeks were pale and the dust of freckles across her nose stood out more prominently than ever.

"Here," Gerald took her by the shoulders and pushed her into a chair. "You're all in, chicken."

Natalie smiled at him. "I am, rather."

"What you need is a drink," Gerald said. "I'm going to mix us all one. This is going to be good. I got it from a fellow who used to be at the old Hoffman House." He went to the 18th-century liquor cabinet against the wall and opened squat doors.

Alicia peered at him through the low light. "How many have you had already?"

Her tone was sharp. Charlotte looked at her and then, quickly, at Gerald. Hugh gazed at the fire, his mouth compressed. He was a practicing Aristotelian and believed in moderation in all things. Two cocktails, and only two, were permissible before dinner.

"Drink deep or touch not the Pierian spring," Gerald said, turning around and grinning amiably. "Alicia's my pet prohibitionist, did you know?"

It was family stuff, trivial, unimportant—or so Eve considered at the time. Nevertheless she registered with a sudden sharp flash and a pang of apprehension that it was in Gerald and Alicia too, a brittle unease, as though they were deeply stirred about something but didn't want it to show, wanted it, very determinedly, not to.

She gave herself a mental shake. She was probably imagining the whole business. She took the glass Gerald handed her. The stem was cool between her fingers and smooth and firm; you could hold on to it. Alicia and her father on the low armchair between the sofas, with Gerald on a hassock in front of her, his shoulders against her knees; beyond the warm circle of fire and lamplight the rest of the room was dim, shadowy and empty at last. *Now,* she thought, *now,* and leaned forward a little.

"I've got news for you, Nat."

In spite of herself her voice wasn't entirely level. Charlotte's knitting needles came to a halt; Alicia's cigarette paused in mid-air; her father adjusted his pince-nez. Gerald said lazily, "Ah-ha—I thought so when I saw you here. Out with it, my girl."

Natalie was looking at her with all her eyes. "News, Eve? Good news?"

Eve thought, with a bitter pang of self-reproach. *She's afraid. How terrible! I have hurt her in the past—but never again.* Aloud she said, "I hope you'll think it's good. Jim Holland and I are going to be married."

It wasn't what her father or Alicia or Gerald had expected to hear. She didn't glance at Charlotte. Natalie jumped up and gave her a quick kiss. "Oh, Eve, I'm so glad," she cried. "This is wonderful. I do like Jim and he's been crazy about you for ages. When did you decide? When's it to be?"

"Almost immediately," Eve answered. "Probably in a couple of days. We've gotten the license, taken our tests. You see, Jim's—"

Her voice stopped. She sat very still. Blackness was swimming up around her. She had waited too long. The man who shouldn't have been there had entered the house unheard while she was talking.

Bruce Cunningham was back from Washington. He stood on the top step looking toward the group around the fire, looking past Natalie, at Eve. The gold buttons on his uniform winked. Nothing else about him moved.

Eve thought despairingly, *Why did he have to come now? Why couldn't he have stayed away until it was over and I was gone?* And then like a warning bell close in fog—*Charlotte.*

Charlotte was beside her on the couch. The others hadn't seen Bruce yet, their backs were to the hall and to the archway leading into it, but Bruce was within Charlotte's field of vision.

Eve tried to fight clear of destroying panic. They had noticed her pause. She must make the best of it. She raised her head, said in a clear light voice, "It's Lieutenant Cunningham, just in time to hear my news," and wondered, desperately, what was going to happen.

Chapter Two

A Cunning and Malignant Mold

Nothing happened, absolutely nothing. Eve had stumbled up a whole flight of steps that wasn't there. Natalie got up and went toward Bruce, her face radiant—she hadn't expected him for another twenty-four hours, and they kissed and the rest called greetings, and Bruce strolled to the hearth, an arm around Natalie's shoulders. He felicitated Eve: "I hope you'll be very happy, Miss Flavell. I have no doubt at all that Holland will. Lucky fellow."

His lean dark face, with which his light eyes were in such contrast, was quiet. His smile was pleasant, agreeable, not sardonic or bitter. He looked as he usually did when he wasn't particularly interested, except that the line of his angled jaw was a ridge, which might have been an effect of light. The others added their good wishes to his. Charlotte's eyes expressed a grudging approval. Hugh was openly pleased. He had known Jim for years, had tutored him for his entrance exams at Yale and evidently considered him an excellent husband for, if not a black sheep, at any rate one of a very dark shade of brown.

Eve settled back in her corner, drank the cocktail Gerald had mixed, and listened to voices that were far away. She felt like a spent swimmer fighting tumultuous seas who suddenly finds himself floating in a land-locked lagoon without knowing or caring how he got there. Her work was done. It was all over. She was empty, drained, and in pain, yet content. She could go in peace.

She was mistaken. Before she could begin her leave-taking, Jim Holland arrived in search of her and, a little later, Charlotte was summoned to the phone to answer a long-distance call.

When Eve was interrogated afterward as to precisely what took place in the house on that bleak December afternoon, where people were at given intervals, what was said and done, it was hard to be exact. There was a good deal of confusion and stir and moving about. Jim had known the family since he was a boy and they were all fond of him and interested in his new job as production engineer at a factory in Bridgeport. He was very pleased about it himself. (His bad knee, injured in a car smash when he was thirty, had kept him out of the Army, and he had raged like a tiger deprived of its kill.)

Talk, laughter, questions, a drink for Jim—perhaps five minutes after he got there, one of the maids came in and said that Charlotte was wanted on the telephone. It was while Charlotte was out of the room that Eve had her brief and dreadful encounter with Bruce. She made no mention of that to the police, until the time came when she didn't have to, when it was too late, when they already knew.

Then, at the moment, her blood ran cold at the chance he took. The others were standing in a knot near the piano, at which Gerald was seated plucking idly at the keys; she had gone to get the purse she had left on a coffee table at the hearth. She was picking up her purse when Bruce spoke. His voice was almost at her ear. She hadn't heard him follow her and her heart hammered, furiously.

What he said, musingly, almost indifferently, was, "You couldn't wait, could you, Eve? Perhaps it was asking too much. Are you in love with Holland? He's too old for you—and too fat."

Eve was indignant and angry and frightened and wildly amused. Jim wasn't any older, in relation to her, than

Bruce was to Natalie, or not much—and Jim wasn't fat. He was a big man, naturally; it was simply that he couldn't get enough exercise with his stiff knee. As for waiting—what good would it have done? Bruce was engaged to Natalie, had been engaged to her for more than a year, and she was passionately in love with him; you had only to see them together to realize that. There wasn't the slightest chance of her terminating the engagement of her own accord—which was the only way it would matter.

Bruce was mad to talk to her like this, here. She said in a voice as low as his own, "Don't, Bruce. I've made up my mind and nothing can change it. I'm going to marry Jim. It isn't any sacrifice. I'm very fond of him. Besides, we've had all this out before. We're in perfect agreement on one thing: Natalie mustn't be hurt. And Charlotte suspects."

"Charlotte—what does she suspect?"

The need for reticence had vanished. "That you—that I—"

"How do you know?"

"She came to see me at the shop the day before yesterday. She told me so."

"Then it was Charlotte who made you do this?"

Her "No," wasn't emphatic enough. She added hurriedly, "I would have done it anyhow. Jim's a swell guy." She turned her head. No one was looking at them. The others were listening to Jim telling a story, gesticulating with his stick. He told a story well. His voice was big, sure. The boom of it was reassuring, like the rest of him. She glanced up sideways at Bruce and a wave of sickness went through her. His mouth was clamped tight, and his eyes were narrowed and intent and smolderingly bright on nothing. He was unhappy, tortured—and in a dangerous mood.

She had seen him like that only once before, on the night he came to the shop to get some books for Natalie, and they found out suddenly and without words what had grown up between them, unbidden, almost unrecognized, until it was too late. There was nothing they could do about it. They both realized that, or seemed to. They, or she rather, for Bruce had been strangely silent, had stamped on the sudden and terrible knowledge, denying its existence, pretending it wasn't there. A week later Bruce had thrown up his job and gone into the Air Force.

If only his wound hadn't sent him home, if only they had met when he was free. Well, they hadn't, and wishful thinking was stupid and purposeless and a waste of time. She had cut the knot of an impossible situation by engaging herself to Jim. Her announcement had effectually squashed Charlotte's suspicion. It mustn't be reawakened. Charlotte mustn't find them together like this, apart from the others. She was at the telephone in the booth under the stairs but she would be back at any moment. . . .

Fear unlocked Eve's weary paralysis. She tucked her purse under her arm, started pulling on her gloves. "I'm going now, Bruce," she said quietly.

He didn't pay any attention. He remained as he was, staring down into the fire. "Charlotte," he murmured thinly.

He had never liked her aunt. Eve was afraid of his tone, his expression; she was more afraid of their isolation, of the shadowy corners, the unseen eyes that might be raking them speculatively.

She said, "Don't, Bruce. Think of Natalie. She's the one we've got to think of," and on that, without waiting for a response, she walked away, arranging her face, buttoning her glove, putting on a smile.

Her back was to the fireplace and to the door beside it, a door leading into the dining-room beyond. The door had been open a few inches. Eve didn't hear it close. Going into the dining-room a few minutes later, Gloria Fox, the parlor maid, found Charlotte Foy there, her face white, her hands gripping the back of a tall carved chair. The girl was frightened at her appearance but Miss Foy wouldn't let her call anyone. She sent her upstairs for medicine, took it, and then said brusquely, "I'm all right now. Go back to your work." When she returned to the living-room, Bruce Cunningham was gone. He had an engagement with a fellow officer. He left after arranging to have dinner somewhere with Natalie.

Eve didn't speak to him directly again. She said good-bye without looking at him. She didn't need to look. The feel of him standing there beyond the archway, tall and straight in his uniform, was all through her. It was Thursday afternoon. She was going to be married to Jim Holland probably on Saturday. The anguish of farewell gripped her devastatingly. It wiped out everything else, so that for a while incidentals were blurred. She heard and saw, spoke and was spoken to, mechanically, in another world that had no real existence.

Jim talked about Lordship Beach, said they thought of taking a house there. It was a swell place with a cliff coming up out of the sea. "It's rather like Cornwall, isn't it, Eve?" She said yes. Her father was pleased when he heard that she intended to give up the shop. "Now that's what I call a good idea." She said the wedding was going to be quiet but she and Jim wanted them all to come.

"But of course, darling," Alicia exclaimed. Natalie said wild horses wouldn't keep her away. Charlotte said suddenly and harshly, "I can't. I've got to go to Boston tomorrow."

She spoke in a loud voice as though she were making a declaration of faith before piled fagots. The others stared. In spite of her detachment, Eve felt a stiffening in them. It was mostly in her father but—did Gerald glance quickly at Alicia and did Alicia's face tighten, so that for a moment she looked hag-ridden, ugly?

Eve was puzzled. She could understand her father, but not Gerald or Alicia. Boston in that household meant the Coreys. Natalie's mother, Virginia, had been a Corey. The old and extremely wealthy Boston family had strenuously objected to Virginia's marriage to Hugh, who, at that time, even if he was a young and brilliant professor of economics was also penniless and a widower with two children to boot. After Virginia's death, the Coreys had tried to obtain custody of Natalie in the courts. Hugh had very properly fought them and had won, but he had never forgiven his wife's people and he hated the yearly trips Natalie made to her maternal aunt and cousins, trips on which Charlotte occasionally accompanied her.

Jim was disappointed at Charlotte's announcement. Unlike Bruce Cunningham, he was rather fond of her. He had known her when she was a good deal younger and she had been kind to him, as a boy. "Can't you put off your trip?" he asked.

She said no without explanation. Hugh made no attempt to hide his displeasure. The paper he was holding crackled sharply and he turned and walked away. He was in a towering rage; he did get into them sometimes, very suddenly. Ordinarily Charlotte was sensitive to his reactions, but not then. She repeated, "I've got to go." Her face was gray and there were brownish pockets under her eyes.

There was an odd little pause. Eve felt it again, more strongly, the presence of queer undercurrents in a family with which she had lost touch. What was worrying her aunt and Alicia and Gerald—and even Natalie? The whole thing was disturbing, disagreeable. She welcomed the interruption when it came.

The phone in the hall rang. This time the call was for her. It was Clara Long, her assistant, talking from the shop. A prospective buyer had turned up, was there now —would Miss Flavell come?

"At once," Eve said. It altered her plans. She and Jim had intended to go to Tony's for rubbery spaghetti and red wine; she left the house almost immediately, alone.

Natalie was cross. "Oh, Eve. I was making all sorts of plans," she said. "I thought you and Jim would have joined Bruce and me somewhere later on this evening and we could have gone to El Morocco, they've got a marvelous new dancer, or to the Casablanca or to the Stork and talked."

"No, my pet," Eve said firmly. Natalie loved to spend money on people and didn't like to be thwarted, but Eve ignored her little pout of disappointment, kissed her and explained that it was impossible. She couldn't afford to lose a chance of disposing of the business. "I'll call you tomorrow." She said good-bye to the others, and to Jim, "There's no reason why you should hurry away. I'll be busy for a while. Ring me in about an hour."

She didn't encounter anyone in the hall. The door of the little writing-room under the stairs was shut. She opened the front door, closed it behind her, and was swallowed up instantly in fog. The fog was thick, impenetrable; it blanketed the entire Square. It was cold and very dark. The lamp above the door shed a feeble glow on the drenched bricks of the steps. Beyond them there was nothing but blackness and moisture and a bone-piercing chill.

Eve was glad to be alone. She drank in solitude as a thirsty man drinks water. The Square was quiet, but then it always had been. Set down in the heart of New York, with the city sprawling away from it in every direction, it managed to hold itself apart and to produce a fictitious air of space and privacy and freedom from walls. Beyond it somewhere horns blasted feebly, and out on the river whistles blew. Eve descended the steps, one hand on the rail. She reached the pavement and turned left. Before she had gone more than a few feet she bumped into someone, violently.

Arms steadied her. A man's voice said, "Oops—sorry. Are you all right?"

Eve said, "Quite all right, thanks," and proceeded more cautiously on her way.

The park, locked and silent beyond its tall iron gates, was completely invisible. Her father wouldn't take his walk that night. Or perhaps he would, with rubbers on and a coat of just the proper weight. He had always taken extraordinary care of himself. She could imagine him crossing the street and unlocking the gate and methodically pacing the paths through the thickets of the artificial wood behind the tall iron railings for the requisite length of time to the dot.

She dallied with the thought of her father deliberately, putting aside thought of Bruce and Jim and herself. Natalie's future was assured, and she had peace with honor; that was all that mattered. Meet other problems as they arose. As far as Jim went he was no romantic, love-sick boy. He was a man of thirty-seven and a realist. He wouldn't demand the impossible. She would make him a good wife, could give him all he needed, a home, companionship, an intelligent interest in his work. Their minds were in tune, they were friends, laughed at the same things. . . .

She collided with a lamp post, blinked wetness that wasn't fog angrily from her lashes, and went toward the pale glimmer of two enormous eyes that were the lamps of a cab in front of the apartment hotel on the corner. As she got in, slammed the door and gave the driver her address, a clock somewhere struck a quarter of six.

There her actual knowledge of what further took place among the people in the red brick house with the blue shutters on that December day ended. Nevertheless she had in her possession then, without knowing it, the groundwork for murder. Certainly on that late afternoon

and early evening, between half-past four when she entered the house and twenty minutes of six when she left it,
the die was cast, irretrievably, into a cunning and malig-
nant mold of planned destruction that very nearly, within
a hair's breadth, defied detection.

It was almost the perfect crime. A tiny shred of green
stuff invisible to the naked eye was what finally broke the
case—that and a man's shoes that didn't fit and a speck of
pink china dug from between the floor boards of a country house miles away. Christopher McKee, the head of
the Manhattan Homicide Squad, exploring in the same
sort of fog that filled the Square that night, had to learn
where to look for these things and how to interpret them.
Before that much had happened.

Chapter Three

Twin Discoveries

CERTAIN FACTS WEREN'T DIFFICULT to establish later. Shortly after Eve went, at approximately ten minutes of six, Jim Holland left the Flavell house with Alicia and Gerald Flavell, and on Gerald's invitation went home with the couple for a final drink. The younger Flavells lived only a stone's throw away in an apartment hotel on the east side of the Square. Alicia didn't second her husband's invitation with any enthusiasm. It was maid's night out, she and Gerald were dining with friends, and in her opinion Gerald had already had quite enough to drink. But Gerald was insistent, so Alicia shrugged graceful shoulders and submitted.

In the Flavell house itself quiet succeeded the departure of the guests. Hugh Flavell retired to his study on the third floor, where he dined frugally from a tray and gave orders that he wasn't to be disturbed before, presumably, settling down to work on his book.

Charlotte Foy, who still looked ill, went to her room to pack, and Natalie, complaining of a headache, went to hers to lie down for a while before dressing. Bruce Cunningham wasn't calling for her until half-past seven. She told Annette, the older of the two maids, not to let her oversleep. "Call me at a quarter of seven." There was no danger of her oversleeping.

When the maid went in she found Natalie clinging to the foot rail of the bed doubled up with pain, her face as white as the soft batiste negligée that wrapped her slender twisted figure.

The maid was alarmed. "Oh, Miss, you're *sick!*" She ran and got Charlotte Foy and they put Natalie on the chaise longue and propped her with pillows.

But once the spasm passed Natalie made light of it, sitting up and throwing her head back and laughing at their worry. "It's just my wretched stomach—I shouldn't have had that drink with Gerald. He mixes such awful concoctions, and liquor always upsets me. That was what was making my head ache. I'm better already."

She wouldn't have the doctor and she wouldn't put off her engagement with Bruce. "The air will do me good, and I won't be late," she promised her aunt. "If your lights are on when I get back, I'll come in and talk to you."

She was as worried about Miss Foy as Miss Foy was about her and tried to persuade the older woman to defer her trip to Boston. "Don't go tomorrow," she pleaded, holding one of Charlotte's hands in both of hers. "You're not fit to travel—and I'll worry about you. . . . If you'll wait until next week I'll go with you. But I can't leave before Eve's wedding."

Charlotte Foy was determined not to postpone her journey. "I've got to go, Natalie," she said austerely. "Everything has been arranged. You can come up on Sunday or Monday. I'm not satisfied with Hendricks. I want my Boston man to see you. And you oughtn't to go out tonight."

Natalie was hurt and more than a little ruffled by her aunt's refusal to listen to her. She didn't like to have her proposals brushed aside in such an unceremonious fashion. She drew herself up stiffly, her mouth quivering and her eyes sparkling frostily. Then she glanced at the little gold clock on the table beside her and gave a cry. "Heavens, the time—and I've got to have a bath and do my hair and dress." She jumped up and threw off her negligée with such haste that she tore the delicate embroidery on the wide bishop sleeve. She let the filmy garment drop to the floor and started pulling off her stockings.

Charlotte repeated, looking down at her gravely, "I *wish* you wouldn't go out tonight," but Natalie didn't pay any attention. She said with bright impatience, "I'm all right now, darling, really I am, I haven't a pain or an ache," and Charlotte shrugged and left her and returned to her packing, and the maid went too, after drawing a tub for her young mistress and shaking in the perfumed salts she wanted.

But Natalie's attack was more serious than she had pretended because when the cook mounted to the first floor to admit Bruce Cunningham at half-past seven she noticed that, although Natalie ran lightly down the stairs in a new black evening dress that had arrived that morning, she was pale and peaked-looking and there were shadows under her big brown eyes.

The cook, whose name was Joan Adams and who had been with the Flavells for years, also noticed that his fiancée's condition made no apparent impression on Lieutenant Cunningham. He kissed her, said briskly, "Hi, Nat—Ready?" took the mink coat from her arm and put her into it and they went out.

Fog blew in when the door opened. Miss Adams closed it, extinguished some of the lights and presently went to bed. If there were any visitors later, she didn't see or hear them; her room was at the top of the house. So that was all for the night, as far as independent witnesses were concerned.

It wasn't until twenty minutes past nine on the following morning that the terrible discovery was made. It took place under particularly distressing circumstances. It was a child of five in pursuit of a bouncing ball who made the gruesome find—with an assist by Patrolman Crothers.

The morning of December 3rd was clear and bright. The fog of the night before had been blown away by a brisk wind out of the northwest, and the sun shone brilliantly in a high blue sky without a single cloud. Patrolman Crothers was completing the last leg of his beat in a pleasant mental vacuum induced by the change in the weather and the peace of his surroundings. The streets bounding the Square were quiet. He liked Henderson Park. It was a swell neighborhood, and everything was neat and prosperous and orderly. Overhead tall trees creaked in the fresh breeze and children's voices rang inside the shrubbery beyond the tall iron railings, but not in any volume. It was a bit early yet for the nurses to have assembled their charges in force.

Crothers was in the middle of the south side of the Square when the uproar began. Beyond the iron fence, inside the park, a child was running and screaming as he ran. His feet clip-clopped rapidly on cement. The screams were loud, frantic. The patrolman came to a halt. He had heard plenty of kids holler before but not many as bad as this. He peered through two black iron uprights rimmed with frost. A boy of five or six in tweed shorts and a tweed overcoat was flying down the path toward the south gate. Some distance away an elderly nursemaid charged in pursuit of him, her hat over one eye, her face red and angry.

"Charles," she called pantingly, "Charles, you *naughty* boy! Stop! Come back here to me. Don't you dare try to unlock that gate! Don't you *dare.*"

It was exactly what the child was trying to do. He had evidently done it before. His screams had stopped. He was crying steadily, in gasps, and wrenching at the lock. Tears streamed down his face.

"Now, young man, that's enough of that." Crothers reached through the bars and put a big restraining hand on the boy's two small fumbling ones. He drew his hand away. There was a stain on his palm. The boy's fingers were reddish-brown and sticky.

The patrolman gazed at the child. His mind worked quickly and well. He was an intelligent officer and he had recently attended a lecture on blood stains at the Police

Academy. The red stickiness on the boy's hand was blood.
He hadn't cut himself. The blood wasn't fresh. It had
been exposed to the air and was partly coagulated.

Crothers used his head. There was an alarm box on
the telegraph pole at the corner. He said to the nursemaid, "Stay where you are," went to the box, called the
precinct, gave his location, asked for help and went back
to the gate. The nurse admitted him. He knelt beside the
crying child. "Come on, big boy," he said to the little
fellow, "what's the matter?"

"In the leaves," the child stammered through hiccough-
ing sobs. "She looked at me. She didn't move. The leaves
did. They blew."

"Where?" Crothers demanded. The child gestured
vaguely and the patrolman began his search. It didn't
take long. He found what the child had stumbled on a
few minutes earlier, near the north gate, off the path and
in among a planting of bushes. The bushes were broken
and had partially closed in over the weight superimposed
on them, with force. Crothers looked down. The hair on
his neck prickled.

A woman was lying on the ground in the middle of the
miniature thicket. Her posture was disorganized. One leg
was doubled under her and her arms were flung out
crazily. Her hat had fallen off. Her face, in profile, plowed
the damp earth. Her eyes were open. Yellow leaves covered her with a light blanket. The wind blew and the
leaves danced, some of them. Others were held in position by the vari-colored stickiness that was blood from a
gaping wound in her breast. A glance was enough without the touch. The woman was dead. She had been dead
for some time. Rigor had already set in.

Crothers lurched to his feet. The few occupants of the
park drawn to the spot by his appearance within those
decorous precincts stared curiously, from the mouths of
various paths. They couldn't see the dead woman, but if

they ganged up on him they would—and some of the spectators were children. He said peremptorily, "Move back, please, all of you. Take the kids away. There's been an accident. . . ." He straightened and wiped sweat from his forehead with relief. The wind blew. Above the wind a siren wailed and two radio cars swung out of Lexington at a smart clip.

Shortly thereafter, that call went streaming out from the golden bowl at the top of police headquarters on Centre Street: *"Homicide, Charlotte Foy, in Henderson Park. Homicide, Charlotte Foy of 22 Henderson Park West. . . ."*

Christopher McKee, the man at the head of Manhattan's Homicide Squad, was in his office when the phone rang. Crothers discovered the body at 9:21. McKee reached the Park at 9:40. His stenographer Kent, Captain Pierson, and three of his own men were with him. The precinct detectives had already been at work. The park had been evacuated, a sizable area near the north gate had been roped off, and there was an officer at each of the other three gates.

Doctor Benson, a tour man from the Medical Examiner's office, was down on his knees examining the body. Off to one side on a broad cement path, where they could do no harm by messing up the surface, the second Commissioner and Assistant District Attorney Smith were talking war and peace. They greeted McKee. Smith said genially, "One more for the undertaker, another little job for the cemetery man. Nasty piece of work."

The Scotsman nodded and went around a sycamore. Feet in stout black shoes moved big bodies out of the way at his advent. The initial facts were given to him by Patrolman Crothers and Radio Patrolman Anders. Kent wrote busily and McKee listened and looked down into the recesses of the winter thicket.

Crothers had recognized the victim at once. He was familiar with the Square and its denizens. He had often passed the time of day with Miss Foy, with her niece, Miss Natalie Flavell, and with Miss Flavell's father.

Charlotte Foy had been shot. There was a wound of entrance just over her heart, a wound of exit between the shoulder blades. The bullet hadn't yet been found. It might be anywhere within a considerable radius. The death didn't appear to be suicide. There was no weapon in evidence.

"Have a look, Inspector?" Pierson asked.

"No," McKee said absently. "We'd better wait until— Where's Dalligan?"

"Here I am." The gangling photographer from Head-quarters pushed forward, laden down with camera cases. McKee said, "Good. I want plenty of wide-angle shots— *look out!*"

Dalligan brought the soles of number twelve oxfords to an abrupt halt and rocked back on his heels. He had been about to tread on a cigarette sodden with moisture that lay at the edge of the thicket that was the dead woman's impromptu grave. When its position had been photographed, McKee retrieved it. Its tip was just barely blackened. No more than a puff or two had gone through the tobacco. He found the match that had companioned it.

The cigarette was a Lucky Strike. There was a package of Lucky Strikes in Charlotte Foy's purse. McKee examined the purse. The only things of interest in it were a large iron key and a piece of paper with the word *Spencer* and what appeared to be a telephone number written on it, in pencil. He studied the position of the body, the surrounding terrain and added up the facts as far as they went.

"Backward, turn backward, oh, time, in thy flight—" Mute evidence accomplished this to a limited extent. The park, one of New York's few private parks, was locked at

all times. Keys were in possession of property owners fronting on it. In the case of apartment hotels the doorman locked and unlocked the gates for guests desiring park privileges. Charlotte Foy had entered the park at an unknown hour with her key. She was some distance from her home and within 20 feet of the north gate when she was shot.

The Medical Examiner couldn't give an opinion as to the time of death. McKee could and did. He said that Charlotte Foy had been killed before 11 p.m. the previous night. The blanket of leaves covering her body proved it. The wind had risen at around 11:00. The 40-mile gale out of the northwest had stripped the last of its leaves from the beech under which she lay, sending them down in showers.

Assistant District Attorney Smith was puzzled. The night had been foggy and the visibility was zero. Yet Charlotte Foy's assailant had sent a bullet crashing into flesh and bone in the exact location where it would do the most good.

"I don't get it, Inspector."

McKee said grimly, "Miss Foy herself provided the necessary illumination when she lit the cigarette. The bullet was fired then. She never completed her smoke. No, she went crashing down into those bushes."

Pierson whistled. "Whoever plugged her must have been a hell of a good shot."

The Scotsman shrugged. He would have nothing to do with guesses about the bullet, its caliber, the weapon from which it was fired, the direction and distance from which it came; that was for the experts after the autopsy had been performed. For the rest, there was only one other important physical clue. Bleeding from the wound in Charlotte Foy's chest had been extensive. It was confined to the thicket in which she lay. A good three yards from it, near the edge of a cement path, shorn grass was stained with an irregular dark patching that was blood. Vague marks led from the thicket to this spot. There was none away from it. The conclusion was obvious. Someone with blood on his or her shoes had wiped them repeatedly on the grass to get rid of telltale stains. Someone who had stood over the dead woman, perhaps to see that life was extinct, perhaps to search her person, her purse. At any rate, it was someone who had had access to the park, who either had a key or had been admitted by Charlotte Foy herself.

McKee stood erect. The ballistics squad was arriving. Kent, who had been doing a little research on the Flavells, came back. The scene here was under full control; accompanied by the birdlike stenographer, McKee left the park by the west gate and crossed the street to the red brick house with the blue shutters and the white fan-lit door.

"Mr. Flavell? Yes, sir, if you'll wait here?"

Sunlight slanted through half-drawn venetian blinds, between sweeping sea-green draperies, and lay down in bars on the polished floor and on the exquisite faded mosaics of a very old Bokhara in the beautiful sunken living-room into which the maid ushered the two men. A clump of stock was fragrant under the sharp black and white of a Dürer; all was order, beauty, and peace. Almost from the first moment of his contact with it, there was something in the atmosphere of the house that the Scotsman found disturbing. It came, of course, from the people who lived there—and one who had died. Its emanations were so subtle, its deviations from the normal so slight, that its true essence continually eluded his grasp.

It began with Hugh Flavell, twice a widower, a former professor of economics, an authority on bees, and the father of a very wealthy daughter. Flavell was fifty-odd and didn't look it, handsome, collected, polite and crisply interrogative, a man of substance and affairs. "Inspector McKee? Yes, Inspector. Sit down. What can I do for you?"

He smoothed thinning fair hair with a nervous hand.

No word of what had happened had apparently reached the late Charlotte Foy's brother-in-law, the Scotsman reflected, yet he was braced for bad news of some sort. His lean body was tight under a dark-blue brocaded robe, gray slacks and a white silk shirt.

McKee told him.

Flavell stared, said, "Charlotte? . . *No* . . . I—" He opened his mouth wider for air, gave a gasp or two, turned livid and crumpled to the floor. He had fainted. His head struck the edge of a chair as he went down.

They put him on one of the two couches inglenooking the fireplace, and Kent used a bell pull vigorously. The maid who had admitted them came quickly, and then an older woman who was the cook, and then Natalie Flavell. Natalie heard the maid telephoning for the doctor. She called down to know what was wrong. The maid said, "It's your father, Miss. He's been taken sick. In the living-room. . . ."

There was a cry, footsteps ran lightly down the stairs and Natalie came through the archway. McKee turned. A negligée of jade-green velvet draped the girl's slender height. Her narrow face, framed in soft hair that swept her shoulders, was frightened. Her features were delicate and firm with an antique cast to them. She had no eyes for McKee and Kent. Her concern was all for her father. She hurried to the couch, dropped on her knees beside it, and looked down at him anxiously. "What is it, Joan?" she asked the cook. "What happened? How did it come on? Oh, look—he hurt his forehead. Get water, get some bandaging, get his medicine. . . ."

The cook soothed her. "Now don't you take on, Miss Nat. It's just one of his attacks. He'll be all right. . . . There now, you see?"

Flavell was stirring. His color began to return. Natalie covered him with a blanket the maid brought, put a pillow under his head. His eyes remained closed but his breathing was normal and his pulse stronger. He was coming out of it. It was only when Natalie was sure that he was better that she gave McKee her attention, and a puzzled frown.

"You were with my father? On business?"

The cook was gone, with Kent. McKee said, "Yes, Miss Flavell. You'd better sit down. I'm afraid that we have bad news for you."

Natalie sat, suddenly. "Is it—Bruce?" She waited for a blow, hands clasped tightly in a green velvet lap. The shadows in her paper-white skin were faintly green. A dust of freckles across the bridge of her long straight nose stood up in speckles of cinnamon.

"It's Miss Foy."

"Charlotte. . . . She's been taken sick. She wasn't in her room. . . ." The girl's wide darkly brown eyes raked his face. Her quivering lips firmed. "She's—is she dead?"

The Scotsman nodded. Natalie didn't seem surprised. There was a quality of numb acceptance in her stricken glance. It blew into a thousand pieces when McKee continued without further preamble, "Miss Foy was shot, some time last night, in the park across the street."

The girl's reaction was not unlike her father's. "No, no, no. Oh, *no.*" She jumped up and backed away from him, her hands out. For a moment it looked as though they were going to be presented with two patients. But Natalie didn't faint. In spite of her appearance of fragility she was young and strong. She was disciplined, too. Tears rolling down her face, she fought with shock, grief, incredulity, horror and fear. The fear was very evident. It came last. Watching it was like watching a tide sweep in. It showed itself in a sudden checking of her sobs, a caught breath, a glance at the Scotsman, stabbing, fearful, and sharply withdrawn.

Doctor Hendricks arrived then. He was a stout gray-haired middle-aged man with a pontifical presence. He had heard about Charlotte and was appalled. He had attended the family for years. He ordered Hugh Flavell taken upstairs and put to bed. When this had been done he had a word aside with McKee.

"I'm afraid you won't be able to talk to him for awhile, Inspector. There's no immediate danger, but excitement's bad for him, with that pump of his. He's liable to go off in one of these attacks."

Hendricks clarified Charlotte's position in the household. He said she was the sister of Hugh Flavell's first wife, Elizabeth, who died when the two children of that marriage, Gerald and Eve, were small. Charlotte had lived with Hugh and taken care of them until Hugh married again, a few years later. His second wife, Virginia, was one of the Boston Coreys. But Hugh was unlucky in his marriages. Virginia died shortly after Natalie was born, and Charlotte had returned and had taken up her interrupted task, with three, instead of two, children to care for.

She was a woman of exemplary character. The pattern hadn't followed the familiar shape. Charlotte Foy hadn't favored her own nephew and niece to the exclusion of Virginia's child; she had given Natalie the same or even more care and devotion than she had given—the other two.

McKee registered the doctor's slight pause. Charlotte Foy's death wasn't robbery. There were $27 in her purse and a ring on her finger; another motive had to be looked for. "Flavell's children by his first marriage resented Miss Foy's attitude, Doctor?"

"No, no," Hendricks said testily, "nothing of the kind. Charlotte was extremely fond of Gerald. . . ."

It was then, under McKee's continued questions, that Eve Flavell erupted. Eve hadn't gotten along with her aunt. As soon as she was out of college she had removed herself bag and baggage from the house on the Square. Hendricks was a reluctant witness. He said that Charlotte was dominating in a quiet way, and Eve was naturally independent. There wasn't anything more to it than that. He returned with relief to Charlotte Foy herself. In his opinion, Charlotte wasn't a well woman and hadn't very long to live.

She had been failing for more than a year. From her color and general symptoms he had suspected something grave, but she hadn't consulted him professionally, she had gone to a specialist in Boston in the spring and later to a farm she owned in Vermont for change of air and scene, separating herself from Hugh Flavell and Natalie for the first time in more than twenty years. The change hadn't done her any good. She was perceptibly worse when she returned to the Square shortly before Thanksgiving.

"Until the time she went away," the physician said, "she was completely wrapped up in Natalie and, to a lesser degree, in Hugh Flavell. After her return, she seemed to have lost interest in everyone and everything. Where she had been cheerful and brisk and competent before, she was morose and brooding. She didn't approve of Natalie's engagement to Bruce Cunningham, and showed it plainly, and that in turn made Natalie miserable. She's a sensitive high-strung girl—"

"With plenty of money, who likes her own way," the Scotsman interjected.

Hendricks smiled. "Don't we all, Inspector?—And as far as money is concerned, I've appealed to her plenty of times for help with some of my poorer patients and never in vain. No, Natalie wasn't at fault, or Hugh Flavell either, for that matter; it was Charlotte. She was a different woman when she came back from Vermont and not a happy person to be with. Naturally, living close to her had a depressing effect on the entire household. I

felt it myself, on several occasions, when I was there. . . .
So did others. Her bitterness toward—toward people she
had never been fond of was simply the result, in my opinion, of a growing lack of control produced in turn by her
physical condition."

Hendricks frowned and was troubled. He had something on his mind he didn't produce. All in good time,
talk to him later, when they knew more, McKee decided.
After the doctor was gone, McKee spoke to the Medical
Examiner's office and asked for a thorough examination
of Charlotte Foy's general physical condition prior to
death, and then questioned Natalie and the three servants. They were routine questions designed to establish
the immediate past of a woman who had no future, on
earth.

Charlotte Foy had been shot and killed before 11 p.m.
the previous night—but how long before? An analysis
of the contents of the stomach matched with the hour
when food was last eaten would give them an approxi-
mation, when the autopsy was completed. The Scotsman
didn't want to wait for that. The *res gestae* of the crime
put uneasiness into him; a dark and foggy night, a shot,
and the swift and quiet flitting of the perpetrator—more
than ten hours had elapsed since Charlotte Foy had been
killed and that was plenty, for escape, for concealment of
the gun and the smoothing of all incriminating traces.

No one knew at what time Charlotte Foy left the house
the night before. Natalie and the upstairs girl, Annette
Lebrun, had last seen her when she went to her room at
ten minutes of 7:00. By 7:00 the two maids were on their
way to a neighboring movie house. Hugh Flavell was presumably in his study on the third floor, and the cook
was in the basement, except for that moment in the hall
at 7:30 when Bruce Cunningham called for Natalie. The
girl said she didn't get home until almost 12:00, too late
to stop and talk to her aunt.

McKee was keenly interested in Charlotte's trip to Boston. An incompleted journey was always of interest in a murder case. If the journey was significant, if, for instance Charlotte had been prevented from making it, with a bullet, knowledge of her plans in advance would have been a necessity to the perpetrator.

Natalie said wearily that a Boston call had come through for Charlotte late the previous afternoon, at a little after 5:00. "Aunt told us then that she had to go, today, and wouldn't be here for Eve's wedding."

"Us" comprised herself, her father, her brother Gerald, Gerald's wife, Alicia, Eve, and Jim Holland, the man to whom Eve had just become engaged. McKee got the story of Eve's visit the day before and its purpose, savored its rarity. He asked exploringly whether there was anyone with whom Miss Foy had quarreled, anyone with whom she was on bad terms and Natalie said, "No, oh, no," with too much emphasis. He showed her the slip of paper, scribbled with the word *Spencer* and a number, that he had taken from the dead woman's purse.

Spencer was Spencer Gorham, Natalie's lawyer and one of the executors of her mother's estate; he had also done some legal business for Charlotte. *Savoy 4-3016* was his telephone number.

McKee asked if she knew the purpose of Charlotte's trip and Natalie said no, flatly. He didn't believe her. She kept looking at him haughtily from under drooping eyelids. She evidently wasn't used to being questioned by anyone and she resented interrogation with the restraint of a young princess, but her angry displeasure was thinly concealed. He had a fantastic notion that she was going to reach for her checkbook in a moment and try to buy him off. She didn't—but she was anxious to get away from him, that was clear; *give her her head.*

"I won't keep you any longer just now, Miss Flavell. I'd like to see Miss Foy's room, if I may?"

The girl jumped up out of the chair, in which she had been unable to sit still, with an impetuous movement. Her velvet skirts swirled. "Why do you want to see Aunt's room?" she demanded icily. "She wasn't killed here."

A shiver went through her, and her brown gaze blurred, and she smiled at him contritely with a sudden change of mood, her lashes wet. "I'm sorry, Inspector. I'm afraid I'm not myself. . . . Come. I'll show you. . . ."

She took him to the door of a bedroom on the floor above, left him and went along to her own room on the same floor at the front of the house. As soon as her door closed, McKee went to it. Inside the room a dial clicked. Natalie was at the telephone. It wasn't her fiancé Bruce Cunningham, or her half-brother Gerald she called first; it was her half-sister, Eve. Her voice was low but audible.

"Eve," she said around a dry sob. "Eve, Charlotte's dead. , . . I don't know how to tell you. . . . It's frightful. She was shot—last night, in the park. The police are here. . . ." At the other end of the wire Eve Flavell asked questions, to which Natalie said yes and no a couple of times, then, "After you left here last night, after you went back to the shop, you were with Jim, weren't you?"

The answer was evidently in the affirmative because Natalie said, "Oh, thank God. . . ." McKee lost the rest. The thud of the knocker filled the lower hall. The maid opened the door and a woman came in. It was Alicia Flavell, Gerald's wife. Mrs. Flavell asked where Natalie was; the girl told her, and she started up the stairs. McKee stepped backward into the gloom of a landing that led to the floor above.

Alicia Flavell didn't see him. She was in a hurry. She went straight to the door of Natalie's room, opened it without knocking. She didn't close it behind her. She was a woman in her thirties, very smartly dressed with smooth dark hair under a small hat. Natalie was at a desk on the far side of the room. She dropped the telephone into its cradle and turned, her face pinched and tear-stained and woebegone in its window of fair hair. Her nerves were on edge. She was startled and not too pleased by her sister-in-law's abrupt entrance. "You—heard, Alicia?"

Alicia Flavell said, "Yes, I heard. I saw them taking Charlotte away. . . ." She put her handkerchief to her mouth. "Someone said she was shot. It doesn't seem possible. . . . Did she—kill herself?"

Natalie's "No" was small, desolate.

Alicia Flavell's back was to the Scotsman. It was a handsome back but uninformative. Her voice was enough. It was harsh and vibrant around the edges as she said, "Eve was here last night, Natalie. In the Square, in the house. She said good-bye when she left in the afternoon. Why did she come back? She didn't like Charlotte—Charlotte was watching her yesterday afternoon and Eve has a pistol. . . . Oh, Nat—I'm frightened."

She wasn't the only one. Natalie said "Shush," with white violence, leaping to her feet. It was too late for shushing. McKee was already in the room. It was shortly after that, before he had time to do more than ask a few preliminary questions, that the twin discoveries were made.

For one thing Charlotte Foy's room had been searched during the night, and, for another, decorating the mauve broadloom at the foot of the stairs, there was a long brown stain that was undoubtedly blood, blood that in all probability had been carried from the pool under the dead woman in among the bushes in the park across the street.

Chapter Four

A SMELL OF DANGER

McKEE LOOKED AT MRS. GERALD FLAVELL thoughtfully and tried to remember where he had seen her before. He had just come up from the lower floor after a brief survey of the smeared stain at the bottom of the staircase. It could have been made by a shoe slipping, a shoe that had been cleansed on grass, but not well enough, with attention only to the soles when the uppers were also splashed. A square had been cut from the carpet and removed for tests. Charlotte Foy's room could wait for a detailed examination later.

Natalie sat on a dressing-table stool. Her long slim hands plucked at each other in her lap. She looked white and exhausted and furiously angry. Alicia Flavell was calm. She stood near one of the front windows, fixing her face. She was handsome in a smooth dark way, not tall, all curves and very well turned out. There wasn't a spontaneous bone in her body. Everything about her was calculated, arranged. There was greed in the sullen mound of her mouth and in her stubby fingers. They were busy with compact and lipstick. Now where—ah, he had it—an advertisement for creams or powders in a magazine; Alicia Grand, postdebutante of New York and Southampton, winner of . . . some blue ribbon at some dog show. She wasn't married to Gerald Flavell then; she must have been "post" for some time, she was in her middle thirties.

"Mrs. Flavell, if you please. You were saying to Miss Flavell a few minutes ago—"

"Yes, Inspector." Alicia snapped the compact shut, dropped it into her purse. Her words had been intended for Natalie's ear alone. Finding that he had heard her, she didn't attempt to retreat. She was too shrewd for that. She went at it in another way, consolidating her losses and taking a temperamental plea.

"I was upset—naturally, Inspector—one does jump to conclusions, stupidly. It couldn't have been Eve I saw down here last night. Natalie says Eve was with Jim Holland all evening. I was thinking about Eve and Jim and how sudden their engagement was. That's how I came to make the mistake, I imagine. So—"

Pinned down, she admitted that the evening before, at around twenty minutes or a quarter of 8:00, she had seen a woman who might have been Eve Flavell, who looked like her, certainly, and walked like her, cross the street from the direction of the park and enter the house.

When McKee said, "You were in the park yourself, Mrs. Flavell?" she gave him a faint smile, heavy lids at half mast over her full brown eyes.

"No, I wasn't in the park. I was walking Dum-Dum, my bull, around the Square. One does use it sometimes."

She was offering him insolence as a red herring—for what? She had regained her composure. Underneath it she was badly rattled and not, McKee surmised, because of her implication of Eve Flavell. Her voice was cold when she spoke of her sister-in-law.

He got her story of the afternoon and early evening up to a quarter of 7:00, when Jim Holland left the Flavell apartment on the other side of the Square. After that? After that, except for her stroll with Dum-Dum, she and Gerald had spent the remainder of the evening quietly at home playing the radio and reading.

Natalie had listened in silence, a white manikin frightened and angry at both Alicia and the Scotsman. She said suddenly, turning on the older woman, "But I thought you and Gerald were dining out, Alicia. You said so when Charlotte wanted you to stay here for dinner."

Alicia Flavell flushed. She became embarrassed, prettily. She said, "I didn't want to mention it but—but, well, the truth is, Gerald had had too much to drink and wasn't fit to go anywhere. It isn't really his fault; it's just that he's worried about business, poor boy. So I made him lie down on the couch and got him to bed as soon as I could. That's why I took Dum-Dum out myself. . . ."

Charlotte Foy had been killed at some time between 6:50 and 11 p.m. on the previous night. A man or woman who knew she was dead had carried her blood from the thicket where she lay into this house. The visitor hadn't been admitted by a servant, which left Hugh Flavell or a key. Alicia Flavell had been out in the Square, alone. As far as an alibi for either herself or her husband was concerned, her story was worthless.

McKee left the two women without further comment. Before he got into the Cadillac parked at the curb and drove away he gave orders to Kent, who had been reinforced by Wileski and McGill, that there was to be no more telephoning for the next twenty minutes.

Eve Flavell's shop on East 19th Street was a tiny building crushed down between a garage on one side and an electrical supply house on the other. It had a tiled roof like an immense eyebrow above timbered plaster stained a faint pink. The single window held a pair of cobwebby stockings flung across an ottoman, pigskin gloves thrown down on a Chippendale table, and an array of bright-jacketed books. Behind them, crisp white-dotted swiss curtains concealed the interior. The blue door, of heavy planking, had a latch and wide strap hinges. McKee lifted the latch and walked in.

The shop was long and narrow. The walls were green. White shelves covered with flat boxes lined the front half; at the back the little building broadened out into a small room with a worn Persian rug on the floor, low bookcases on the left, a beautiful Sheraton desk opposite, several comfortable chairs, and in the rear wall, between two simulated windows that were mirrors, a mantel of white brick.

Fire burned redly in an iron basket under the mantel. Eve deposited a lump of cannel coal on the fire with tongs, turned, and stiffened.

McKee studied her as he continued to advance. She wasn't at all like her half-sister Natalie. She was lovely. Hair that was bright on the crests and a warm shining chestnut in the hollows waved away from a face that would have delighted a sculptor with its sweep of brow and cheekbone, the modeling of the jaw and chin.

Like her father and Natalie and her sister-in-law Alicia, Eve Flavell was frightened and on her guard. Odd to find a fear that was individual in each of them when apparently they had nothing to be afraid of, he reflected. They couldn't all have killed Charlotte Foy, but they could all be concealing important and incriminating knowledge.

McKee said pleasantly, "Miss Flavell?" and Eve said "Yes," and moistened dry lips and swallowed. "You've come about Charlotte? . . . Sit down, Inspector. I'd better lock the door so that we won't be disturbed."

She did so and came back, and they both sat and lit cigarettes. Light from a lamp over a bookcase fell on the curve of Eve's cheek, on a string of pearls around her white throat, on the buttons of her yellow cardigan.

"You know how your aunt died, Miss Flavell?"

"Yes, in the park. She was shot. Poor Charlotte." Eve passed a hand across her eyes.

The better not to see you with, my dear? There was something very charming about this girl, and for the first time in a long while McKee found himself disliking the work he had to do. Yet, according to Doctor Hendricks and the servants and a neighbor or two, Eve Flavell was not on good terms with her aunt. . . . He didn't attempt to trap her. He told her what Alicia Flavell had said about her being in the house the night before.

Eve looked at him steadily, the pupils of her beautiful gray eyes large and dark. She said "Alicia," with a wry smile and looked away from him at the fire. The fear, at which the Scotsman had guessed, was hard and tight inside of her, an iron ball crushed up under her ribs, so that the pain was physical. *Think fast, Mr. Moto,* she told herself shakily. *This is no ordinary policeman. For all his good manners, his courtesy, he's an astute, a clever, and a ruthless man.* Aloud she said quietly, "Yes, I went back to the Square last night, Inspector, and I was in the house. But I didn't kill Charlotte. I didn't know she was dead until Natalie told me a few minutes ago."

McKee's heart sank. "Why did you go back, Miss Flavell?"

Eve's own heart was pounding. *He must never know that—never.* She forced herself to speak slowly. "I went back because, like an idiot, I forgot my purse. I left it behind me in the afternoon."

The Scotsman's brows rose. "You came all the way here without missing your purse, although I presume you took a cab? Yes—and then, instead of telephoning, and in spite of the fact that it was a nasty night, you returned to get it, through the fog?"

Eve let him finish. "I did miss it. I missed it when I got into the cab, but there was a woman here I had to see, so I paid the man off when I arrived. I didn't phone later because I knew the servants were out and I didn't want to disturb Father or Charlotte."

Her statement was very thin. There was no way of disproving it. The cook had been in the basement, the two maids were at the movies, Natalie was out with Bruce Cunningham and Hugh Flavell presumably in his study on the third floor. Unless Charlotte Foy had admitted her. . . . "Who let you in, Miss Flavell?"

"I still have a key."

"And a gun?" She was obviously suffering. Anger at her and at himself for having to go on with it made him curt.

"Oh, yes." Eve produced it, calmly, from a drawer in the desk, handed it over. It was a Colt .32. The chamber was full. It bore no traces of having been fired recently. Such traces could have been removed by cleaning. The rifling on the barrel, compared with the marks on the lethal bullet—when it was found—would tell the tale. McKee pocketed the weapon.

Eve said she hadn't been in the park at all; she had no key for that, and the gates were always locked. She reached the Square at around a quarter of 8:00 and went directly into the house. She hadn't seen her father, or anyone else. Her purse was in the living-room, behind one of the couch cushions. She retrieved it and—left.

McKee pounced on her hesitation. "At once?"

Eve thought swiftly. Bruce was with Natalie, so it couldn't have been Bruce who— She told the truth.

"No, not at once, Inspector. I went upstairs to Charlotte's room. I thought she might have heard me, might wonder who it was. Charlotte wasn't there, her door was locked, I tried it—but there was someone in her room." Eve's hands tightened in the lap of her tartan plaid skirt. It had been bad enough when it happened, but now— murder had been abroad in the blackness and the silence of the fog-filled Square the night before—coldness spread through her. "I rapped on the door and I called."— *Charlotte,* she had whispered so as not to rouse her father. *Charlotte, it's me, Eve.* Her life, more than her life, had depended upon getting an answer to a single question. There had been none forthcoming—"Whoever was inside the room stopped moving around, didn't speak. I'm sure it wasn't my aunt, Inspector—or she would have said something."

She had no clue to the identity of the person in Charlotte's bedroom. She admitted that the vague stirrings and rustlings behind the locked door had upset her. The house had seemed curiously empty and, yes, frightening —but not enough to make a fuss about. She could still feel the constriction between her shoulder blades when she ran down the stairs, without looking back, and let herself out into the open air.

McKee was pleased. His eyes began to shine. They were getting to it. If this girl was speaking the truth—and he thought she was, up to a certain point—Charlotte Foy had gone out of the house on the Square before 7:45. Her death hadn't been long delayed after she left the house. The soles of her shoes, protected by the branches which had closed in over them, were not much more than damp—which meant that she had been killed between ten minutes of 7:00 when Natalie and the maid last saw her, and a quarter of 8:00, when Eve entered the house.

Anyone with an alibi for those 55 minutes could be struck off the list of possible perpetrators. So far there were no complete alibis. Hugh Flavell had none, he was alone in the upper part of the house all evening; the cook had none, she was in the basement; Natalie had been with the lieutenant she was engaged to, but only from 7:30 on; Alicia Flavell was confessedly out and about Henderson Square from 7:30 until almost 8:00, which left her husband, Charlotte's nephew, uncovered. This girl certainly had no alibi.

He didn't mention the blood stain on the carpet in the Flavell hall. A roundup of shoes was being unobtrusively begun; *have Eve's wardrobe examined.* He didn't believe for a moment that she had killed her aunt in cold blood, but what about hot? He was engaged in probing for the root of her controlled terror when the phone rang.

Eve sat facing him, an elbow on the flap of the desk.

She turned, lifted the instrument, said, "Yes? . . . Sorry, wrong number." Her profile, silhouetted against a stretch of green wall, was a medallion in ivory.

The Scotsman made a long arm. He took the phone from her. He said, "It may be for me, Miss Flavell," and spoke into the mouthpiece. Instead of an answer there was a click. Whoever was at the other end of the wire had hung up on finding that Eve Flavell was not alone.

McKee replaced the receiver without comment. It wasn't Natalie, and it wasn't Alicia; Kent was taking care of them. It wasn't Eve's fiancé, either. A stick rapped smartly against the closed door and a man called the girl's name in muffled tones.

"That's Jim," Eve said, jumping up as though movement of any sort was a relief. She let Holland in. He kissed her and she said something inaudible to him and they both came toward the fire. Jim Holland was a big man in his middle thirties with a strong rugged face that was massive without being fat, thick brown hair, a high forehead, and intelligent blue eyes. He looked solid and dependable and clever. He walked with a slight limp, using a cane.

Holland was shaken by the tragedy in the Square. There were lead-colored marks under his eyes and his big mouth was grim. "I've known Charlotte since I was a kid. It's a horrible thing—horrible. . . ." He took out a handkerchief and blew his nose resoundingly. "Has anything important been discovered, Inspector?"

The news that Eve had returned to the Square the previous night rocked him backward. She hadn't confided in the man she was going to marry. Holland grew roots in the floor. He jerked himself out of stillness to say, turning to her frowningly, "Ha—well, did you see anything that helps, Eve?"

His devotion to her was obvious; he was evidently head over heels in love. He had been in the house when

Charlotte Foy announced her impending trip to Boston, a trip that had been cut down in its youth. According to Alicia he left the Flavell apartment on the east side of the Square at 6:45.

Jim Holland corroborated her. "It must have been around that, I should say. I got back to my place on Kossuth Street at seven, did a little work to pass the time and then came up here to the shop."

He had arrived at 8:30. Eve had fixed scrambled eggs and bacon and made coffee and they had been together until 11:00, when he went home. He hadn't seen Charlotte after he left the Flavell house at a little before 6:00; he hadn't heard a shot while he was negotiating the Square. He began to look angry. He had a formidable jaw. Eve Flavell might not always find him as easy to handle as she did now.

Holland had no alibi for the crucial hour. He could have killed Charlotte Foy; he had no motive, showing. Neither had anyone else. Holland could have been the person in Charlotte's bedroom, if he had been able to procure a key to the front door—which to a man familiar with the house would have presented no particular difficulty. Search his rooms for a weapon, for shoes with telltale stains on them, the Scotsman decided. Meanwhile— Eve Flavell was even more anxious to get rid of him than her young half-sister had been. Oblige her, by all means. She was evidently contemplating action of some sort, and the sooner the basic facts were established in the sudden, violent, and motiveless death of a middle-aged woman of excellent character and good family, the better. Too many people were concealing too many things. There was a smell of danger about the case he didn't care for; someone was likely to get hurt.

Five minutes later he left the shop. He didn't turn as he crossed the pavement to the Cadillac parked at the curb. He had a shrewd idea that Eve was standing behind the dotted-swiss curtains watching him with those long gray eyes. He drove away, but not far. Around the corner he stopped the car, got out, found a convenient doorway and waited for what he was sure was going to happen— and was right. Three minutes later Eve emerged from the shop, alone. Holland was evidently playing storekeeper for her. She glanced quickly up and down the street, crossed it, and began to walk rapidly south.

Chapter Five

At first, following Eve's slender hurrying figure into the subway at 14th and out of it at 8th, McKee thought she was going to the house on Henderson Park, but at 4th Street, she swung east, then south, then east again into Eldon Place. Midway along the short block she mounted the steps of the first of a row of three brownstone houses and entered the vestibule.

McKee was in time to hear the click of the latch, the soft closing of the inner door. He entered the vestibule in the girl's wake, scanned the names on the letter boxes. *Gram, Visniski, Tennerfly, Graham, Violet;* none of them had so far been connected with the case under investigation. He pushed the top floor bell labeled *Violet,* hoping the girl hadn't gone there, got an answering click and entered the dim lower hall. Footsteps mounted in the obscurity above. McKee followed them without noise. Halfway up the stairs leading to the third floor he looked through banister rails in gloom at Eve's pretty legs in nylons and red calf sandals, motionless in front of a door. The door opened and a man's voice said, "Oh—hello, Miss Flavell," with enthusiasm.

"Is Mr. Cunningham in, Mr. Graham?" Eve asked, and the man she called Graham answered, "No, he's not, right now. He went out about three-quarters of an hour ago. I don't think he'll be long. Won't you come in and wait?"

"I think I will, if you don't mind." Eve's feet and ankles moved forward and the door closed.

Outside of it, pressed close to the fine old paneling, McKee listened as well as he could, to what went on inside. It wasn't much. "Don't stay with me, Mr. Graham.

I'll be quite all right in here." Graham murmured some-thing indistinguishable and Eve said—she had a very definite voice, low and a little husky and with a soft ring to it—"No, nothing, thanks. . . . Yes, I have cigarettes."

Inside the apartment a door closed and typewriter keys rattled. A woman on the floor above was playing the piano; a cat meowed plaintively somewhere; the Scotsman tried the door of the apartment absently. To his surprise and pleasure it wasn't locked. He eased it out of its frame. A corridor stretched right and left in dimness in the light of a single lamp with a heavy shade. There was no one in sight, but someone was coming up the stairs from the street.

McKee stepped into the hall, shut the front door be-hind him, opened another at random on darkness, and found himself in a windowless bath. He left the door there a little ajar. He was only just in time. A man in a trench coat was entering the apartment. It was Bruce Cunningham. McKee recognized him at once; there was a large framed picture of him on the dressing-table in Natalie's gold-and-white bedroom in the house on Hen-derson Square.

Cunningham went in the direction of the living-room. He opened the door, and paused. Eve Flavell said, "Bruce," on a breathless note.

"*Eve*—what are you doing here?" Cunningham an-swered blankly as though he couldn't believe his ears, harshly, peremptorily, as though he didn't want to believe his eyes.

McKee abandoned his position between what felt like a wash basin and a metal clothes hamper and moved un-ostentatiously out into the corridor. He had a fair view. The living-room was straight ahead and the door was open.

Cunningham stood just inside of it, tall and wide-shouldered, his lean dark face in profile, his peaked cap pushed to the back of his head. He took the cap off and went on staring at his visitor. Eve was on her feet in front of the chair from which she had risen. Her raspberry tweed coat made a high spot of color against a window. One hand was at her throat. Above its round white column her head was a little bent. Her white triangular face was cold, expressionless.

She was saying in an icy little tone, "You heard about —Charlotte, Bruce? You know what—happened to her." She looked ill. The hand hanging at her other side was clenched.

"Yes," Cunningham said quietly, "I heard. Natalie called me—that was when I gave you a ring at the shop."

"I couldn't talk to you," Eve said. "There was a Police Inspector with me."

"I gathered as much," Cunningham said drily. "That's why I think— Wasn't it rather stupid of you to come straight here?"

His cool question appeared to infuriate his fiancée's sister. She said, her eyes blazing, "I didn't come here because I wanted to. Disabuse your mind of that idea. I came because I had to. There are certain things I've got to know. . . ."

Bruce Cunningham balled the gloves he had drawn off, tossed them into the air, caught them. "Exactly, my angel—and there are things *I* want to know. You were in the shop all last evening with the estimable Mr. Holland, I presume? At least Natalie told me you were. You're sure about it? I'd like to hear you say so yourself."

There was more than the width of the room between them. They were antagonists, eyeing each other warily. Eve thrust her hands into the pockets of her coat and faced Cunningham more directly. "No," she said, "I wasn't in the shop all evening. I went down to the Square. I wanted to find out what happened. When I saw nothing of you, I went into the house to talk to Charlotte. Charlotte wasn't there." Her hand was at her throat again, a fold of soft flesh between tight fingers.

"So you think I killed her?" Cunningham said softly. He was smiling. It wasn't a pleasant smile.

"I don't think anything," Eve cried out at him. "I don't want to think. Except about Natalie. She's my sister. She loves you. You're going to be married. I didn't tell the Inspector about last night. You mustn't either, for Natalie's sake."

"For Natalie's sake," Cunningham reflected musingly. He was still smiling, his eyes narrowly bright.

"Yes," Eve told him on a full breath. "For Natalie's sake—and for hers alone. I don't care about anyone else in the world. But she mustn't be hurt. Nobody knows about last night but us. . . . I didn't say a word to the Inspector. You mustn't either. If the police were to find out—"

A dog whined somewhere and claws scratched wood. A door at the other end of the apartment opened and an English setter bounded along the hall. He caught sight of the Scotsman and let out a howl.

McKee sighed. He didn't do much field work these days; as a general rule his place was at the center of a battery of phones directing an investigation rather than taking an active part in it. So far his luck had been good. The string had run out. It was no part of his plan to antagonize these people at this stage. He did a lightning shift. He was at the outside door, had it open and was standing in the opening when Bruce Cunningham appeared.

The Lieutenant was something less than pleased to see a visitor who had walked in unannounced. He controlled anger at the interruption with difficulty. "Yes? Who are you, what do you want?" he demanded curtly.

"The door was unlocked," McKee said. "I'm sorry. I knocked but no one answered." He introduced himself.

Cunningham's manner changed. The savagery went out of him, he became brisk, civil. He said, "Come in, please, Inspector." He was a quick thinker. "It's about Miss Foy, I suppose? Miss Flavell, Miss Eve Flavell, is here now. We were just on the point of starting for the Square. This way."

They went into the living-room. Eve Flavell was sitting in a chair near one of the two tall windows. Her back was to the light. Her position was comfortable. The face she raised to McKee was white, tight, the scarlet of her mouth the only color in it. She smiled at him.

"Hello, Inspector. We meet again."

"Yes, Miss Flavell." Cunningham was as taut as his prospective sister-in-law, but his powers of dissimulation were better. He had an interesting face, not handsome but definite and well-planed. Women would take to him instinctively. There was humor and gentleness in his firm mouth with indentations at the corners, and his light eyes under dark strongly marked brows, were intelligent. So was the shape of his head.

Play it straight, the Scotsman decided, and see what he got. "You understand the questions I'm going to ask you are purely routine, Lieutenant? We're interviewing all Miss Foy's relatives and friends. Now—do you know anything that will shed any light on her death?"

Cunningham took off his trench coat, folded it and threw it over the back of a sofa. His uniform molded a lithe hard figure. "Nothing whatever, Inspector. It's a complete mystery to me. I was dumbfounded when I heard about it. It just doesn't seem possible."

The Scotsman nodded, showed regret. "I see. . . . I had hoped— well, we go on trying. From present indications Miss Foy appears to have been shot and killed between ten minutes of seven and, say, eight o'clock. Would you mind telling me what you were doing, where you were, during that time?"

Bruce Cunningham struck a match, held it to a ciga-rette. In the small flare his face was bleak. He didn't look toward Eve. He dropped the match into a tray, inhaled smoke, and said musingly, "Ten minutes of seven. . . . I was here at ten minutes of seven, changing. I had an en-gagement with Natalie—Miss Flavell—for dinner. I got to the house at half-past exactly; I remember, because on account of the fog I was afraid I might be late, but I looked at my watch when I got there and I wasn't."

McKee watched smoke rising in spirals. Cunningham and Natalie had been together from 7:30 on, according to separate and independent statements. What had Eve Flavell been referring to when she said, *I didn't tell the police about last night?* Whatever it was it must have taken place before 7:30. These rooms weren't more than three or four minutes' walk from the Square. . . . "What time did you leave here, Lieutenant?"

The setter licked a paw and rolled over on his side. Cunningham sat down on the arm of a chair. He stretched his long legs out in front of him, thrust his hands into his pockets, and threw a bombshell in the most casual of tones. "I left here early. I think it was at about ten after seven. I had an appointment to meet Charlotte Foy at the north gate of the park in Henderson Square at seven-fifteen."

A gasp from Eve as he began to speak was instantly suppressed. Her face was a little death's-head, with black-ness for the eyes, in the hollows of the slender cheeks, and beautiful temples. McKee stared fixedly at the imper-turbable lieutenant. He himself had already predicted a meeting between Charlotte Foy and someone else in the darkness and the fog the night before. It was this man she had gone to see. She had never emerged from the tryst. Cunningham was alive, she was dead, with a bullet hole in her.

McKee made no attempt to hide the gravity of the lieutenant's disclosure. Eve Flavell, at least, was fully cognizant of it. Question and answer after that, clipped, cold, impersonal. Gradually the full story emerged. On the previous day Bruce Cunningham got back from Washington earlier than he expected and went directly from the station to the house on the Square. He arrived there at around 5:00, left in about half an hour, after making arrangements to spend the evening with Natalie. He had had no private conversation with Charlotte; she had been called to the telephone shortly after he got there and he was under the impression that she wasn't in the room when he left.

He hadn't come straight here from the Flavell house; he had an appointment with a fellow officer, Hilary Fenn, for 5:30-ish at the Harvard Club, where they had a couple of drinks together. He got home at about half-past 6:00, maybe a little later. Meanwhile Charlotte Foy had telephoned.

Bruce Cunningham explained that he had lived in the apartment before he went into the Army, sharing it with a writer, Philip Graham. An artist friend of Graham's, Joe Buchanan, had taken his place when he joined up, but the two men had insisted on his staying with them while he was on leave. Philip Graham had answered Miss Foy's call.

Graham was summoned. He was a plump man in his forties with thinning auburn hair and thick-lensed glasses over weak eyes. He looked his bewilderment at McKee's questions, didn't get any explanation of them. He said that Miss Foy rang up at ten minutes of 6:00 the previous evening. He remembered the time because he had been expecting another call and was watching the clock. Miss Foy asked for Bruce. When Graham told her he wasn't in and wanted to know whether there was any message she said yes. Would he ask Lieutenant Cunningham to meet her at the north gate of Henderson Park at 7:15. She repeated the location twice. *The north gate. Tell him I want to speak to him, but that I won't keep him long.*

Years of experience at interrogation convinced the Scotsman that Graham was speaking the truth. He had no ax to grind, no connection with the Flavell family. Back to Cunningham again, "You kept the appointment with Miss Foy, Lieutenant?"

Cunningham lit a fresh cigarette. "Yes, Inspector, I did —but Charlotte didn't. When I got to the north gate she wasn't there. The mist was heavy and it was very dark; I've never been out on a night that was any darker. I looked through the gate. I even called. There was no sign of her. I walked up and down the pavement in front of the gate for a while. Then it began to rain and I decided that the weather had kept her indoors. It was getting late by that time, so I went round to the house, collected Natalie, and we went out to dinner."

"Did you mention your appointment with Miss Foy to Miss Flavell, ask her where her aunt was?"

Cunningham shook his head. "No. Charlotte was ill and Natalie was worried about her; anyhow I didn't want to bother her. If Charlotte had changed her mind, I figured she'd see me later."

McKee took a turn up and down the big comfortable living-room, a man's room, bare of ornament, cluttered with books, pipes, golf clubs, a skiing kit on end in one corner, a collection of fishing rods in another; the three men who occupied the rooms had sporting tendencies in their hours of ease. Charlotte Foy's telephone call to Cunningham was, to say the least, peculiar. He had been in the Flavell house that afternoon, was going to be there again in a matter of minutes. Charlotte Foy wasn't content to wait. She wanted to see him alone, out of doors, in the darkness and fog of the wooded Square where they couldn't be seen or overheard. The flavor of secrecy about the proposed meeting was arresting. Cunningham was, or professed to be, in complete ignorance of what Charlotte wanted to see him about.

"You have no idea, Lieutenant?"

"Not the slightest."

"Did Miss Foy approve of your engagement to Miss Flavell?"

"I don't think she did, at first. But later, yes."

"What was her objection, in the beginning?"

Cunningham shrugged. "I wasn't a favorite of hers, and Charlotte was a woman who played favorites. She was very good, you understand, but she was narrow and stubborn and liked her own way. Cross her in anything and you were at once a villain of the deepest dye."

Was this a reference to Charlotte Foy's relationship with her niece, Eve? The girl had scarcely moved since Cunningham made his disclosure. She was locked up inside of herself, tension in every slender line. If Cunningham hadn't mentioned his appointment with Charlotte to Natalie, he had to her. She had said to him when he first came in, *No one knows about last night but us.*

Leave it, the Scotsman thought. Neither of them was giving freely. Get at it another way.

Eve stirred, she came out of her long winter's nap to say, "It wasn't that Aunt had anything against Lieutenant Cunningham personally, Inspector. But she had another man picked out for Natalie. She wanted her to marry Everett, a cousin of the Corey's. She was disappointed about it, but I'm sure she got over her feeling."

What Eve Flavell was sure of, even if she was telling the truth, wasn't necessarily so. If Cunningham hadn't pulled the trigger of the gun that had blown a hole in Charlotte Foy—and while the testimony was damaging it was by no means conclusive—the perpetrator would have had to know that Charlotte would be in the park, at the north gate, at 7:15. The people in the house when she made the call included Hugh Flavell, Natalie, Gerald,

his wife, Alicia, Jim Holland and the servants. The afternoon that had preceded the slaying in the misty darkness
of the Square was becoming more and more important.

Cunningham declared he had neither a pistol nor a
revolver, offered to let himself, the apartment, be searched
then and there. McKee waved the offer aside. It would
be done later as a matter of course. Cunningham's uniform was too trimly fitted to conceal the bulge of an
iron he would scarcely have been stupid enough to carry
about with him, and it could have been more than adequately disposed of in—a clock in a near-by tower struck
one—the 18 hours that had elapsed since Charlotte Foy
was killed.

Get men here to search the apartment, not only for
a gun but for other things, blood-stained footgear, letters,
papers, evidence of any sort that would lay bare the real
picture with which they had certainly not, so far, been
presented. Meanwhile keep an eye on the Lieutenant
and Eve Flavell; he said pleasantly, "You were on your
way to the Flavell house when I arrived. I'm going there
now. We may as well go together."

Eve stood automatically, a robot in raspberry tweed
operated by a hidden mechanism. Cunningham put on
his trench coat, tightened the belt, picked up his cap.

In spite of these preparations for departure, they didn't
immediately leave.

The front doorbell rang. Before anyone could answer
it the door opened, a voice called "Bruce" softly and a
woman came along the hall and paused on the threshold
of the living-room. She was a tall woman in her middle
forties with a quantity of fair hair under a small gray hat
with a red wing in it. Sables were slung across the shoulders of her gray cloth suit. She exuded an air of vigor, of
richness and of shock. There was strain, grief, in her
generous red-lipped mouth.

She didn't see either Eve or the Scotsman; they were

partially concealed by the door that swung inward and she was looking at Cunningham. She said with a little rush, "Bruce, I want you to do something for me, get me something—"

Eve Flavell said "Sue," sharply. Cunningham said quietly, "Hello, Susan. You heard about Charlotte, I suppose?" He waved toward McKee, in shadow to the left of the door. "Inspector McKee of the Homicide Squad. Inspector, Mrs. De Sange."

Susan De Sange had been in the Flavell house the afternoon before. Her name was not down on the list of guests. She told the Scotsman so, herself. With her appearance on the scene the roster of people intimately connected with the life, and with the death, by violence, of the late Charlotte Foy, became complete—with one notable, and tragic, exception. The Scotsman couldn't know that then. He felt it instinctively in his bones.

Chapter Six

SOMETHING NEW UNDER THE SUN

"YOU'VE BEEN A FRIEND OF THE FLAVELLS for a long time, Mrs. De Sange?"

"For more than twenty years, Inspector. I knew this infant when she was a young woman of four." Susan De Sange laid a hand on Eve's, linked tightly together in her lap.

The two women were on the back seat of the cab they had picked up outside Cunningham's rooms. The lieutenant was with the driver in the front seat. McKee occupied one of the stools. The light outside the windows was cold, gray. The sun had vanished and clouds pressed down threateningly. It looked like snow.

When she had heard that they were on their way to the Flavell house, Susan De Sange had said she'd go with them; she wanted to tell Hugh and Natalie how sorry she was, find out whether there wasn't something she could do.

She went on explaining her link with the Flavells. She had lived next to them, in a little cottage close to their big house in Eastport, where the three children had been born and where both Hugh's wives had died. They had been difficult days for her, too. She had lost first her husband and then her only child in the fall and winter of '21-22. The Flavells—and Charlotte—had been extremely kind. The intimacy that grew up between them then had lapsed when the Flavells moved to New York and she left Connecticut. It had been revived after almost two decades when she ran into Eve at a party early that spring. She had entertained and been entertained by both Hugh and Natalie; Charlotte was in Vermont. She met her for the first time after her return to New York in late November.

Listening, the Scotsman made various mental notes. Like Hugh Flavell and Natalie, Alicia and Bruce Cunningham and Eve, Susan De Sange was deeply stirred by Charlotte Foy's death. She lived in the Trianon, an apartment hotel on Henderson Square less than a hundred yards from the spot where Charlotte had been shot down.

Eve Flavell was surprised to hear that she had been in the house the afternoon before. She opened her long gray eyes. "I didn't see you, Sue. Were you there when I—"

Mrs. De Sange said tranquilly, "I didn't go into the living-room. I wanted to talk to Charlotte alone, about a wedding present for Natalie. I'm going away in a week or two and I hadn't much time."

She said it too casually, not looking at McKee but into the darkening streets, abstractedly. Charlotte Foy's appointment with Bruce Cunningham for 7:15 at the north gate of the park had been made at ten minutes of 6:00. "What time were you in the Flavell house, Mrs. De Sange?"

"What time? I'm afraid I can't remember exactly, Inspector. It was quite late. I'd been to a bridge at the Pierre and I was going on for cocktails at the Jacobys'."

"You did see Miss Foy?"

"Oh, yes. She came to me in the little writing-room. We were only together for a few minutes. I didn't want to keep her."

Had she told him, the Scotsman wondered, because she thought the servants would? Kent had talked to them, talked to them himself. He put a smile around his request for an alibi. "We're trying to establish the whereabouts of Miss Foy's relatives and friends and acquaintances for the hour from ten minutes of seven until approximately eight, Mrs. De Sange. During that time you were—where?"

"Dining in my room in the Trianon. I went out later for a short walk, but as far as I can recall it was after eight."

The apartment people would probably know. The cab swung into the Square, turned right and pulled up before the mellow red brick house with the blue shutters. It was after they went in that McKee got a fresh slant on affairs in general. Hugh Flavell was in love with Susan De Sange, and his daughter-in-law, Alicia, didn't approve of his very obvious devotion. His cold, high-nosed face lit up when the older woman entered the room. "Susan. My dear, this is very kind of you." He got up impetuously from the chair in which he had been sitting moodily before the fire.

"Hugh, I'm so sorry. . . ." She took his hand. He patted hers and shook his head. "I'm still dazed."

Alicia watched them thoughtfully from behind the smoke of a cigarette in a jeweled holder. Her nod to Susan was cool. Natalie had put on a long-sleeved black dress. Her face was drawn and colorless between the wings of her soft fair hair. "Bruce," she went swiftly to Cunningham. McKee joined Kent in the hall.

Spencer Gorham, the Boston lawyer Charlotte was going to see and to whom she had talked over the phone a few hours before she died, was coming to New York some time that evening. There was no report yet from the Medical Examiner's office, nor had the lethal bullet been recovered. Men were busy searching the Park for it inch by inch. Gerald Flavell had been at the house but had gone; he was expected back later.

Mrs. De Sange had arrived at the house the previous afternoon at around 5:30. She had said to the maid who admitted her that she wanted to see Miss Foy alone and was ushered into the writing-room. Charlotte was then talking to Boston. The little writing-room was next to the booth that housed the phone and a comfortable chair.

Mrs. De Sange could have overheard both the conversation with Boston and Charlotte Foy's call later to Bruce Cunningham. The maid didn't know what time she left. McKee mounted the stairs thoughtfully, with Kent.

The dead woman's room was on the same floor as Natalie's, at the back of the house. It was a big bare room austerely furnished with a bed, a dresser, a bureau, a desk, several tables, and two chairs. A small bathroom led out of it. There was a luggage rack at the foot of the bed. A pigskin suitcase on it was open. The suitcase held a change of underlinen, a flannel nightdress, two pairs of rolled stockings, a brown bathrobe, and a small wooden box with a brass handle in the lid. The things were tumbled this way and that. The box was old and empty.

Kent said, waving at it and at the desk, also open and with the papers in it in considerable disorder, "When the maid came in here early yesterday evening everything was okay. She says Miss Foy was a very tidy woman and that she'd never have left her stuff like that. Someone went through the desk and the suitcase after she went out."

"Yes, I think so." McKee told the secretary of the stirrings Eve Flavell had heard when she was standing outside the locked room, of the silence that followed her knock and her call to her aunt. Whoever had been in the room knew that Eve was there. . . . He didn't like it. "Fingerprints, Kent?"

"Belloni and Knox just left. They got a mess of them. Nothing doing on the shoes." He had examined every shoe in the house. There was no blood on any of them and no indications of a hasty cleaning. "Of course they could have been thrown out."

McKee's nod was somber. "What's in the desk, Kent?"

"Oh, a lot of junk. Letters, canceled checks, postcards, receipts—some stuff I haven't sorted."

McKee ordered the lot sent to the office for a detailed

examination, looked into the room's two closets—and
stared.

The first closet was full of expensive clothes in cello-
phane bags and protective wrappings, with shoes in racks
and a variety of hats in boxes on the shelves. There was a
smell of camphor and a faint almost impalpable dust
over the entire collection. Voluminous folds and deep
pleats stamped most of the gowns as pre-war. The second
closet held a black skirt and a black jersey blouse with
a Bennington label in the collar. These were apparently
the only clothes, besides the dress she had on when she
was killed, that the dead woman had brought with her
from Vermont.

Charlotte Foy's life had suffered a sharp sea change
within the year, he reflected. It was natural enough that
a woman who discovered that she was mortally ill should
become indifferent to what she ate and drank and what
she put on. Yet—was there more to it than that? McKee
had an unpleasant sensation of missing something significant, of depths he couldn't plumb, dark recesses in
whose subterranean windings the truth about the dead
woman lay concealed.

He had felt it all along. He felt it more keenly standing there with a doorknob in his hand, looking from the
full closet of abandoned luxuries into the almost empty
one. He tore himself loose from conjecture without a·
focus, stared into the old-fashioned wooden box in the
suitcase that might have held jewels, old letters, keepsakes, wondered whether the intruder of the night before
had removed the contents of the little chest, or whether
it had some other significance, and presently left Kent
sorting through the desk, and descended the stairs. He
was half way down the top flight when he pulled to a halt.

Mrs. De Sange was crossing the lower hall. She didn't
see him. She paused near the foot of the staircase, looked
over her shoulder at the living-room archway, and then

moved on out of sight.

McKee reached the main floor in time to see the door of the writing-room close. He opened it without noise. Susan De Sange was so absorbed in what she was doing that she didn't hear him. Her back was to the door. She was down on one knee at the trash basket beside the Empire desk.

McKee said, "Looking for something, Mrs. De Sange? Can I be of any assistance?" and Susan De Sange turned. She smiled up at him and rose with a single twist of her strong supple body. Her color was high and her eyes were bright; otherwise she was perfectly at ease. "Thanks, no, Inspector. I *was* looking for something—but it doesn't seem to be here. Yesterday afternoon Charlotte gave me the name and address of a mutual friend of ours that we used to know up in Eastport. I left it behind me when I went. It must have been thrown away."

She pulled out a chair, sat down at the desk, opened a gray snakeskin purse with a silver monogram and silver corners, and extracted a sheet of paper with a list of names on it, explaining that she was going to let people, friends, and distant connections of Hugh's, know about Charlotte's death.

McKee left her to her task and sought out the maids. The trashbasket had been emptied that morning. The papers were in a receptacle at the foot of the cellar stairs. Kent joined him and they sorted through empty cigarette packages, advertisements, and letters of no importance. Almost at the bottom of the small stack Kent found the only object Mrs. De Sange could possibly have been looking for. It was a three-cornered fragment of double-weight paper jaggedly torn from a photograph. The outline of what might be an arm, in what might be a dark coat, was bordered for two inches one way and three the other by a small white margin.

The Scotsman turned it over curiously. A photograph

had cropped up during the little talk between Charlotte Foy and Susan De Sange at between half-past 5:00 and 6:00 the night before; somehow or other it had gotten torn. Try and find out whose photograph it was and which woman it belonged to—but not by asking. Certainly not. Meanwhile have the paper tested for prints.

Kent returned to Charlotte's room to begin a photographic survey, and McKee talked to Hugh Flavell first in the dining-room and then in his study. To his surprise Flavell was remarkably pleasant. "Come upstairs, Inspector, where we can be comfortable." Mrs. De Sange—something—had made him a different man. He could be attractive, likeable, when he wanted to. A weight seemed to have fallen from his shoulders and he had completely recovered from his attack of the morning. He offered McKee a drink from a tantalus in the handsome book-lined room on the third floor. "Not so early? It is a good rule, I think. Prohibition ruined this generation, most of us oldsters, I mean." Yes, he said, it was a habit of his to walk in the Park morning and evening, but he hadn't left the house last night; the weather was too bad. He couldn't imagine what had taken poor Charlotte out into the fog on such an evening.

McKee told him about her appointment with Bruce Cunningham, and Flavell showed surprise and bewilderment. "Now what—" he threw himself back in his chair behind the streamlined mahogany desk. He sat erect, drummed fingers on the polished wood. "To tell you the truth, Inspector, I'm beginning to wonder if Charlotte wasn't getting the least little bit—queer."

The woman lying in among bushes in the Park across the street hadn't looked it. The Scotsman waited patiently for enlightenment. But Hugh Flavell didn't pursue the subject except to say, "Perhaps I'm wrong, but she, well, during the last year she took fancies. I never approved of her going up to Vermont alone—and then there was her anxiety to hurry on Natalie's marriage, when at first she opposed the engagement. I suppose it was simply that she was ill."

McKee asked whether a date had been set for the wedding and Hugh Flavell said no. "Natalie's too young." As she was in her twenty-second year this didn't seem a very valid objection. Flavell added, "Bruce feels, and I agree with him, emphatically, that it's better for them to wait until he's over his wound and out of uniform."

His own whereabouts between 6:50 and 8:00 the night before? He had been in his study, working. No one had disturbed him. From the study he had gone directly to bed in the bedroom beyond at, perhaps, eleven o'clock.

McKee thanked him and went downstairs. He was in the lower hall, wondering if Charlotte Foy had approved of Mrs. De Sange and her brother-in-law's third drift toward matrimony, when Kent poked a head over the banister railing. The blond, birdlike secretary was excited. The Scotsman joined him, and Kent said, "Something I want you to take a look at," and led the way through the dead woman's bedroom and into the bath.

The upstairs girl, Gloria Fox, was standing beside the sunken tub looking scared. The door of the medicine cabinet was open. Kent pointed to an empty space between a bottle of mouth wash and the cabinet wall. "There's a box of medicine gone from there, Inspector."

"What was in it?"

Gloria Fox answered, "It was pills Miss Foy brought down with her from the country. She took them whenever she got a pain. She sent me for one yesterday afternoon."

The box was small, of blue pasteboard and had been more than half full of little capsules. It wasn't in the dead woman's purse. Someone else must have removed it. It could have been taken at any time between late the previous afternoon and less than ten minutes ago, when Kent had been with McKee in the cellar. McKee looked grimly at shining chromium, at a green shower curtain. Question the people here now? It would be useless. There had been no check on their movements during that quarter of an hour's search in the basement, and no one was going to step forward as the thief. The best thing to do was to get in touch with Charlotte Foy's doctor in Vermont and find out what the capsules were. They might be harmless. And then again—Doctor Hendricks had said that Charlotte was probably suffering from a serious internal condition—they might not. A sedative to quiet pain, to quiet— The discovery had the opposite effect on the Scotsman.

He swung on his heel, descended the stairs, got the name of Charlotte's Vermont doctor from Natalie, and went to the telephone. He called Headquarters. He used the word *urgent* gently, as a curb on his own nerves. After Headquarters, the Medical Examiner's office; the post-mortem on Charlotte Foy was in progress. "Look for a drug, a sedative of some sort, will you?" he asked. "And let me know as fast as possible." He hung up.

Men from the Ballistics Squad and two homicide detectives, Davidson and Peak, were still searching the park for the bullet that had crashed through Charlotte Foy's body to bury itself in the ground, in among thickets, under piles of leaves or in the branches or trunk of some tree. They had to have the weapon that had killed her. To search for it adequately they had first to get hold of the lethal slug.

McKee left the telephone booth and the house. It was ten minutes of 3:00 when he entered the park across the street. It was five minutes of 5:00 when the bullet was finally found. It was embedded in a small hillock crowned with a statue of Niobe weeping for her children that was at least 80 feet from the thicket into which the dead woman had crashed. Sergeant Wennikoe of the Ballistics Squad unearthed it.

Big men in a ring stared at the battered bullet on Wennikoe's palm under a darkening sky. There was something new, or comparatively new, under the sun. In all of the Scotsman's experience it had happened only once before within the precincts of Greater New York.

Charlotte Foy had been shot and killed, not with a pistol or a revolver, but with a high-powered bullet from a hunting rifle.

Chapter Seven

UNAWARE OF THE DANGER

THE MURDERER, AND THE MURDERER ALONE, knew the weapon with which Charlotte Foy had been eliminated. He or she knew, too, that the police would eventually uncover the make and caliber of the death-dealing gun. Until a thorough search had been accomplished, the longer they withheld their knowledge the better chance they had of discovering the rifle's ownership and whereabouts. It was Sergeant Jabowski of the 4th Detective Division who unwittingly made the premature revelation.

Jabowski was in the hall of the Flavell house on the Square when the call came through. Kent took it. He told the news to a small group of officers near the front door. "A *rifle*," Jabowski exclaimed. "My God, the dame shot down like a sick dog . . . What do you know?"

Eve was standing just inside the living-room archway. The sergeant had a carrying voice. She heard him. The blood drained away from her heart, and the walls and floor shook. "No," she whispered soundlessly to herself, frozen into a terrible immobility. "No. . . . Oh, *no.*"

She stared blindly at a blue horse in watercolor treading yellow sand in front of a blue sea. It had been a long and dreadful day; the night before had been almost as bad. She hadn't expected Charlotte's death—no, never; she had expected—something. When Natalie told her that Charlotte was dead; her first sensation had been one of release, and for a moment she had been able to breathe. When she heard what had actually happened, she had been flung back into darkness. The inner darkness had never quite left her since.

After Bruce had called her the night before at around

7:00, telling her that Charlotte wanted to see him, and where, she had tried to reassure herself. He had said, "I don't know what she wants. It may be nothing at all, but I thought you'd better be prepared. If it's unimportant, I won't call you back."

It could so easily have been nothing. Charlotte was naturally secretive. She could spend hours of brooding, of mysterious comings and goings, of complicated figuring with paper and pencil, to announce triumphantly that she'd found a new way of circumventing an upholsterer's estimate or of how Natalie could fit in a round of social visits.

Eve had tried to tell herself this in the shop, holding cold hands to the fire or walking up and down the floor, watching the clock and waiting for the telephone to ring, until she couldn't stand it any longer. If everything was really all right, Bruce would go to the house and get Natalie and they would drive away together. She would know when she saw him. A glance from a distance as they came out would be enough. She wouldn't be seen; the darkness would hide her. So she had gone down to the Square.

But she hadn't taken the fog and the crawling traffic into consideration, and it was twenty minutes of 8:00 by the time she got there. There was no sign of Bruce or of Natalie; there was nothing but blackness and fog and the sickness of agonizing uncertainty. That was why she had gone into the house, opening the door quietly with her key. She had determined to see her aunt and find out whether Charlotte had seen Bruce and herself before the fire that afternoon and, if so, what she meant to do. She hadn't seen Charlotte, or anyone else. Her adventures in the house had been exactly as she described them to the Inspector.

All during the dreadful day she had told herself wearily that whatever was lost, Natalie at least had been

saved. Now she listened to the echo of Sergeant Jabowski's words and the inner darkness rose in poisonous
clouds, filling her eyes, pressing against her eardrums,
stopping the breath in her throat. *"No,"* she whispered
again.

Charlotte had been killed with a rifle—and Bruce's
rifle was in his apartment.

She had seen the tip of the barrel that morning, where
it rested against the wall behind the golf bag. The other
guns, Hugh's and Natalie's, her own little .22 with the
kick to it, Gerald and Alicia's Remingtons, were up in
the house in Eastport. But Bruce's was here, in New York.

Eve knew little or nothing about the science of ballistics. She had never been interested in hunting and
shooting, as the others were, had had a tendency to fire
the pretty little rifle Natalie had given her with her eyes
shut. She had a vague notion that you could tell if a
certain bullet was fired from a certain revolver but no
idea whether this held true of other weapons. She did
know that the finding of a rifle in Bruce's apartment
would be a catastrophe.

It would bring everything out into the open: Bruce's
telephone call to her after he got Charlotte's message, the
reason for it, and the real reason for her journey to the
Square the previous night.

The rifle mustn't be found.

She lit a cigarette and turned round slowly. Firelight,
subdued voices, the tinkle of a spoon, the dull bloom of
the silver pot in Alicia's hand; tea had been brought in a
few minutes earlier. The scene was almost exactly as it
had been 24 hours ago, except that Charlotte's solid un-
bending presence had been replaced by Susan's easy
grace. The red wing in her hat flashed. Hugh was looking
at her and saying something and smiling. On the other
side of the hearth Alicia and Bruce and Natalie were
talking. Natalie's arm was through Bruce's and her

smooth young head was tawny against his uniform.

How, Eve wondered, was she going to warn Bruce, so he could go and get his rifle and put it in a safe place until the one that killed Charlotte was discovered? She couldn't warn him without attracting the attention of the others. Yet the rifle had to be taken away.

Bruce's trench coat was across a bench in the hall. Perhaps his keys were in one of the pockets. She went through the archway. The hall was empty. Its big shadowy emptiness was frightening. Where had the detectives gone? Were they on their way to 11th Street now? She must hurry. She put on her things, went in to the fire and said to the assembled group, "I've got to go. Clara Long will be wild; she's got Christmas shopping to do and I promised to be back early."

Bruce didn't say anything; he didn't look at her. Natalie said, "Oh, Eve dear, can't you stay?" She seemed to feel the need of people around her.

Eve thought with a stab of pain, *She has Bruce, isn't that enough?*—and was appalled by the fierce quick thrust of jealousy. Bruce was Natalie's. As much as one person could belong to another he belonged to her. She looked down into her half-sister's narrow, sensitive face. Natalie's eyes were swollen with crying. Suddenly Eve saw her, not as she was, but as a long-legged child with two thick fair braids, running into the house with her school-books under her arm, or coming in from a ride in her first hard hat on her first pony, and declaring that Eve, home from college, should have one too. "She's got to or I won't. I won't!" She was the most generous, the most open-hearted person in the world. Remorse and tenderness swooped over Eve.

She stooped and put a hand on Natalie's shoulder, gave it a little squeeze. "I'll be back later, Nat dear. And do stop worrying and thinking about things. There's nothing you can do, and if you go on like this you'll make yourself ill."

Outside the front door she glanced along the quiet street bounding the Square on the west. A soldier and a girl, a woman with a pom, an elderly nurse with two children, a man in a polo coat with his back to her, looking through the railings into the hidden park. Eve shivered. There were no policemen in sight.

The light was gray under a pressed-down, heavy sky. The air was cold. Without any particular reason, as she descended the steps and turned left, Eve thought of the man with whom she had collided in the fog when she left the night before. What was he doing there, idling in front of the house? He hadn't stopped to light a cigarette, or anything. He was just standing still.

She gave herself an impatient shake. What did it matter? He wasn't anyone she knew. The Square behind her, she walked rapidly south and then east. Would Mr. Graham be in Bruce's apartment? If so, he would admit her. Suppose the police were already there? Worry about that and about how she was going to get hold of the rifle, what she was going to do with it, when she got there. If Mr. Graham wasn't in—

She refused to think further. Turning into Eldon Place she slowed, approaching the brownstone house in which Bruce was staying, warily. Light traffic was going by in the street, trucks and private cars spaced the curb sparsely at intervals, a scattering of pedestrians with bundles, a street cleaner with a cart, a plumber's van, *McCracken's Plumbing Shop At Your Service—Any Time, Any Place;* there was no one who looked remotely like a detective or a policeman anywhere in the vicinity.

If Eve had turned then, she might have recognized the man in the polo coat who had been peering through the railings in Henderson Square, looking into a florist window at the other end of the block. She didn't turn; she mounted the steps and pressed the third-floor bell.

The latch chattered noisily and her heart gave a great leap of thanksgiving. She ran quickly up the stairs, raking each hall with an exploring and fearful glance. They were all empty, innocuous. Graham opened the door of the apartment.

Eve smiled at him. "Again, Mr. Graham. We *are* making nuisances of ourselves, aren't we? I lost an earring this morning. I wonder if I could have dropped it here. May I come in and have a look?"

Graham was charmed. They searched the living-room together. Eve rose from beside a chair with the missing silver trinket in her hand, where it had been all the time. "I wonder, now that I'm here—the police are simply infesting the house on the Square, my shop—whether I could sit down quietly and rest for a little while. I know you're busy with a story and I don't want to keep you. I think if I just close my eyes. . . ."

Graham threw his work away. There was no rush about it. He fussed, fetching a footstool, a cushion for Eve's head. How was she going to get rid of him? Graham himself helped her. Would she have a Scotch, or he could shake up a cocktail? No, she wouldn't have either, but she would like a cup of tea. There wasn't a pinch in the house? Oh, then it didn't matter.

Graham said it did. It wouldn't take him five minutes to nip round to the delicatessen on the next block. Eve smiled at him gratefully. He was very kind—a cup of tea *would* do her head good; she'd put the kettle on. . . .

As soon as the outside door closed, she locked it and re-entered the living-room. Bruce's rifle was there, behind the golf bags, invisible except for the tip of the barrel. She picked it up, thrust it down in among the sticks, threw the cover over the top, fastened it and slipped the catch into the lock. If she was stopped, if she met Graham when she was going down the stairs, she could invent an excuse for her hasty departure and explain the bag by saying she was going into the country and was borrowing the sticks.

But first, before she left, call Bruce. It would only take a second, and if she didn't call him and the police asked about the rifle he might say it was here. She carried the golf bag into the hall with her, propped it against the wall, took the receiver off the hook and dialed the Henderson Square house.

If Natalie or her father or Alicia answered, what should she say? Her calling Bruce would look decidedly queer. Could she disguise her voice? The idea was both ludicrous and distasteful. She didn't have to put it into operation.

One of the maids said distantly, "Mr. Flavell's residence," and Eve asked for Lieutenant Cunningham. Bruce came on at the end of a long minute. By that time Eve was on fire with impatience. Words tumbled out of her. "Bruce, I'm at your apartment. Charlotte was killed with a rifle. I heard a detective say so. I couldn't talk to you in the house. . . . I didn't want the police to find your rifle, not yet, not till they discover who killed Charlotte."

At the other end of the line Bruce laughed. "Eve, you idiot," he said softly. "Look, my pet, you're playing with dynamite. Don't be so ambitious. Leave the rifle where it is. I didn't kill Charlotte. If you've got any such notion in your head—get rid of it."

He seemed maddeningly unaware of the danger he was in. Eve said desperately, "Bruce, I'm going to take the gun to the shop with me. Then if—"

She paused. The hall was warm, dim; coldness washed along her arms, down her spine. A sound that wasn't Bruce had come along the wire. It was small and fragmentary, a tiny almost imperceptible click. It was, or could be, someone putting one of the extensions in the house in the Square back into place.

Bruce must have heard it too, for he said in a hard

curt voice. "All right, my dear, I'll get in touch with you later," and hung up.

Eve dropped the instrument into its cradle shakily and got to her feet. Fear was around her again, a huge net into which she blundered at every step. She told herself that she might have imagined the click; it might have been made by the operator, by someone calling the apartment. The fear didn't leave her. . . . She had to get out of here at once. She picked up the golf bag and started for the door. She was at it, with the knob in her hand, when she heard the footsteps, and the voices. Men, two or three of them, were coming up the stairs.

Eve had locked the door behind Phil Graham. The shrill ringing of the bell, the knuckles rapping briskly against the panels thudded against her with a physical impact. The police were in the hall outside. They had come to search the apartment for a rifle.

She backed away from the door, clinging to the bag. She had to get out of here. Her shoulder hit the wall— she couldn't get out. There was no rear exit, no other door. In a moment Graham would come back. And then—

Graham did come back. He bounded up the stairs. Voices in the hall were a jumble. They moved closer. Eve stood motionless. There was a roaring in her ears. The sound of the key in the lock pierced the clamor. It was tiny and final. This was the end. She ran her tongue over dry lips and closed her eyes.

Chapter Eight

WAKE UP, WAKE UP!

EVE'S INERTIA, HER PASSIVE ACCEPTANCE of the inevitable, didn't last for more than a fraction of a second.

Outside the door of the apartment a detective said, "What's the matter, Mr. Graham? Haven't you got the right key?" and Philip Graham said, "It isn't the key—the key's all right—that damn night latch has slipped again. . . . This is about the fifth time."

Inside the door the poison of lethargy drained out of Eve. She understood what was happening. Graham had guessed that she didn't want to see the police and was trying to help her. Without being aware that she had moved she was at the door, had her fingers on the brass latch. It fell softly into place.

If the sound was audible to the men outside in the hall there was no immediate reaction. Eve didn't wait for one. The respite was only temporary. The police would be in the apartment in a matter of minutes, one way or another. Her brain was functioning again, coldly and clearly. She had to get out of here. There was no rear door, no other ordinary entrance or exit—but there was a fire escape. She had looked at the black veranda stretching across the living-room windows that morning.

She tightened her grip on the golf bag, sped into the living-room and threw one of the windows up. Out, now. It was almost dark. She knelt on the fire escape, drew the unwieldy bag after her, put it down on black iron bars and lowered the window. There was no clamor from inside the apartment. Evidently the door still held. Sooner or later the police would get it open. She would have to hurry, and she mustn't be seen.

Lighted windows in the backs of other apartment houses hung the darkness with squares and oblongs of green and lemon yellow and apricot beyond clothes lines and acanthus trees and a wildness of poles. An iron ladder led upward. Eve climbed it, her right hand on the railing, her left arm holding the golf bag to her. It was heavy and unwieldy and it bumped enragingly against the treads. She reached the fourth landing. There were milk bottles on it and a row of empty flower pots. The end of the bag hit something and there was a harsh rattle of breakage. A silhouette moved across the shade of the lighted room inside and a hand reached out. Eve didn't wait. She leaped up the next ladder. It seemed to her that the bag was alive, that it had a monstrous existence of its own. She struggled with it pantingly. She was on the top fire escape. Nothing remained but four rungs going straight up in the air. Could she make it? She had to. Gritting her teeth and leaning perilously backward above purple depth she kept on doggedly climbing, and was up and over the parapet at last and on solid flatness. She blundered on a little way, trying to be quiet and putting distance between herself and the route by which she had come. She halted near a vent pipe to get her bearings and her breath.

The last of the daylight was almost gone, except for a handful of sullen light in the west. Vague shapes rose threateningly on every side, but they were motionless, and didn't converge on her. Gradually she was able to distinguish outlines. Number 2, the house she was on top of, was one of three brownstone houses in a row. Off on the left the sheer wall of an apartment house rose toweringly. There was no escape in that direction. She turned right. If she could find the staircase leading down into the third house, the farthest one along, she might be able to get away. Unless the police were lying in wait for her cunningly, ready to spring out from behind the first door she opened.

She did find the staircase and there were no police. She descended in dimness, listening at every step, holding the heavy golf bag high and clinging to the banister rail. Voices talked behind closed doors, someone hummed a tune, a child cried, a radio blared "Oh, Promise Me." Dust rose in little clouds under her pressing feet. If only she didn't meet anyone! She collided with a man on the second-floor landing.

He wasn't a policeman. He made no attempt to stop her, stood aside courteously. She didn't look at him as she went past. She averted her face, horribly conscious of her burden. A golf bag was scarcely the sort of thing one carted about with one in early December. The first floor, the door, outer darkness. Eve stood still in the gloomy vestibule and glanced quickly along the street.

The plumbing truck was still in front of Number 2. Two men were beside it. They weren't looking in her direction. She went down the three remaining steps, turned west and began to walk rapidly along the pavement, refusing to glance back, fearful at any moment of a hand on her shoulder, a voice calling to her to stop. Ten yards, twenty, there was no hue and cry; she drew a long breath, let air out of her lungs in a tearing sigh of relief and quickened her pace.

Behind her, on the other side of the street, a man in polo coat detached himself from the shadow of a high, brownstone stoop and drifted along in Eve's wake. Two blocks to the north she signaled a cab. She noticed the man in the polo coat then, standing on the corner below, without thinking anything of him.

She drove straight home, ignorant of pursuit, of the eyes fastened curiously on her peculiar burden from the interior of another cab near the garage. Inside the shop, with the batten door closed securely behind her, she put the bag down unobtrusively and walked forward.

Clara Long was seated at the desk at the back, making out bills. She greeted Eve with quiet sympathy. "Poor dear, you look all in." She didn't appear to have seen the golf bag. At any rate, she didn't ask any questions. She knew about Charlotte. Jim had told her before he left that morning. She said the police had been there. They had poked around the shop and had gone upstairs.

When she saw that Eve didn't want to talk about her aunt she added briskly that there had been a half dozen calls, from Mr. Holland and Mrs. De Sange, from customers, and one from Natalie. There were no messages. They said they'd call back.

Pulling off her gloves and hat, hanging up her coat, putting coal on the fire, Eve reflected wryly that she had left herself wide open. She said she was coming straight back here from the Henderson Square house, and Susan and Natalie knew she hadn't. Philip Graham must know there was something wrong, too, but he was Bruce's friend. Bruce could take care of him. To be a good conspirator was an art, she reflected. She had no natural aptitude for it; she would have to learn. The first thing to do was to hide the rifle.

Clare was putting her things on. "You're sure there's nothing I can do, that you don't want me to stay?" she asked. Eve said no. "You're right. I am pretty well all in. It's been rather dreadful. . . . As soon as you're gone I'm going to lock the door and go to bed. I've got a ghastly headache."

She went to the door with Clara, closed the door behind her, and slid the bolt. The shade was drawn. There was no danger of being seen from the street. There was no other means of entrance to the shop, except the little mirrored windows at the back, and they were both latched securely. The last time she had mislaid her key she had come in through one of them by breaking a latch, but it had been fixed and was solidly in place.

She unlocked the golf bag and took out the rifle. It was hard and cold and smooth and so beautifully balanced that it didn't seem heavy. The bag she put under the curtain masking the lower shelves. What should she do with the rifle, where could she conceal it so that it wouldn't be easily found? If only, she thought, she could get up to Eastport and leave it in the game room or slide it into one of the gun racks with the others, but to leave New York would be dangerous—until later, any-how. Perhaps she could make it tomorrow. Meanwhile—

The phone on the desk rang. She jumped, and glared at it angrily. Why couldn't people leave her *alone?* Let it ring, she decided; she had no intention of answering it. But the shrill summons filed at her nerves, and it was a tremendous relief when it stopped.

She looked around frowningly. The police had already been here and she had handed her revolver over to the Inspector. It was scarcely likely that they would search the shop again, soon. But they might. Under the stairs was too obvious a hiding-place; so were the closets. She tried the rifle in among stocking boxes and it stood up like a sore thumb. Behind the bookcase was just as bad. She couldn't put it under her mattress or in a bureau drawer.

The decision was taken abruptly out of her hands. Someone was rapping on the front door. The rifle joined the golf bag behind the flimsy curtain. Eve stood erect and tried to stop shaking. She hadn't answered the phone. She wasn't going to answer the door, either. She smoothed damp palms against the wool of her skirt, pushed hair back from a throbbing forehead.

Who was outside on the pavement demanding admit-tance? A truck was going by. The singing of tires, the squeal of brakes—someone called her name. "Eve." It was Jim. He wasn't alone. Gerald and Alicia and Susan and Bruce and Natalie were with him. Standing close to the door she could hear their voices. "She *must* be in," Jim said. "I'm worried about her." Natalie said, "If she's not here, where *can* she be?" Her father was there, too. "Isn't there a back way in, Nat?" he demanded impatiently. "Knock again, Gerald."

If she didn't open the door they might— Suppose they got really upset and sent for a policeman? That would be nice. That would be lovely. Eve retreated soundlessly and came on, making her footsteps loud. "Coming," she called, and turned the key in the lock and opened the door.

They surged into the shop in a body. Jim kissed her. "Where have you been all day? I've been trying to get you for the last hour?" She murmured something evasive and greeted the others. They had come to tell her the news that was no news. The police were searching the house on the Square, Gerald and Alicia's apartment, for the rifle with which Charlotte had been shot and killed. Had she by any chance brought hers down from the country. If so—

She said she hadn't.

Natalie's slim height was buttoned into a black Chesterfield. Her skin was very white and her eyes were enormous. She looked frightful. So did Gerald. Their father was scornfully amused. "They can look the house over and welcome. I simply prefer not to be there. But if they break anything, they'll pay for it."

Eve played hostess with what energy she could summon: "Come on back. Let's sit down." She pushed chairs into position, put coal on the fire, offered cigarettes. Jim helped her. She tried to respond to the warmth in his eyes, to the pressure of his fingers on her arm, tried to answer him coherently.

Bruce was with Natalie on the little sofa in front of the hearth, sitting close to her, an arm along her shoulders. She was leaning against him as though she were cold. Eve thought despairingly, *I've got to talk to him. He's got to find some way to get that rifle out of here. But how can I talk to him with all those people around?* At her elbow Jim said quietly, "What is it, darling? You're worried about something. Have the police been at you again?"

Eve threw him a smile and turned a little and tried to catch Bruce's eyes, but he was looking down at Natalie playing with her engagement ring, twisting it to and fro.

Eve tried to deny the pain which assailed her. Weariness and fear put a nightmare quality into the lights, the shifting figures, the warmth and comfort of the familiar little room, with the fire glowing under the white mantel on which the clock ticked unheard. She could feel Jim beside her, loving her with a devotion that was big and solid and sure, and across the rug, less than five feet away, the man in whom she was absorbed, wrongly, dreadfully, was talking in a low voice to Natalie, the sister she loved, no matter what her faults, and would rather die than hurt.

Her eyes moved. They touched the curtains behind which the rifle was hidden—and Charlotte had been shot with a rifle. Standing there, leaning against the mantel, Eve had a sudden sensation of seeing them all as animated masks, secretive, unreal, acting out preconceived roles that had no connection with what was actually taking place. The suggestion of strangeness where no strangeness should have existed was queerly frightening. It shoved back the barriers of the known and sent her spinning into a lost world of terrible surmise, incredible conjecture. Could one of them, her family, her friends, have killed Charlotte?

Alicia was roaming about beyond Susan. Eve recalled idly that, according to Jim, there had been a marked hostility between Susan and Charlotte in their one meeting, a chance meeting in the Square a day or two before

Charlotte died. Alicia picked up a satin bra and held it out admiringly. "Why doesn't someone tell me these things?" she said vivaciously. "I didn't know you had stuff like this, Eve. How much?"

Eve said out of a dry throat, "Seven-fifty." Her charming sister-in-law was standing not three feet from the particular curtain behind which the gun was thrust, insecurely, and showed every intention of continuing her explorations up the counter. She had to get her away from there. She said, "Come and look at these," and took a box of lacy slips from the floor under the desk and opened it.

There was talk after that, a discussion of rifles in general, of wind velocity and angles and distance; they didn't stay much longer. Before they went, Gerald insisted on mixing a cocktail. He always did. A visit to anyone, anywhere, would have been incomplete without it. He busied himself with glasses, with liquor from the cabinet in the corner, ice from the tiny chest upstairs.

When was she going to be able to talk to Bruce, Eve wondered dully, as she found some crackers and cheese and speared olives out of a bottle. She mustn't give the impression of wanting to hurry them away. If only they'd go, she thought, and she could speak to Bruce alone and get him to take the rifle and throw it in the river. It was impossible. He was engrossed in Natalie, didn't give her so much as a glance, and she couldn't call him aside and start whispering to him in a corner.

Gerald's cocktail was awful but she drank it down. Alicia was in a conversational mood. She said, balancing her glass and a cigarette in a long jade holder and looking from Eve to Jim, "What about you two? What about your plans? Are you going through with your marriage, or are you going to put it off?"

There was a small silence in the green-walled room with the fire glowing redly and sending up little tongues of blue flame. Jim said with a shrug of his big shoulders, pushing hair back from his high forehead, "Well, after all, it's hardly decent to—Charlotte isn't buried yet and—"

Eve said quickly, looking at an intricate design in the border of the worn Bokhara near a chair leg, "I don't see why we need to wait. Of course, yes, I suppose, for a day or two, but after that—"

Natalie roused herself and sat up. "I think you're quite right, Eve. No girl likes to have her wedding put off." She looked accusingly at Jim. "I don't understand you men," she said to him sharply. "You rush a girl off her feet and then when the weather changes you change your mind with it." Her voice was edged with hysteria. She was beginning to shake a little. The day, and all that had happened, had been too much for her. Her freckles were miniature copper pennies and her mouth was a blur.

Bruce put a hand on her arm. "Hold it, baby," he said and grinned down at her. The smile didn't go any farther than his lips. He didn't look at Eve. Jim had turned very red. Alicia said with a little laugh, "They're trying to make an unwilling bridegroom of you, Jim. Don't pay any attention."

Jim didn't answer. His eyes sought Eve's and she gave him a nod of understanding. Natalie was beginning to recover her composure. She said contritely, with a quick rush, "I'm a fool, Jim. I didn't mean that. It's just my nerves."

Eve shoved her glass in from the edge of the table. That was Nat all over, she thought, with irritated tenderness; she was as volatile as quicksilver, down one minute and up the next.

Jim said gruffly, "Don't give it another thought, kid."

Bruce put an end to it. He got up and pulled Natalie to her feet. "Far be it from me to break up this gathering.

I don't know about the rest of you, but I'm starving. Come on, young woman."

Alicia did her lips and Susan threw furs over her shoulders. They were dining at a quiet place Gerald knew of where they wouldn't be stared at. They wanted Eve to go, but she refused. Jim asked her to go somewhere alone with him. She pleaded a headache. "I'm going to have a cup of soup and go straight to bed."

He looked at her quietly and agreed. "You are tired. You need a rest. I'll be around first thing in the morning and we can talk."

It dawned on Eve then that they were to have been married tomorrow and she had done nothing whatever about it, had scarcely given her wedding a thought all day long. She couldn't worry about it now. Tomorrow was another day. But her heart twisted when Jim kissed her lips lightly, without insistence. He was so *good*. Tears moistened her lashes. She blinked them away. The good-byes were endless.

Gerald touched her cheek with a gloved forefinger. "Not too hot, are you, baby? Take it easy."

"I will, Gerald. Good night, Father. Good night, Natalie dear. Good night, Sue, Alicia."

They were gone. Once more the door was closed and locked and bolted. Eve leaned against it wearily. The visit had been nerve-racking, and a lot of valuable time had been lost. Detectives were searching the house on the Square, Gerald and Alicia's apartment. Suppose they came back here? They might, at any moment. She must hurry.

She got the rifle out from behind the curtain and rested again, against the shelves. It was good just to stay still and do nothing. A curious lethargy weighed her down. How still the shop was after the voices that had filled it. The street outside was quiet too. The garage, the electrical house, the business buildings across the way were

all closed. Distant traffic was a faint roar, rising and falling, rising and—Eve's chin hit the button of her sweater
and she jerked her head up and moved out into the
middle of the floor, her skin prickling.

She had said that she was tired; she was righter than she
knew—she was actually falling asleep on her feet. How
ridiculous, with work to do, important, imperative work.
Go upstairs and throw water on her face and open the
windows there, she decided, the place was too hot. Her
forehead was wet and the rifle was heavy in her hands.
Her fingers didn't seem to have any grip to them. She
was still half asleep. *Fool*, she raged at herself, *wake up,
wake UP.*

The water helped but only for a minute or two, then
fatigue was back over her again, a paralyzing cloak that
wrapped her in thick clinging folds. She picked the rifle
up from the bed where she had laid it, looking longingly
at the bed's flat white surface and turned away. She
couldn't sleep until she had disposed of the gun, safely.

Where could she put it? The shop had no cellar, no
convenient pile of coal. An umbrella stand, a deep one,
would be good. She could wind tape around the barrel
and make it look like a stick and leave it out in the
open. There was an umbrella stand in the hall closet
in the house on Henderson Park; there was no umbrella
stand here.

Cellar, umbrella, cellar, the words went round mean-
inglessly in her aching head. Tears of rage and frustration
stung her eyes. What was the matter with her, why
couldn't she think. The chair beside the dressing-table
was coming toward her. The flowers on peach-colored
chintz grew larger and larger and then retreated to pin
points in the oddest manner, as though they were on a
trolley and the trolley was running away on tracks.

She went to the basin and threw more water on her
face and the fog of weariness lifted a little. There was no

hiding-place up here; downstairs was better. The mouth of the staircase yawned blackly, the door at the foot of it was closed. She was tumbling down the staircase; no, she was going down mincingly, the rifle absurdly clasped to her breast, a cold hard doll with one long leg.

She stumbled out into the shop, hit a metal stand with sweaters suspended from it. They were flat, brightly colored bodies swaying emptily on a gibbet. The lights hurt her eyes. Sit down for a moment to rest, she thought, and she would be all right. It was only seven. The clock on the mantel burred and struck seven wheezy strokes. She dropped into the nearest chair and closed her eyes. The darkness was lovely, a deep swinging bed. She lay back on it to rest for just a minute and fell soundly asleep in the armchair beside the desk, Bruce Cunningham's rifle clasped loosely in the crook of a relaxed arm.

Chapter Nine

CLIENTS, OLD FRIENDS, AND A PATIENT

IT WAS ALMOST EIGHT O'CLOCK that night when the reports, for which Inspector McKee had been anxiously waiting, came through from the Medical Examiner's office and from Charlotte Foy's doctor in Vermont. Meanwhile, McKee knew nothing of Eve's activities, where she had been, or what she had done. He was busy elsewhere.

Spencer Gorham, the Boston lawyer Charlotte had been going to see, arrived in New York early in the evening. His train was late. Due at 5:33, it didn't get into Grand Central until 6:20. Kent and the head of the Manhattan Homicide Squad met Gorham at the gate by arrangement.

The lawyer was a small spare man with a dry manner, an immense bony forehead, and frosty, twinkling blue eyes. "I thought I ought to come down to look after Miss Natalie Flavell's interests, you know," he said, shaking hands with the two officials. "Her mother's people, Jane and Alex Corey, who are also clients and friends of mine, are pretty much upset—not to speak of the young man she left behind her. Hah—I mean young Everet Corey. Pity that match didn't go through, pity Natalie engaged herself to this fellow Cunningham. But there it is. Young people—when they take the bit in their teeth—what can you do?"

Gorham hadn't dined and the three men proceeded through the great lofty waiting-room, crowded with the usual traffic, to the Commodore Grill. Seated at a table near the bar the lawyer discoursed, at length, over a plate of scrod and a hearty dollop of scotch. He had been surprised and shocked at Charlotte Foy's death—but not as much of either as he might have been under other circumstances.

"I knew there was something up, Inspector, something in the wind. Yes." He squeezed a lemon and nodded.

He said that Charlotte had first gotten in touch with his office at around the beginning of November. Unfortunately, he wasn't there; he had spent the entire month West, on business, and he didn't return to Boston until yesterday, the morning of the 2nd. In the meantime Charlotte Foy had called twice. His secretary said she wanted to get in touch with him as soon as he got back, that the matter was urgent, so late the afternoon before he called her at the Flavell house on Henderson Square.

Charlotte hadn't said a great deal over the phone. What she had said was rather startling. "She had seemed," Gorham pursed his lips, "I don't know just how to put it, Inspector—not so much afraid to talk because of physical circumstances such as, for instance, that she might have been overheard, but because—well, it was as though she were picking and choosing her words, so as more or less to prepare me for information of some magnitude, without coming into the open with it, then and there."

As far as the lawyer could recall Charlotte's actual words, she had said, *"I've got to see you, got to tell you something. It can't go on any longer. It mustn't. It's very terrible. You will have to help me."*

Gorham put down his fork and reached for the salt. "Naturally, I was alarmed. I tried to get her to speak more freely. I asked her questions. I asked whether the communication she had to make, whatever it was she had discovered, had anything to do with Natalie. She said, 'Yes—yes,' and then she added, 'I'm—frightened,' in a disordered sort of fashion that had me genuinely worried. But I couldn't get another word out of her. No— she seemed to pull herself together after that. She said she had to go to the bank in the morning and that she would take the one-fifteen from Grand Central and would drive straight from the station to my office as soon as she reached Boston. She asked me to have her will ready because she intended to make changes in it, and hung up. That was about all. Well, Inspector, what do you make of it?"

McKee took a sip of dry sherry and dragged at a crumpled cigarette. The long, low-ceilinged room was blue with smoke. He looked beyond it, at Charlotte Foy at the telephone and in the beautiful hall of the house on Henderson Square, and the unplaced group of men and women who could have overheard her. The call, the prospective trip, were important. He had felt it all along. He was sure now. He said, "What was your own reaction, Mr. Gorham? What did you think? You know these people, I saw them for the first time today."

Gorham ordered another scotch and communed with the pale amber liquid in his glass through half closed eyes.

"Well, Charlotte's reference to Natalie was pretty disturbing." He quoted her. " 'I'm—frightened.' What was she afraid of? Whatever it was, it wasn't for herself. It had something to do with Natalie, with a threat to Natalie. Charlotte was crazy about the child, you know, her whole life was wrapped up in her. That's why I came down. Hugh Flavell may be Natalie's father, but I'm in charge of her affairs and I've known her since she was born."

He explained the girl's circumstances. Natalie had been independently wealthy before the war, with the estate left to her by her mother. With the war, her holdings, a good many of them in munitions and airplane parts, had quadrupled. From a comparatively modest eight or nine hundred thousand, she now had properties worth four or five millions. In spite of taxes and the law of diminishing returns, she was an exceedingly rich young woman. The entire estate had become her own on the 10th of the previous April, when she reached the age of twenty-one, but she had retained Gorham to take entire charge of her affairs.

"What was the financial arrangement before last April, during her minority?" McKee wanted to know.

Gorham said that, as Natalie's duly appointed guardian, Hugh Flavell had been allowed an annual income of $15,000 a year for her care and upbringing. He said shrewdly, "There could have been nothing wrong there, Inspector. Accountants went over the records regularly. I'll be fair. The Coreys, Jane and Alex, have always considered that Hugh Flavell feathered his own nest very well indeed. Of course he benefited by Natalie's income —but you could scarcely expect him to separate himself from a daughter of whom he's very fond and set up an establishment of his own. No, no, whatever Charlotte was going to tell me, I don't believe it had anything to do with a misappropriation of funds. As I said, Natalie's her own mistress and can do as she pleases. And even if such a state of affairs did exist, she would never prosecute."

The sherry was bitter on McKee's tongue. "In case of Natalie's death, to whom would her money go, Mr. Gorham?"

Gorham coughed. He lit a cigar. "Entirely unethical, Inspector, entirely—but in view of—yes. In strict confidence, of course? Well, at my insistence, Natalie made a will on her twenty-first birthday. In the event of her death, half her estate would go to Bruce Cunningham, the fellow she's engaged to, and the other half would go to Hugh Flavell for life with a handsome allowance for Charlotte. On Hugh's and Charlotte's death, their half would be divided equally between Gerald and Eve Flavell. But—good God, Inspector, you don't think—"

"Certainly not," McKee assured him. "It's just to get the picture clear. And now Charlotte Foy's will, the will she spoke of changing when she reached Boston?"

"One-third of her property goes to her niece, Eve Flavell, two-thirds to her nephew, Gerald. How much would it have come to? Not more, I should say than, oh, perhaps forty thousand all told. Originally Charlotte had nothing of her own, but she came into a nice little property through a distant cousin in, let me see, back in '35, I believe. The farm in Vermont where she spent the summer was part of it."

McKee looked fixedly at a row of bottles; Eve Flavell again. Charlotte had been going to change a will under which Eve stood to benefit to the tune of $13,000 or $14,000. He threw the implication away. Whatever else might or might not induce Eve to commit murder, money would have nothing to do with it. He was sure of that. Her brother, Gerald Flavell, however, was another kettle of fish.

He went on shuttling back and forth between the present and the past. What had Virginia, Natalie's mother and Hugh Flavell's second wife, died of?

"Pneumonia following an influenza, following on childbirth," Gorham said. "She had never been very strong. Like Natalie, she had been very slender and with a tendency toward anemia. She never really got on her feet after Natalie's birth."

Could Gorham remember a Susan De Sange, a young widow? Gorham could and did. "Tall, handsome creature with fine eyes. Lived next door to the Flavell's in Eastport, in the little cottage at the foot of the lawn. Yes, yes."

"Hadn't there been some sort of"—the lawyer swirled ice and drained his glass—"unpleasantness between Charlotte Foy and Susan De Sange in those days?" There had been, he was positive of it. On a visit to the house in Eastport following Virginia's death, he had been struck with Susan. Later he asked Charlotte about her and Charlotte had been grim. She had said that Susan De Sange was not the sort of woman she cared to have around the house, that she wasn't a good influence for the children.

"To tell you the truth," Gorham said, his eyes twinkling, "I thought at the time that Mrs. De Sange was too attractive. Naturally, Charlotte wouldn't have been pleased to have Hugh Flavell marry again. She was fond of the children and to have them, and perhaps Hugh, taken away from her by a younger, and a very handsome woman, wouldn't have been pleasant."

The lawyer also knew Jim Holland, the man Eve was going to marry. Holland's mother had come from Boston and was a friend of Virginia's. Hugh Flavell had tutored the lad for his entrance exams to college. "I remember young Holland as a great gangling lump who was always getting under foot and turning a fiery scarlet. Good Lord, he's not mixed up in this?"

McKee shrugged. He pointed out that the only glimmer of a motive for Charlotte's murder that they had so far been unable to unearth was inherent in what she had been going to disclose when she reached Boston. She had been shot down less than two hours after she announced her impending journey. The people who were in the house when she made the announcement were all automatically under suspicion. They would remain so until the rifle that had killed her was found and its ownership and possession, from 6:50 until 8 p.m. on the night before, were firmly established.

At the thought that his call might have been instrumental in bringing about Charlotte's death, Gorham was appalled. He offered to do anything he could to help. McKee accepted his offer. The Boston lawyer was familiar with Charlotte's financial affairs. There was a chance that if he looked over the contents of her desk he might be able to tell them what the secret visitor to her room was after, and whether anything had been removed. Spencer Gorham agreed to the suggestion as soon as it was made. Kent closed his notebook and the three men left the Commodore and drove downtown.

McKee was glad to get back to the office. A feeling of pressure, of the need for haste, dogged him naggingly. Yet everything possible was being done.

He was wrong. He had no sooner entered the long narrow inner office than the joint and agreeing reports arrived, from the Medical Examiner's office and from Dr. Steven Harris, in Bennington, Vermont.

There was morphine in Charlotte Foy's body. It had been prescribed by Dr. Harris. Each pill in the missing box contained 0.15 gram. The dosage was heavy. Anything less would have done Charlotte Foy no good, Harris said; the poor lady had acquired a high tolerance.

Fernandez, the Chief Medical Examiner and McKee's friend, said, "A couple of those pills would put a normal man or woman out of the running—for good, Christopher. The lethal dose is from two-tenths to five-tenths of a gram. The effect? Diminishing body temperature, coma, and death due to respiratory paralysis. If you know anyone who's liable to get any of them, you'd better go to work fast."

Chapter Ten

BLUE BOX OF DEATH

McKEE DID GO TO WORK. He used the telephone, talked to a half dozen different men and raced through reports. Detectives searching the Flavell house on the west side of Henderson Square, Alicia and Gerald's apartment on the east, Jim Holland's rooms and Bruce Cunningham's temporary domicile for the rifle that had killed Charlotte Foy, had been ordered to look for the blue pasteboard box that had contained the morphine. In each instance the results were negative. The same thing went for Eve Flavell's shop, which had been gone over earlier in the day.

What now had to be done, the Scotsman decided grimly, was to search these people individually. It wasn't a pleasant job, the effects of not doing so might be still more unpleasant—the morphine had not been removed for fun.

According to the latest bulletin, the Flavell family, accompanied by Bruce Cunningham, Susan De Sange, and Jim Holland, were dining at the Cedars, a small and very ultra restaurant on East 52nd Street. Eve Flavell wasn't with them. At least she hadn't gone with them when they left at a little after 6:30.

McKee rang Eve's number. There was no response. He called the local precinct and told them to send a man around to see whether the girl was there and deliberately not answering the phone for any reason, or whether she was out. If she was out the detective was to wait until she got home and call back immediately.

He blamed himself furiously afterward for not going to the shop then and there, at once, in person—but, as

Commissioner Carey pointed out, he had no reason to suspect what had happened. Philip Graham had successfully thrown the homicide detectives off the track in the search of Number 2 Eldon Place, during the later afternoon. His hocus-pocus about the latch had sounded convincing. He had explained that it was a trick arrangement that had been installed by a former woman tenant following a murder in an adjoining street, and that it was continually giving trouble. He had finally gone up the fire escape from the apartment below and had opened the door from the inside, all of which had given Eve Flavell plenty of time in which to get away.

As far as the men watching the house from the interior of the plumbing van parked at the curb went, they didn't know Eve Flavell by sight, and although her entrance had been noted, they had supposed her to be visiting one of the tenants. If she had come out with her burden she would have been spotted and stopped. She didn't come out.

Nevertheless, in spite of his lack of information, when McKee left the office on the third floor of the 10th Precinct at a few minutes before eight that night, he was uneasy and on edge. He didn't at all care for the way the case was going. More than ten hours had elapsed since Charlotte Foy had been found shot to death inside the high railings of a small private park in the middle of the city, and they had made remarkably little progress. It was true that they had uncovered a number of leads, but these would take time to follow, and with the box of morphine tablets abroad, *and* the lethal gun, time was the one commodity they couldn't afford—not if a second tragedy, following hard on the heels of the first, was to be prevented. Murder bred murder as naturally as a guppy spawned eggs. No one knew that better than the Scotsman. He drove straight to the Cedars, accompanied by detectives Wise, Visniski, Peterson, and

Gish, and by two policewomen. They waited within call, in the shadow of the two tall trees that gave the place its name. McKee went inside.

The Cedars was one of those elegantly quiet places that made its innings on the staggering check. McKee had been there before, in dinner clothes and with an innocuous front, on several unostentatious missions. The head waiter hurried into the small square hall shedding greetings and smiles. The Flavells? But *"Oui, Monsieur, certainment."* McKee said, "Where," and was told. He waved aside an escort and paused in the doorway of the long stately inner room dim in candlelight and looked over men and women's heads and the sparkle of jewels, at the people he had come in search of. The Flavells were at a table to the left of the fireplace at the far end.

It was not a festive occasion for them. Of the lot Hugh Flavell was the only one who seemed moderately cheerful. Natalie, her pale head hatless above a black gown, sustained herself with obvious effort. She was between Bruce Cunningham and her brother Gerald. Jim Holland was next to Alicia, who shared Hugh Flavell with Susan De Sange, on his other side. Flowers, candles in antique silver holders, the soft clash of knives and forks, the discreet hum of voices; it was the first time McKee had seen Gerald Flavell and he studied Charlotte's nephew curiously.

Gerald Flavell had his father's features; he had Eve's eyes with the extravagant dark lashes. He was strikingly handsome and—a little soft? A man who paid his way with charm ("that's the only thing I've plenty of, baby")? It was a quality that could be a curse to its possessor, as well as to the recipients. Gerald was younger than Alicia by perhaps four or five years. She adored him. Bruce Cunningham was moody and abstracted. Jim Holland was bored.

McKee's gaze moved, and his brows rose. A man at a

neighboring table was watching the Flavells. The man was alone. He was short, middle-aged and thickset, with powerful shoulders and a clever, dissipated face. The Scotsman detached himself from the doorway and started forward.

The members of the Flavell party were not, with the possible exception of Jim Holland and Natalie, glad to see him. He was direct. The corner of the long narrow room was secluded—except for the man at the next table. McKee kept him within his field of vision while he told them, in a modulated voice, of the disappearance of Charlotte Foy's pills, pills that contained morphine.

"For your own sakes," he concluded quietly, "I'm sure you'll agree to the personal search that has been suggested."

The police were invariably handicapped in making such a proposal. The disentanglement of an endless amount of red tape would have been necessary before it could have been legally enforced. On the other hand, a point-blank refusal would in itself be suspicious. They all agreed, with various expressions of alarm, surprise, wonder, and indignation. When would the search take place? At their convenience, as soon as they had finished dinner. McKee said he had matrons and detectives waiting.

Dessert had been served but appetites were destroyed. Natalie stared at McKee, flushing and paling. She knew something, he decided, not necessarily about the morphine but something she hadn't told. Susan De Sange was openly shaken. Chairs were pushed back, cordials lowered, napkins flung down. The check was paid by Hugh Flavell, out of Natalie's black suede bag, at her insistence. "There are two fifties there, Papa."

Hugh Flavell looked at the Scotsman icily, a spot of color high on each cheek. He was a man in a fever, holding himself in check in the face of an illegal, impertinent, and altogether outrageous intrusion on their private lives. "I suggest, Inspector, that we return to the Square."

McKee shook his head. "It will be simpler and easier if the search is made here, Mr. Flavell. I can assure you that you will be treated with courtesy—and I'd like you to realize that this is as much for your own protection as for anything else." He didn't add that there were too many ways of getting rid of a small blue pasteboard box in a drive of more than two miles.

They rose in a body. McKee moved aside to let them pass, and stared. Mrs. De Sange knew the man at the next table who had been watching the one in the corner. She was startled, and for the fraction of a second, angry and frightened at seeing him there; her back had been toward him while she was seated. She nodded stiffly in his general direction and moved on with Hugh Flavell, the red wing in her hat making a bright flash in the gloom. The others, Cunningham with Natalie, Jim Holland with Alicia, and Gerald Flavell lighting a cigarette and bringing up the rear, obscured McKee's view of the stocky man with the heavy shoulders and the keen, knowing eyes. It was a pity, in the light of ensuing developments. The other diners couldn't give him any information later. They hadn't even noticed what was taking place, the whole scene had been so quietly concluded.

There were detectives waiting to receive the party in the hall. As Gerald Flavell passed him McKee turned and surveyed the luxurious disorder of the abandoned table. A cherry tart, ice cream in silver goblets, a glass of chartreuse, another of brandy, coffee cups; there was nothing informative. He let a glove fall to the floor, stooped to retrieve it, glanced at the taupe carpet under the folds of damask and remained in a motionless crouch.

There was no longer any need to search the Flavells or Mrs. De Sange or Bruce Cunningham or Jim Holland, the man Eve Flavell was going to marry. The blue pasteboard box was lying under the table, almost in the exact center of the loose grouping of pushed back chairs.

McKee reached. He picked up the box with his glove. He opened it. It was half full of the deadly little pills. It had been dropped or thrown to the floor by some member of the Flavell party, because the thief who had removed it from Charlotte Foy's bath cabinet knew it would be found in his or her possession in the course of a search—and because the purpose for which it had been taken had already been—

The shadowy candlelit room faded out. McKee was through it and in the hall. There was no sign of the Flavells or their guests. Peterson and Wise were standing at the foot of the stairs. The Scotsman threw them orders in passing, including a summons for Medical Examiner Fernandez. The air beyond the door was cold. A few snowflakes twisted down. He crossed the pavement, jumped into the waiting Cadillac, gave the address of Eve Flavell's shop and said carefully, his voice flat, expressionless, "I've got to get there in a hurry. Step on it, will you, Edwards?"

Edwards stepped. The journey that would ordinarily have taken a full quarter of an hour consumed only a few minutes. The street outside the little building between the electrical supply house on one side and the garage on the other was dark and silent when the Cadillac slowed around the corner and slammed to a stop. McKee was out of it while it was still in motion. The precinct man detached himself from shadows. "Miss Flavell ain't here, Inspector. I knocked and—"

The Scotsman brushed him aside. He rapped and waited, rapped again and didn't wait. He took out his pistol and smashed a hole in the plate-glass window. Edwards helped make the hole larger. McKee went through it, paused only to unlock the door and raced toward the back of the shop.

The lights were all on. Eve Flavell was lying in front of the burned-out fire, half on and half off the armchair beside the desk. She had fallen sideways. Her head hung down. Her face was blue, engorged. Her breathing was heavy, monotonous, mechanical. It filled the little room, bounced back from the walls. The long shining barrel, the chestnut stock of a rifle, lay stretched out on the rug at her feet.

The Scotsman didn't look at the rifle. He bent over Eve. He said harshly, "Coma," and gathered her up in his arms. The door at the front of the shop opened. The Chief Medical Examiner, Fernandez, hurried in. He was a slim, dark, elegant man with bright hazel eyes. He strode the shop's length. He took a look at the unconscious girl McKee was holding. He lifted an eyelid. Eve's pupils were pin points. He touched her cheek. It was cold, clammy. Her breathing had slowed. Respiratory paralysis had set in. He said, "Morphine, yes. . . . She's dying, McKee. I don't know—we can only try. . . . Give me that bag."

Chapter Eleven

WAITING AGONY

"GOOD NIGHT, DARLING."

"Good night, Nat, dear."

At the foot of the steps in front of the house on Henderson Square Natalie looked up at the tall man in uniform beside her, the gold insignia on his cap flashing in the faint light coming through the fan above the door. She raised her face and Cunningham bent and kissed her, lightly. At a step on the pavement they drew apart.

It was Hugh Flavell, on his way home from seeing Susan De Sange into the lobby of the Trianon around the corner.

The four of them had driven down in one cab after that terrible and distressing scene at the Cedars; Jim Holland had taken another with Gerald Flavell and Alicia. It was twenty minutes of 10:00. The night was nasty. Sleet was beginning to fall and wind wailed through the black trees across the street.

Natalie laid a gloved hand on Bruce's sleeve. "You're sure you won't come in?"

"No, dear," he said firmly. "You're desperately tired. What you need is a good sleep. I'm going straight home to bed and I want you to do the same." He touched her shoulder, said good night to Hugh Flavell, and walked away into the icy darkness.

Hugh Flavell stood where he was for a moment, looking after the flier's retreating figure. There was a peculiar expression on his handsome, high-nosed face. It wasn't exactly friendly, the watching detective noted from the shadows a few yards farther along. Natalie was at the open door above, her tall slenderness framed in a narrow oblong of apricot. She said, "Coming, Papa?" and her father joined her and the door closed behind them.

Across town, in the shop on 19th Street, the Chief Medical Examiner was busy with the stricken girl. Fernandez said afterward that he never worked harder over anyone in his life than he did over Eve Flavell on that stormy December night.

In the beginning he held out very little hope. The unconscious girl was carried to the bed in the long narrow bedroom on the floor above, and nurses and an oxygen tank were sent for. Hypodermics of strychnine in small doses were given, and a heart stimulant was administered.

Eve had been discovered by the Scotsman in a dying condition at a little after 9 p.m. At 10 o'clock there was no change, but at any rate she wasn't any worse. By 11:00, her heartbeat had picked up slightly, her breathing had eased and her body temperature was beginning to rise. But Fernandez said warningly that she was by no means out of the woods. It was still touch and go.

Meanwhile the rifle that had been lying on the rug in front of the hearth at Eve's feet had been sent to Headquarters. Before it was removed, McKee examined it. The model was familiar to him. It was a .351 self-loader, manufactured by the Winchester Repeating Arms Company and was used extensively by the FBI, as well as for deer and other four-legged game. McKee ran his eye over the plate attached to the oddly shaped stock. The patent marks were there: *August 27, December 10, '01; Feb. 25, '02; Feb. 17, Dec. 22, '03; Aug. 21, Oct. 30, '06; July 5, '10.* It had been purchased subsequent to 1910. There was no difficulty in establishing the .351's ownership.

The rifle belonged to Bruce Cunningham. It was registered in his name in the Permit Bureau at Headquarters.

McKee talked over the phone to the detectives who had been sent to search the rooms on Eldon Place where Cunningham was staying while he was on leave; he also talked to Philip Graham. The golf bag in which Eve had carried the rifle was unearthed. The manner of her exit from the third-floor apartment via the fire escape while Graham, with mistaken chivalry, had pretended to fumble with the key in the hall outside the locked door didn't detain the Scotsman. Why she had gone to so much trouble, did. He shoved conjecture impatiently aside. Charlotte Foy had been killed with a bullet from a rifle— but there were plenty of them in existence and there was no proof, yet, that the lethal bullet had come from Bruce Cunningham's gun. They would know in a short time. Until then there were certainties closer to hand.

Eve had been put out of the running by the man or woman who had dropped or thrown the box of morphine capsules under the table in the restaurant on 52nd Street. Whoever had poisoned her in all probability had eliminated Charlotte Foy. So the killer had to be someone who had been (1) at the shop earlier that evening and (2) at the Cedars when McKee reached there.

The list wasn't extensive. Seven people, and seven only, fitted the requirements. They were Hugh Flavell, Natalie, Gerald and Alicia, Susan De Sange, Jim Holland, and Bruce Cunningham.

Empty cocktail glasses stood about in the room at the back of the shop: on the desk, on a table under the window to the right of the fireplace, on the mantel, on the top of the bookcase. In no other place in the building was there a sign of Eve Flavell's having eaten or drunk anything else. McKee used the telephone, and Daligan and Grant, a fingerprint man, came up from Centre Street. The unconscious girl's prints were taken and her glass was isolated. It was one of the two on the table under the window. Dried sediment in the bottom would have to wait for a qualitative and quantitative analysis, but during a pause for rest and a quick drag at a cigarette Fernandez put the tip of a scooping finger to his tongue and said, "No doubt about it, Christopher. She got the stuff in this. Someone dumped the contents of a couple of those capsules of Charlotte Foy's into the girl's cocktail and gave it a whirl with the cherry on the end of a toothpick. Who fixed the drinks?"

McKee didn't know. He found out a few minutes later.

Jim Holland had called the shop around 9:30, during those first anxious minutes when both Fernandez and McKee were afraid Eve was going out. Acting on the Inspector's directions, a detective told Holland, "I'm sorry but Miss Flavell can't come to the phone just now." The engineer muttered something indistinguishable in reply and hung up. But he didn't accept the dictum. He drove from his rooms on Kossuth Street to the Henderson Square house, where he picked up Natalie. They arrived at the shop together in a state of thorough alarm at 11:15.

Natalie's narrow white face was distracted between wings of soft pale hair. She hadn't stopped to dress carefully. She was hatless, and under the mink coat she had thrown on, the silver buttons of her lime green suit were fastened crookedly.

"What have you done to Eve?" she demanded imperiously, walking up to the Scotsman and pausing squarely in front of him. The nostrils of her delicate nose flared, freckles stood out on her white skin. Her pretty mouth was a red line.

Holland was equally upset. "Yes," he said, anger thick in him, "what has Eve done that the police—why couldn't she come to the phone?"

It would have served no useful purpose to conceal the girl's condition from her half-sister and the man Eve Flavell was going to marry. McKee told them what had happened. He said, "Miss Flavell was poisoned with morphine taken from the cabinet in Miss Foy's bathroom in the house on Henderson Square."

Natalie stared at him blindly, her eyes round black stones. *"Poison!"* she whispered, *"Eve!"* and fumbled for the nearest chair unsteadily and dropped into it, her self-possession stripped away. She wasn't a smart streamlined young woman with a fortune tied to her apron strings and a habit of command; all at once she was a bewildered child, knocked topsy-turvy and fighting ghosts in the dark.

Jim Holland gripped the back of the chair in which she sat huddled. He glared redly at McKee. He seemed to have difficulty with his breathing. "Where is she—Eve?" his stick rapped the floor sharply. "Where is she now?"

Holland started walking around aimlessly. "Is she going to get better? . . . She *has* to." His big face, ordinarily ruddy, was putty-colored.

McKee shrugged. "She has an even chance. If she recovers she'll recover fast. We'll know within an hour."

Natalie gave a cry and hid her face in the crook of her arm.

McKee said quietly, "If you want to help Eve Flavell, you'll pull yourselves together," and began asking them questions. They answered dully, lethargically, ears tuned to footsteps and voices on the floor above. They had seen nothing suspicious here in the shop earlier that evening nor in the restaurant on 52nd Street, so they declared. It was Gerald Flavell who had mixed the cocktails before they went to dinner. Natalie raised her fair head and looked pallidly at McKee. There was terror in her eyes. "Oh! But Gerald wouldn't—" she faltered. "No, never. . . . Why, he loves Eve. . . ." Holland swore steadily, his eyes heavy-lidded, half closed.

Certainly if either of these two had given Eve a dose that had so nearly proved fatal, they were remarkable thespians, the Scotsman reflected—but it meant nothing. One of the seven people, and only seven, could have dumped the morphine into Eve Flavell's glass. . . .

Outside, wind blew and sleet slapped thinly down.

The whisper of starched skirts intruded. One of the nurses was coming down the stairs. At what she said, weight took itself away from McKee; and Natalie sat up, her face illuminated with a light that made her look slightly mad; and Holland said hoarsely, his voice a croak, "Thank God—oh, thank God."

Eve wasn't out of danger, but she had taken a turn for the better and Fernandez was more sanguine. After a word with him, McKee let Holland and Natalie see her for a moment.

Eve's sleeping-quarters were in striking contrast to Natalie's gold-and-white bedroom in the house on the Square. The shop's upper floor was one long narrow room with a diminutive bath opening out of it. A maple bed, a bookcase, a highboy, a small vanity case, and two chairs were adequate but not luxurious. A reproduction of Sarnoff's Winter Wood was sharply black and white against one wall, where Eve could look at it when she woke in the morning.

It was then just short of twelve o'clock, and while Fernandez was beginning to hope, he was by no means fully satisfied. Eve might or might not look at the Winter Wood again. Her eyes were closed. Thick dark lashes were half moons of shadow on her lovely worn face. Its contours had been accentuated by the near approach of death. One lax hand protruded from under the blankets. A nurse held a finger on the wrist and eyed a watch.

Fernandez stood close by with a hypodermic in readiness. He gazed with interest at the stricken girl's half-sister, at the man she was engaged to. Natalie approached the bed slowly, as though she were afraid of what she was going to find. She looked down and gave a sudden hard, dry sob that was like a cough and dropped to her knees. Holland stood just behind her, big and solid, transfixed. His lips opened but no sound came through. He looked as if he were being torn apart.

Eve was stirring. Fernandez nodded, and the Scotsman touched Natalie's shoulder and motioned to Holland, and all three of them walked toward the stairs. McKee went down first, Natalie following slowly on Holland's arm. The Scotsman stepped out into the long narrow shop. It was empty and still as it had been when they left it a minute or so earlier. The door and the windows were all closed. The curtain across the alcove under the stairs moved a little. He glanced at it and then away as Natalie went past him and sank into a chair and began to cry. Sobs shook her long slender frame, doubled forward over fingers that wrenched at each other in her lap. "I can't *stand* it," she said in a broken voice. "First Aunt Charlotte, and now Eve. She looks so dreadful—what does it mean? Why should anyone want to hurt Eve?"

Holland leaned heavily against the mantel and stared down into the replenished fire. The clock on the shelf, a ridiculous little clock with a loud tick, struck twelve. He raised his eyes and looked at the clock. The whites rolled. They were threaded with tiny red veins. He said in a low voice, "We were to have been married tomorrow. . . ."

McKee told them that the worst was over. Fernandez corroborated him a couple of minutes later coming down for a puff of a cigarette. When he crushed it out and returned to the second floor, McKee said, "There's nothing more either of you can do here. Miss Flavell will probably sleep for hours. What she needs most now is rest and quiet. And so," he smiled at Natalie, "do you. Will you take this young woman home, Mr. Holland?"

Natalie rose obediently and drew her mink coat around her and wiped her eyes. She opened her purse. "Money?" she said. "What about money? Those nurses—Eve will need care. Suppose I leave a check. I haven't more than a hundred dollars in bills with me—"

But McKee waved the check aside. "It's on the police, Miss Flavell."

Holland took her arm. "We can see Eve tomorrow, Inspector?"

"The first thing in the morning," McKee promised, and on that they said good night.

McKee watched them through the door. It closed behind them. The untenanted little room at the back of the shop was warm and quiet. The curtain across the deep closet at the foot of the stairs hung in straight, unstirring folds. McKee looked at it. He said, not moving, "You can come out now, Lieutenant Cunningham."

Chapter Twelve

BLUFF AND FATIGUE AND STRAIN

"THANKS, INSPECTOR."

The curtain was lifted, and Bruce Cunningham, First Lieutenant in the Army Air Corps, uncoiled his length from the wall against which he had been propped, dipped his head for the lintel, and walked out into the shop. The flier's tanned face was tightly planed and his eyes and mouth were narrow, grim, but he wasn't abashed or nervous or in the slightest degree discomposed. He shrugged his Army overcoat into place, went past the desk to the hearth, took off his cap, knocked wetness from it, laid it on the mantel and turned.

McKee moved an ash tray an inch on top of the bookcase beside which he stood. "You came here to get your rifle, didn't you, Lieutenant?" He studied the flier thoughtfully.

Cunningham nodded without haste. "That's right."

"You knew Eve Flavell took it from the rooms on Eldon Place and brought it back here with her early this evening."

"Yes," Cunningham said, "she told me so over the phone late this afternoon, while I was in the Henderson Square house." He looked around. "Where is it?"

"It's down at Headquarters being tested," McKee answered pleasantly. "Charlotte Foy was killed with a bullet from a rifle."

Cunningham smiled. One eyebrow went up crookedly. "Not with a bullet from my rifle, Inspector. I didn't kill Charlotte. When I went to meet her on Wednesday night, the rifle was in the Eldon Place living-room, leaning against the wall beside the bookcase. It was some other gun that put Charlotte out of the way."

The Scotsman let the assertion pass. There were plenty of rifles in the world and there was no proof that Cunningham's .351 was the lethal weapon. The Lieutenant moved to a chair, hitched it closer to the fire, sat down, and leaned toward McKee.

He said in a steady voice, "I was stunned when I overheard in there—" he waved at the curtained closet— "what happened to Eve. I didn't know she was in any danger. . . ." He looked into the fire. "When the doctor came downstairs and said she was going to be all right—" He gave his dark head a shake, squared his shoulders and drew a long breath. "This is the point—" he turned more directly toward McKee—"Eve did a very foolish thing when she went to my place this afternoon and took the rifle and brought it back with her. But there wasn't anything I could do to stop her. When I was here with the others earlier this evening, I had no chance to talk to her alone or to get the rifle from her then. That's why I came back a little while ago."

McKee said, "Yes, I see. But would you mind telling me why you didn't come out in the open, Lieutenant? Why you hid in there in that closet under the stairs?"

Cunningham examined the toe of a polished brown shoe. "When I walked in here the shop was empty. Then I heard Natalie upstairs, heard her coming down. . . . I didn't know what happened. Natalie had nothing to do with this gun episode. I didn't want to pull her into it anyway. She's had enough to bear as it is. My intention was to get my rifle and take it to the police myself. The simplest and easiest thing to do when I found that Natalie was here was to get out of sight until she and Jim Holland went. Then, while I was in there, I heard about Eve."

The Lieutenant turned away. "I was in a spot. I didn't know quite what to do. While I was thinking it over,

Natalie left." He got up, propped an elbow on the mantel, faced McKee squarely. "That rifle of mine didn't kill Charlotte, Inspector. You can count on it. I repeat, it was in the living-room on Eldon Place when I left to go and meet Charlotte at the north gate of Henderson Park on Wednesday night."

The Scotsman started to answer and stopped. Instead, he asked Cunningham a number of questions. The flier's answers were straightforward and jibed with what he already knew. In spite of himself, the head of the Manhattan Homicide Squad was impressed. Here, he thought, was a man who had risked his life, day after day, for months, battling Zeros over the Pacific. He had carried out dangerous missions with daring and skill. He wore the Order of the Purple Heart on his breast. Was such a man likely to have shot down an elderly and defenseless woman out of the dark? It didn't ring true; it was neither logical nor convincing. On the other hand, this was a crime in which murder was wearing a mask, and an extremely clever one. Someone in that group of people around the table at the Cedars had discarded the box of morphine capsules when its usefulness was at an end. . . .

The wind kept on blowing and the sleet kept on coming down. Without warning one of the little mirrored windows, the one to the right of the fire, flew open and let darkness and a slam of icy particles in. McKee raised his eyes. He stared at the black oblong open on the night. He got up and went to the window and looked out. Less than two feet away the walls of the building in the rear rose sheerly. But there was a narrow alley behind the shop that on investigation angled crookedly to the street farther along the block. The catch of the window was released from the inside. The only thing that held the little casement in place was the tightness with which it fitted into its frame.

McKee pushed it open and shut it a half dozen times

without a word. Behind him, Cunningham said, "What is it, Inspector?"

"Oh, nothing, nothing at all," the Scotsman said airily. But he had received a blow. It was a hard one. The air-tight case involving seven people, and seven people alone, had broken down with a crash. Now it was anybody's game. Eve Flavell's glass, the glass into which the morphine had been dropped, had been standing on the table below the sill. He touched his fingers to the green wood.

Cunningham got it. He looked from the window to the table to McKee's face. He said, "The morphine could have been dropped into Eve's glass by someone standing out there. . . . There was a lot of confusion and noise here and people moving around."

McKee didn't answer. He stood erect and abandoned the window, but not its implication. He wanted the man who was watching the Flavell table up there in the restaurant on 52nd Street. He reached for the phone.

Wanting wasn't having. In the turmoil attendant on the finding of the box of morphine tablets the man who had roused the Scotsman's interest earlier had slipped away. It wasn't of any real importance, or it didn't seem to be, then. While McKee was in the middle of orders to have the man traced, the other call came through and with it, except for minor details, to all intents and purposes the case was washed up, finished, and at a successful conclusion.

The experiment with Bruce Cunningham's Winchester, the results of which Sergeant Cutts of the Ballistics Bureau communicated to McKee at 1:15 a.m. that morning, had taken time. It wasn't the first of its kind in the Henderson Square murder. Before the discovery of the bullet that had killed Charlotte Foy, other weapons had been collected from the various people involved.

There was Eve Flavell's Colt, and a museum piece, a

revolutionary blunderbuss that had been removed from over the mantel in the Gerald Flavell's apartment; there was an old Army revolver belonging to Jim Holland that had been his uncle's and that had been recovered from the bottom of a trunk in his rooms; and there was a curious and interesting weapon belonging to Hugh Flavell, a walking-stick shotgun of European manufacture that Flavell had picked up in the Pyrenees in 1930. All these weapons had been duly discharged as a matter of routine. They were automatically discarded after the discovery that Charlotte Foy had been killed, not with a shotgun or a pistol or a revolver, but with a bullet from a rifle.

Bruce Cunningham's .351 was checked in at Headquarters at 10:30. At around 11:00 it was tried out. The procedure was simple in its early stages. A test bullet from the .351 was discharged into the open end of a long wooden box, packed with three feet of cotton, backed up by another six feet of cotton waste. The lid of the box was unhinged and the bullet dug from the waste at the far end, encased in a clinging cocoon of cotton in which it had wrapped itself.

It was lifted out tenderly, tagged, and conveyed, with the .351, to the room on the floor above with the bright lights and the microscopes, where Sergeant Cutts went to work. The lethal and test bullets stood side by side under twin microscopes. The Sergeant's all-seeing eye moved from one series of lenses to the other. He revolved the leaden slugs gently, and peered and made notes and peered again. Men wandered in and out of the room at intervals. Cutts paid no attention. He was one of the best ballistics experts in any police department in the world and his word was practically law on the witness stand—but you couldn't hurry him.

He made his announcement at the end of almost three hours of study. Charlotte Foy of Henderson Square West had been shot and killed with a bullet from the .351 Winchester repeating rifle that belonged to Lieutenant Bruce Cunningham.

Cutts sewed it up so tightly that there wasn't a hole a midget could slide through. There was no question of any fooling with the barrel, any trick. Whole and complete and entire, just as it stood, Bruce Cunningham's .351 was the murder weapon, beyond the possibility of a doubt. Cutts talked to Inspector McKee himself.

In the shop on East 19th Street, with the fire low and sleet tapping at the now closed casement windows with squares of mirror for panes, McKee listened and dropped the instrument slowly into its cradle. He looked past the gold eagle on the cap on the mantel at a pink china shepherdess leading a mild brown cow into infinity on top of a bookcase, and then he looked at Bruce Cunningham.

"I'm sorry, Lieutenant," he said, "but I'm afraid you'll have to come with me."

"I congratulate you, Inspector, I do indeed. It was nice work—and, for once, quick. I couldn't ask for a prettier case, I really couldn't. It's just about perfect."

John Francis Dwyer, New York's short, chunky, dynamic District Attorney, blue-eyed and with hair the color of May butter, rubbed his hands together happily in the big room at the end of the corridor in the long gray building on Centre Street. It was 10 o'clock on the morning following the attack on Eve Flavell. Commissioner Carey sat behind his desk and nodded his agreement. McKee stood at one of the windows looking out.

The facts were simple, and damning. The rifle with which Charlotte Foy had been killed not only belonged to Lieutenant Bruce Cunningham, but Cunningham, and Cunningham alone, had had access to it at the time the crime was committed.

The flier had been taken into custody at 2:15 that

morning. After a quiet denial of having given morphine to Eve Flavell and a reiteration of his innocence about Charlotte Foy, he had made no further statement.

The Scotsman's continued silence began to get on Commissioner Carey's nerves. "Well, McKee?" he rapped out at last.

The Inspector turned from the window. "It's all been said, hasn't it?"

"You're convinced Cunningham is our man?"

"My conviction is neither here nor there, Commissioner," McKee answered. "It's a question, now, of proof. The ownership of the rifle isn't the important thing—or not the most important. Guns have been stolen before and used and thrown away or replaced. As far as this case goes, there's just one loophole. Graham, one of the two men with whom Cunningham has been staying, says that the .351 was in the apartment on the day Charlotte Foy was killed. That's a lot of hours to cover. The defense will undoubtedly be that the gun was removed by another person prior to the shooting and returned after it had taken place."

Dwyer snorted genially. "Nothing doing. No, sir. . . . Wait a minute, Graham's outside. Would you like to talk to him, Commissioner? Good." He pressed a buzzer and Philip Graham, Bruce Cunningham's unlucky friend, was brought in, tired and unshaven and in a fog. A writer by profession, he had handled crime for years, in fiction; he had found fact something else again. He retold his story for the hundredth time. Boiled to its bones it was simple and damning for the Lieutenant.

The .351 had been in the apartment for months. Graham had noticed it particularly on Wednesday morning because the dog knocked it to the floor. As McKee pointed out, there was a possibility that it might have been removed later on that day. Graham and Joe Buchanan, the man who shared the apartment with him were in and out; how it could have been returned was another matter.

Bruce Cunningham had said in a previous statement that he left home at a few minutes after 7 p.m. on Wednesday evening in order to keep his appointment with Charlotte Foy at the north gate of Henderson Park. Apparently he had lied. He did leave the Eldon Place apartment at a few minutes after 7:00 but he returned unexpectedly, perhaps a quarter of an hour later.

The writer squirmed in his chair. He hadn't exactly seen Cunningham come back, but he had called to him. After a couple of minutes Cunningham left once more. At that time 20 to 25 minutes past 7:00, Graham and Joe Buchanan were both in the apartment. At around 8 o'clock Graham went out for the evening, but Joe Buchanan remained in the apartment all evening, working on a drawing, and when Graham got back at a little before 12:00, Buchanan told him that the evening had been quiet and that there had been no alarums and excursions and *no callers*.

A statement from Buchanan himself was unavailable at the moment. On the morning following the murder, before Charlotte Foy's body was discovered, he left New York to visit his aunt. Graham didn't know where this aunt, a Martha Denham, lived. He had said he would be back at the end of the week.

After a few more questions Graham was dismissed and then Bruce Cunningham was brought in. The flier entered the room with a confident step, between two detectives. The Commissioner nodded at them and they withdrew. He said, "Sit down, Lieutenant," and Cunningham dropped into the indicated chair.

He bore the marks of what he had been through since 3 o'clock that morning. His lean dark face was tired, the jaw and sensitive clean-cut mouth were sternly set and eyes, straight-looking intelligent eyes under a good forehead, were narrow with strain.

He would have been a fool if he hadn't been worried. He wasn't a fool. He had acted like one in not disposing of the rifle immediately after he had killed Charlotte Foy with a bullet from it, McKee reflected. This was one of the peculiar features of the case that made him uncomfortable, irresolute.

Innocent or guilty, the flier's composure was genuine. There was no bravado about it. He sat in an easy attitude, knees crossed, shoulders relaxed, a long tall figure in uniform, his head up. He drew a cigarette from his pocket, tapped it thoughtfully on the back of a brown hand and lit it without asking permission. He admitted his return to the Eldon Place apartment after he had, he said, failed to find Charlotte Foy at the north gate of Henderson Park.

"Yes, I went back there."

Dwyer moved in on him. "We know you went back. You went back to put the rifle you killed her with in what you considered, for the moment, a safe place."

"No, Mr. District Attorney," Cunningham answered with a quirk of his strongly marked dark brows, "I went back because I forgot my wallet."

Dwyer laughed. "Well, well, well, so you forgot your wallet? Now isn't that nice?"

Bruce Cunningham remained cool. "I didn't think so at the time. It was a nuisance."

"But what a convenient nuisance," Dwyer purred. "Where were you when you made this—interesting discovery about your wallet?"

Cunningham looked at him. "At the north gate of the park. I had decided that Charlotte Foy wasn't coming and was just about to start around the Square to pick up Miss Flavell when I found that in changing my clothes I had left my wallet behind in my other pocket."

The District Attorney was openly incredulous. "It was raining, then, I believe. . . . Yes. And your coat was presumably buttoned, your overcoat and the jacket of your uniform. Yet standing there in the fog and the rain, you suddenly remembered that you didn't have your wallet with you."

"That's right."

Cunningham smiled. If there were women on the jury, the Scotsman decided, and he smiled like that often enough, Francis was going to need everything he could get on the ball. Bruce Cunningham's face was introspective and a little aloof in repose; when he smiled, it changed, warmed, was gay, devil-may-care and singularly attractive.

His smile didn't produce a softening effect on New York's choleric district attorney. He said harshly, "The Flavells are wealthy people, Mr. Cunningham. You were due at the house in a short time and you're engaged to be married to Natalie Flavell. Yet you walked ten blocks through the driving rain, five there and five back, rather than borrow what money you needed from your fiancée or her father."

The lieutenant remained imperturbable. "I don't borrow money from women, Mr. District Attorney, and Hugh Flavell is not a wealthy man."

His rocklike composure got under Francis's skin. He waved coldly at the desk, at the two bullets and the rifle laid across it, at the report headed *Ballistics Department* beside the rifle.

"We don't need to listen to any more of your lies, Cunningham. Those things tell the tale. You shot Charlotte Foy with that gun. No one else could have got possession of it, and you have no alibi for the period covering the time within which the shot was fired. You're as guilty as hell. Why don't you come clean? Give us a confession. It will make it easier for everyone. If you won't think of yourself, think of that poor young girl to whom you're engaged, of her family. Think of the uniform you wear."

For a startled moment McKee was under the impression that Cunningham was going to break. He sat forward in his chair staring at the gun, at the bullets, with grim concentration. There was pallor under his tanned skin and his eyes, narrowed on the damning exhibit, had a helpless, almost a hopeless gleam to them. He drew a long breath and sat erect.

"Dilly, dally, come out and be killed," he said in a tired voice. "You know, I've often wondered what sort of argument the police used to get a confession, what it was they offered a man in exchange for his life. I know now it's nothing, just bluff and fatigue and strain and to hear you stop talking. You're a smart man, counselor. I'm going to put something to you. You've provided me with opportunity and a weapon. But what about motive? What possible reason could I have for killing Charlotte Foy? That's what I'd like you to tell me. Just that."

He had placed his finger on the weak spot in the State's case. Nevertheless the question was a mistake. He waited too eagerly for an answer. That he had a motive, even though they didn't know what it was, was now certain. Even without motive the evidence against him was overwhelming. He was taken away. A short conference ensued. The result was a foregone conclusion. Before 11 a.m. on Friday, December the 4th, Bruce Cunningham was under arrest in connection with the murder of Charlotte Foy.

Chapter Thirteen

FRAGMENT OF A PHOTOGRAPH

"NO, PAPA, LET ME ALONE—PLEASE." Natalie rose and walked swiftly to one of the front windows in the living-room of the house on the Square and stood there, looking out. The sweeping sea-green draperies framed the gray light of mid-afternoon. The girl's slim black wool back was as straight as a pikestaff and her soft fair hair fell in a motionless and shining wave to her stiff shoulders.

Hugh Flavell, who had been leaning toward her sup-plicatingly, sank back cross-kneed into the corner of one of the deep sofas at the fire with a gesture of despair. McKee leaned on a yellow satin chair, arms folded along the top, and watched them both.

Immediately following the scene in the Commissioner's office, the Flavells had been informed of what had taken place. Natalie hadn't broken down or had hysterics. After an outburst of tight-lipped fury at the stupidity of the police she had gone into action. Within half an hour she had retained Anthony Burchall, New York's most eminent criminal lawyer, to look after Bruce Cunningham's interests.

Whatever else Charlotte Foy's coddling, the swaddling clothes in which she had wrapped Natalie, had done to her, it hadn't made her a weakling, the Scotsman reflected.

At the window Natalie repeated icily, "I don't care what the evidence is, I don't care anything about the rifle. Bruce didn't kill Charlotte. The idea is too ridiculous for words. Bruce wouldn't kill *anyone*."

It was to her father she spoke. Hugh Flavell didn't say anything.

McKee said soothingly, "Don't worry too much, Miss Flavell. The formalities of the Lieutenant's release on bail will be concluded shortly. After all, he isn't in custody on a charge of homicide but only as a material witness."

He didn't add that it had taken all kinds of persuasion to convince the District Attorney that at this point the material-witness charge was a safer bet than a homicide rap, as a precautionary measure, until the evidence should be complete—and that Bruce Cunningham wasn't likely to be out on bail long.

The moment Anthony Burchall informed Natalie that Bruce Cunningham was eligible for bail she had ordered him to arrange it. The bail was stiff. Natalie had dismissed the $100,000 demanded by the court with a few strokes of a pen.

Dwyer was furious but there was nothing he could do about it. He was convinced that in the Lieutenant they had their man and that no further search was required. McKee didn't agree, which was why he advised going slow. He wanted the whole canvass laid bare. He wanted the man or woman with the blood-stained shoes who had searched Charlotte Foy's bedroom. It wasn't Bruce Cunningham; Cunningham was with Natalie when that search was being conducted. He also wanted the photograph with the corner torn off that had cropped up between Susan De Sange and Charlotte Foy shortly before Charlotte died.

He looked absently at the blaze of a burned-orange Degas above a bookcase. Above all, he wanted the missing Buchanan, the third occupant of the Eldon Place apartment, who had been at home from 8 o'clock on, the night Charlotte was killed and whose testimony that there had been no visitors, unless it was changed, would put Bruce Cunningham in the electric chair.

Buchanan had said to Graham of that evening, "No

alarums and excursions and no visitors," which would seem to indicate that no one except Bruce Cunningham could have replaced the .351. But Graham's report was only hearsay, and until they talked to Buchanan himself they couldn't be sure. He was out of New York, visiting an aunt who was ill. Graham didn't have the slightest idea where the aunt lived, except that it was on a farm within a radius of a couple of hundred miles of the city. The search for Buchanan was already under way. In addition, McKee was interested in the gentleman who had been watching the Flavell table in the Cedars and who had so expeditiously vanished. Susan De Sange knew this man.

Natalie turned from the window and began to move restlessly around the room. She didn't look at her father; she was aware of his lack of confidence in Bruce's innocence. She said, pausing beside a coffee table and shifting a crystal box with tight fingers, "Someone got hold of Bruce's rifle, Papa. That's what we've got to prove. It was there, in Bruce's apartment for months. Anyone could have taken it when the apartment was empty. I had a key. Suppose other people had keys, too?"

Hugh Flavell stepped on her mounting hope, cried it down. "Natalie, my poor darling," he said, "stop and think. You lost your key ages ago and Charlotte had been with us here in this house for more than ten days. If someone wanted to kill her with Bruce's rifle—why wait that long?"

Natalie flashed back at him with an accuracy the Scotsman couldn't have bettered. "If Bruce's rifle was used deliberately, Papa—and that's what it looks like— then the murderer couldn't have used it while Bruce was in Washington. That's why he waited. That's why it was done on last Wednesday night. Because Bruce was home and because—" Yes, she had hold of it. She continued steadily, "Because someone heard Charlotte telephone to

Bruce and ask him to meet her that night at a quarter past seven in the Park across the street."

Hugh Flavell was startled, outraged. "Natalie—what are you *saying?* Think. That would mean that it was someone in this house who—"

The girl refused to retreat. "Yes," she said drearily, "I know. But—" She dashed tears from her lashes and turned on her father, "You don't believe Bruce *did* kill Aunt Charlotte, do you?"

Flavell hadn't the courage to say yes. He threw up his hands. "Certainly not."

"All right, then," Natalie answered, and drove him into a corner with remorseless logic. "Whoever did it had to know where Charlotte was going to be—and how could anyone know who didn't hear her telephone to Bruce?"

McKee interposed. He said, "Someone could have followed Miss Foy when she left here that night."

Flavell seized on the suggestion. "That's it, Inspector, you've hit on it, I believe. The telephone call had nothing to do with it. Perhaps Nat *is* right, perhaps someone did want to make Bruce look guilty. Very well, the idea would seem to be that there was someone hanging around outside the house."

It was a possibility the Scotsman had already considered. He returned to the subject of the key to the Eldon Place apartment. Natalie said that Bruce Cunningham had left a key with her when he went to camp in June. She had used it in July, and in the beginning of August, to send him things he wanted, some books and a heavy sweater and, later, some addresses. Then she had lost it. She couldn't say when. All she knew was that when Bruce came home in November he had asked her for the key and she had looked in the compartment in her purse where she kept it and it wasn't there.

McKee quirked mental eyebrows when she told him, her forehead furrowed with concentration, "It's hard to think back, but Father and Susan were with me once, weren't you, Papa? And I think Jim Holland went with me the second time. I met him in the Park; he was on his way here."

"The third time, Miss Flavell?" McKee asked and Natalie said, "I was alone. . . . No, I wasn't. That's right, Alicia was with me. Yes, she loved the woodwork in the window and doorframes."

So they were back to it again, McKee reflected wryly, back to the same people who, if you excluded Bruce Cunningham, could have discarded the box of morphine capsules in the restaurant on 52nd Street. And they were all at large and there was no proof. . . . He took the thought away with him and didn't like it.

Earlier that afternoon Dwyer had gone to see Eve Flavell in the shop on 19th Street. It was unfortunate that he got to her before the Scotsman did. Eve was still weak from the after-effects of the morphine poisoning. Dwyer didn't know her and he attributed the stricken stillness with which she received the announcement of Bruce Cunningham's arrest, seated in a chair in front of the fire against propped pillows, to physical weakness and to concern for her young half-sister. He was completely deceived by her lovely, expressionless face, turned a little away from him, and by her averted eyes and monosyllabic answers.

"You wouldn't want your sister to marry a man like that, come now, would you, Miss Flavell?"

"No. Oh, no."

"You went to the Eldon Place apartment and took Bruce Cunningham's rifle in order to shield your sister, because you didn't want her to suffer—but you didn't know at that time the purpose for which the gun had been used?"

"No, I didn't know."

Inside herself Eve was summoning every ounce of her

strength to ward off collapse. Dwyer was gentle with her. He said that Charlotte had discovered something about Bruce that made him unfit to be Natalie's husband. She had confessed as much to Natalie's lawyer, Spencer Gorham, over the phone on the afternoon of the day she died. "Your poor aunt signed her death warrant when she went to meet Cunningham that night, probably to tax him with what she knew. She played right into his hands. It was a perfect setup for murder. It was dark, and there was a heavy fog and the streets were deserted. . . . Think of his callousness, Miss Flavell. He shot your aunt down, returned the rifle, temporarily, to the living-room on Eldon Place and then took your half-sister out to dinner as though nothing had happened. That was brutal. That was shocking. Have you any idea, any inkling, of what Miss Foy had on Cunningham that made it necessary for him to kill her?"

"No, I'm afraid not. No, I haven't." That was it, Eve thought numbly, sitting very still and trying to rise above the tumultuous black seas that threatened to overwhelm her. That was the very heart of it. Charlotte *had* seen Bruce talking to her in front of the fire in the house on the Square that day and that brief glance had undone all that she had accomplished by the announcement of her engagement to Jim. Yes, Charlotte knew the truth. But Charlotte was dead. The police must never find out —never.

Dwyer went on putting the framework of motive into words. "Your sister Natalie is a very wealthy young woman. Cunningham wanted to marry her money. Miss Foy threatened the marriage, so she had to die."

It hung together horribly. Eve knew it wasn't true. But terror filled her at the completeness of the State's case. She mustn't let it show. She fought for control fiercely. *Don't move,* she told herself *don't speak. Don't give away. Don't let this man guess. . . .*

It began then, perhaps, the bitterest part of the anguish that covered her like flame, devouring her entity, eating the marrow of her bones—and the bitterness consisted in her aloneness. Natalie could grieve openly for Bruce, hers was the right; she, Eve, could show nothing except solicitude for her sister and a vicarious anxiety. But there were certain positive things she could do so that no one should ever guess the truth. She must go through with her marriage to Jim as soon as possible. That was absolutely necessary. Let one hint of the feeling between herself and Bruce come to the surface, and he was lost. She made a little prayer then, and swore an oath: if Bruce were saved she would never think of him again in that way, never, never, as long as she lived.

Dwyer left after asking a great many questions and without having obtained anything of real importance. He was only just gone when Jim arrived at the shop. He was overjoyed to see Eve out of bed. He knelt beside her chair and took her into his arms. "I was afraid last night that I would never see you like this again, sitting up and talking," he said huskily, his cheek against hers.

His bigness, his solidity, his goodness were comforting. He was so unselfish, made so few demands. But almost at once they were quarreling. Jim knew of Bruce's arrest and what had led to it. He scolded Eve for taking the rifle and trying to hide it. "It was all very well to think of Natalie—but look what happened to you."

He refused to admit that Bruce's arrest was an absurd mistake. He said soberly, "It doesn't seem possible that Cunningham did it, but after all, someone killed Charlotte, and the police don't make an arrest on a charge of murder, or in connection with a murder, unless they've got pretty good grounds. . . . All right, all right, darling —if it will make you feel better I'll swear that Bruce Cunningham is whiter than snow."

Jim's tone was indulgent. But his glance at her was

puzzled and—was there a question in it? Eve said quickly, "It will break Natalie's heart, Jim. Oh, she won't say anything—but it will kill her." A cold little tongue of warning was curling round her own sick heart, and she told herself that she would have to school her eyes and her voice, even her thoughts.

To the consternation of the trained nurse left in charge by the Chief Medical Examiner, Eve announced a little later on that she was going out. Jim understood her better than the strange woman. "She wants to see her sister," he said. "Better let her have her way or she'll drive herself mad sitting there and brooding. I'll be responsible for her. I don't see how it can do any harm. I'll see that she doesn't tire herself out and I won't let her stay long."

He got a cab and helped the nurse put her into it and they drove to the house on the Square. When they arrived, Alicia and Gerald and Susan were there. It was dusk. The curtains were drawn and the lamps lit. Natalie's skin was paper white and her bones seemed to have sharpened. When she saw Eve she jumped up and went to her and took her two hands. "Are you all right? Ought you to be making this effort?" she asked anxiously.

"I can totter about," Eve said and smiled into Natalie's eyes affectionately. "I wanted to see you." They exchanged a wordless look. The conviction of Bruce's innocence was strong in both of them, and in them alone, Eve thought bitterly. It didn't matter. Natalie's calm surety gave her renewed strength. Tea was brought in and Natalie poured with an air of proud self-possession that was oddly touching.

Eve sat beside her, facing the others, in a loose semicircle around the hearth, with the width of more than space dividing them. It was evident to Eve that while Hugh and Alicia and Susan, as well as Jim, paid lip service to Bruce's innocence, they didn't really believe it.

Natalie was talking to her in a low voice about Anthony Burchall, Bruce's lawyer, and what he was doing when the front door opened and footsteps crossed the hall. Natalie was facing the archway. She broke off in the middle of a sentence, gave a glad cry and jumped up and started across the floor. Eve was on her feet too. So were the others.

Bruce was coming down the steps and Natalie was in his arms, laughing and crying at the same time. He disentangled himself presently and Natalie threw back her hair and they came over to the fire. Voices were a high babble congratulating Bruce.

He nodded pleasantly, perfunctorily, turned to Eve, looked at her level-eyed. He said, his voice brusque, "I thought you were in bed. Ought you to be on your feet?"

"I'm getting off them now," Eve said, and dropped into the chair she had vacated, her knees wobbly. Seeing him like this, out of jail and free, made her weak.

Bruce didn't turn away from her. He stood there beside the tea tray, tall and straight in his uniform, light glinting on the wings over the pocket of his breast. He said slowly, "You shouldn't have gone to Eldon Place and taken that gun. Look what happened to you. You might have been killed."

You could hear the clock tick. Outside, a cab went by in the street. Eve put her cup carefully on an end table, grayness swirling up around her. What were the others, what was Natalie thinking? Why had Bruce mentioned the rifle here, now, before them? They had to know, she told herself confusedly. But what explanation was she going to give that would sound even faintly plausible.

She didn't have to give any. Natalie did. She thrust her left arm through Bruce's and reached for Eve's with her right. Drawing Eve close, she looked up into Bruce's face and said in clear ringing tones, "She did it for us, darling. Thank God, she's safe."

Tears rushed to Eve's eyes. The bitter irony of the situation, of Natalie's generosity, her lack of knowledge of the real truth, were burning arrows plunged into her breast. The pain was frightful. She felt she couldn't bear it, and knew it had to be borne. She didn't glance at Bruce. She needn't have been afraid. When she did, he was looking away from both her and Natalie, into the fire.

Listening to Alicia's vivacious babble, to her father's measured tones, to a quip from Gerald, Eve resolved fiercely that there was only one thing for her to do. Natalie's happiness was bound up in Bruce. He had to be cleared and she must help. . . . It was then, standing there, that she thought of the man who had been lurking outside the house the night Charlotte died.

She began to talk in a quick, excited voice. She described her collision with him at the foot of the steps in the fog. She said, "He must have been there for some reason. He wasn't just passing by."

Natalie took fire from her tone. "What did he look like, Eve?"

But Eve didn't know. He was a voice in the dark, nothing more.

She realized afterward that if she had been keener at the time she would have had an inkling then. One voice was missing from the chorus of questions, one face was averted in the loose circle around the hearth. It didn't really matter.

On the following day, on a windswept hill 60 miles to the northeast, under a bleak sky from which snow was beginning to fall, she saw the man who had been lurking outside the house on the Square the night Charlotte died, saw him and heard him, and was beset by pain from a new quarter, and as a result of what she saw and heard she came close to death for the second time within 48 hours.

Chapter Fourteen

BEHIND THE MARBLE ANGEL

SUSAN DE SANGE'S HOSTESS GOWN of a dark shade of American Beauty emphasized her height and grace and the frankly mature richness of her undoubted charm. She shook hands with McKee pleasantly and waved him to a chair in the living-room of her suite on the ninth floor of the Hotel Trianon. It was 11 o'clock on Saturday morning.

It was an ordinary hotel suite, but Susan De Sange had done something to it. She was a woman who would leave her imprint on her surroundings, wherever they might happen to be. Magazines and books were scattered about, there were violets in a low green bowl, and a frost of jonquils in front of a mirror perfumed the air.

She was grave but not unduly cast down by Bruce Cunningham's arrest in connection with Charlotte's murder. She said, "I can speak freely to you, Inspector. I've grown very fond of Natalie Flavell. . . . If he—is that sort of man, how much better that Natalie should discover it now, than after her marriage to him. Poor child, it's terrible for her—but she'll get over it eventually. Everything passes."

The flowers were from Hugh Flavell. His card was lying on the mantel. McKee said, "Mrs. De Sange, the other night, in the Cedars, there was a man at a table beyond you, a man to whom you bowed on the way out. Who was he?"

They were both on their feet. Susan De Sange was standing at a table taking a cigarette out of a sandalwood box. She turned slowly. A frown put vertical lines between arched brows on her broad low forehead. She was a handsome woman and she had lived a full life; wonder touched the Scotsman, not for the first time, that she should be emotionally interested in Hugh Flavell. Flavell was all right. At fifty-odd he was good-looking and intelligent enough and his manners were agreeable, but he was narrow, self-centered, set in his ways, and a terrific egotist. He was also, McKee reminded himself, the father of an extremely wealthy daughter. And Natalie was generous. . . . As Eve had said, she loved to give, and no one connected with her would ever want. He made a mental note to look up this woman's financial situation.

Susan De Sange was watching him covertly through her eyelashes. She said musingly, "A man at the Cedars. . . . Oh, now I remember. That was Edgar—Edgar Bently. Of course I know him. He's a cousin of my husband's. But—why do you ask, Inspector?"

McKee told her. "He was watching the Flavell table closely on Thursday night, Mrs. De Sange, when as you know, the morphine capsules with which Eve Flavell was poisoned were thrown to the floor. It's just possible that Mr. Bently saw something, some slight movement that would give us a clue as to who disposed of the morphine. You were more or less occupied with yourselves, but this Mr. Bently, from the position he was in, had you all more or less under observation. And by the way, there must have been a reason for his—interest."

Susan De Sange shrugged. There was weariness and a flavor of resignation in her faint smile. Amusement left her. She ruffled the pages of a book with a shapely hand and sighed. "Poor Edgar. I'm afraid Hugh was the reason. Yes. You see, Edgar's been wanting me to marry him for years and he—well, he doesn't like my interest in the Flavells. I suppose it's a perfectly natural reaction but it's annoying and a bore. As far as the other night goes, I'm sure Edgar didn't see anything important, Inspector. He was here this morning and if he *had* seen anything he would have told me. In fact, to be frank, he would have been glad to."

She explained that Bently was an architect by profession and lived in Norwalk, Connecticut, and that he was in New York on a visit, but she didn't know, so she said, where he was staying. "If I see him again, Inspector, I'll find out and let you know."

"Thank you, Mrs. De Sange."

He reflected that she might, or might not, be telling the truth. Voice, expression, carriage, bearing were all they should have been. As with those others, it meant nothing, McKee reflected. Of all the cases he had ever encountered this was the most truly Jekyll-Hyde. Behind one of these innocuous façades lay the will and the ability to kill ruthlessly, cleverly, and with the bland face of innocence. Evaluated in general terms, Susan De Sange was no more and no less suspicious than anyone so far involved. She was an old friend of whom Hugh Flavell had become enamored when he met her again in maturity. Eve was very fond of her; Alicia Flavell disliked her intensely. Alicia's dislike was understandable. She was working the same side of the street; she was a favorite of Hugh's and made a fuss over him and over Natalie, and she would resent the intrusion of another woman into that circle of—eight millions.

McKee told himself impatiently not to keep coming back to that. The money was not Hugh Flavell's; it was his daughter's, and Natalie was very much alive. The only concrete thing that singled Susan De Sange out for special notice was the photograph that had been torn during her curious interview in private with Charlotte Foy three hours before Charlotte died. These rooms, as well as the Flavell house, had already been searched in vain for the photograph with a corner missing.

He sprang the scrap of photographic paper on her without warning. "Will you look at this, Mrs. De Sange, please?" He held it out to her with a sudden movement and kept his eyes on her face—and knew he was right. Oh, yes, innocent or guilty, this woman had been deeply involved in some fashion or other with the late Charlotte Foy. Susan De Sange was perceptibly shaken by the little exhibit. But she was a lady of parts; she recovered herself swiftly. "You talk in parables, Inspector. I'm afraid I don't quite—"

McKee stopped her. He said in a tired voice, "On Wednesday morning, after Charlotte Foy's body was discovered in Henderson Square, you went to Bruce Cunningham's rooms to get him to do something for you. I believe you wanted him to recover this bit of paper for you from the writing-room in the Flavell house. I can't urge you too strongly to tell me the truth, for your own sake. Whose photograph was it, Mrs. De Sange? Who produced it? Why was it torn? What significance did it have?"

She wasn't going to tell him. Far from it. She gathered herself together and answered with well-assumed astonishment, "You're wrong, Inspector, quite wrong. I—" she paused, stared and frowned, "Now that you mention it I *do* seem to recall that Charlotte had a picture with her when she came in to me in the writing-room, but I don't know whose it was, or what she was doing with it or what, if anything, it meant."

McKee told himself that this was a lie out of the whole cloth. The effort she put into it and her concealed agitation—and more than agitation—were illuminating. Find the original of the photograph and they would be a good deal further along. Whatever the story back of the photograph, Susan De Sange wasn't going to give it to him.

He went a few minutes later but before he left he listened to a one-sided conversation over the telephone.

Hugh Flavell called Mrs. De Sange and asked her to go up to Eastport with them for Charlotte's funeral. She said, "I will if you want me, Hugh, dear, if you think I can be of any assistance. No, no trouble. . . . I've been intending to go up to the cottage anyhow, there are some things there I want."

The Flavells were leaving on the 12:15 from Grand Central. Late the night before, Charlotte Foy's body had been released by the District Attorney's office and shipped to an undertaker in the Connecticut town. Until Buchanan was found, as long as there was a possibility, however slight, that Bruce Cunningham had been framed, these people would have to be kept under observation. McKee thanked Mrs. De Sange and took his departure.

McKee verified the fact that Edgar Bently had called on Mrs. De Sange early that morning. A man answering his description had arrived at the Trianon at 9:30 and, according to the elevator girl and the doorman, he left at around 10:00.

The Norwalk police corroborated Bently as a consulting architect whose cottage in Silvermine was also his office. He was a man of moderate means and kept no servants, and the cottage was locked up, so no further information was forthcoming from that end. To search New York for him would be a long and possibly an abortive task, and the result, if they did manage to locate him, might be disappointing. His interest in the Flavells might have had an amorous origin, as Mrs. De Sange said, and he might have seen nothing whatever in the Cedars. In spite of this, and in spite of the fact that the Homicide Squad was understaffed and that McKee got not the slightest encouragement from either Dwyer or Commissioner Carey, he decided that the attempt to locate Bently had to be made.

Accordingly, Detectives Gish and Wileski began a tour of the hotels, and McKee had a delayed conference with Spencer Gorham, the Boston lawyer who handled Natalie's affairs. Gorham could find nothing wrong as far as the papers in Charlotte Foy's desk went. Charlotte had never apparently thrown anything away and his task had been as lengthy as it was unproductive. Her valuables, stocks and bonds, personal belongings, etc., were in her safe-deposit box at the Grant National Bank. To complete the picture the box would have to be examined. To do this a court order would be necessary, unless the police wanted to wait until the heirs had taken out letters of administration.

McKee didn't want to wait. "You know what ought to be in the box?" he asked, and Gorham said, "Yes," displaying a little green memorandum book that had been in the dead woman's desk.

The Scotsman had done favors for the Grant National's first vice-president. Twenty minutes later he and Gorham were examining a long drawer behind locked gates in the bank's vault. The lawyer consulted the little green book and looked. He looked again and raised a shocked face. $9,000 in war bonds bought by Charlotte the previous June were not there.

Inquiry revealed that Charlotte Foy had visited her safe-deposit box on Tuesday, the day before she died and that on that day she had removed the small old-fashioned wooden chest that was in her packed suitcase when McKee looked her bedroom over. It was possible the bonds had been in that. They weren't there now. Gerald Flavell had occasionally handled an investment for his aunt, McKee reflected, and the good-looking and increasingly hag-ridden Gerald was hard up and owed bills in every direction.

This deduction was apparently wrong. Back at the office McKee found a message from the Fingerprint Bureau waiting for him. The small wooden chest that Charlotte had been going to take to Boston with her had been tested for prints. It had taken time to get a complete set of the men's and women's under scrutiny. There was one set, and one set only, on the polished wood of the chest. They were Hugh Flavell's. The stenographer, Kent, delivered the message to the Scotsman. It had caused a good deal of excitement. Kent said, "What do you think of it, Inspector?"

McKee didn't answer. He looked at the clock on the wall above the green filing cabinet. It was 14 minutes after 12:00, and Flavell's train left at 12:15. He could never make it. Sitting there staring across rooftops gloomy under a sullen sky, he told himself it didn't matter, that the Flavell's were covered, that no member of the party could hope to slip away for any length of time, that they were returning to New York in a few hours and that, besides, he had things to do here, pressing things. Wileski had called in. Susan De Sange's cousin by marriage had been located. Edgar Bently was staying at a small and inconspicuous hotel on the south side of Henderson Square. McKee swiveled around in his chair, pushed a weight from his shoulders, and reached for the phone.

At about the same time, in the long shed in Grand Central two miles to the north and east, Eve Flavell shared the uneasiness and the vague sense of dreary foreboding the Scotsman refused to acknowledge. The chill was bone-piercing and the lights in the car were dim. Eve didn't want to leave the city. She didn't want to go to Charlotte's funeral. She had an impulse then, at the last moment, to get up and bolt to the door and run along the ramp and up through the great station into the open air and the freedom of the streets. As on that other day, the afternoon of the day on which Charlotte died, she waited too long. Out on the platform the conductor chanted faintly, "All Aboard," the doors slammed, and they were under way.

The trip from New York to Eastport wasn't long; it took only a little over an hour. Outside the windows of the fast New Haven train the city merged rapidly into the suburbs and the suburbs into open country studded with towns. Tawny fields and patches of woodland began to flash past. At Greenwich there was a brief glimpse of the Sound, lead-colored under the leaden sky. The Flavell party had been unable to get seats together. Jim Holland and Eve were opposite each other on the aisle, Natalie and Susan and Hugh were farther to the rear. Alicia had gone up with Gerald early that morning. Funeral services for Charlotte were to be held in the Nye Funeral Home, after which she was to be buried in the little cemetery on the edge of the village.

In New York the murder had produced scarcely a ripple; the great city had a glut of sensation and, except for inquiring reporters after Bruce's arrest, they hadn't been bothered. Eastport was going to be different. Hugh had lived there as a young man, he returned every summer, he had been married to Eve and Gerald's mother in the gray stone Episcopal Church under the elms, where the three children, Gerald and Eve and Natalie, had duly been christened. All of them dreaded the arrival in the small town, the formalities that had to be gone through, and the questions, discreet or otherwise, that would be asked.

If it hadn't been for Natalie, Eve wouldn't have come. She was still weak and more than a bit shaky from the beating her system had taken. But the Chief Medical Examiner, who had developed a warm interest in her, had given his consent. "It won't do you any harm. With a thing like that you come up as fast as you go down. Only, don't let yourself get too tired, and don't catch cold."

Natalie had said forlornly the afternoon before, "I wish you could come, Eve, it would make me feel better—but not if it's going to do you any harm." Her eyes were enough. They were worse now. She had changed a good deal in the last 24 hours. Overnight she seemed to have grown five years older. She was as gentle as ever, but her color was bad, and there was a new stern set to her narrow white face that made her look a little like a Joan of Arc in a severe black suit with a big-brimmed black hat covering her soft pale hair. The effect of her wide brown gaze, no longer bright and eager but stony and withdrawn, traveling over their father's face and Gerald's and Alicia's and Susan's and Jim's, exploringly, marked the distance along the road that had separated her from them since the previous day.

She had broken down only once, when she was alone with Eve for a moment last night. Then she had given way to her fears like a mad creature. "They'll convict him, Eve, for something he didn't do. They'll put him to death. . . . I've read stories in the paper, I know. Don't try to deceive me. . . . I can't *stand* it. Bruce—when I think of him behind bars, in a cell." Eve had succeeded finally in quieting her, taking her in her arms, and holding her tightly until she stopped shaking.

"Nothing is sure," she told her. "Nothing will be sure until they get the man who was in Bruce's apartment all evening. Someone, perhaps that man was hanging around outside in the Square Wednesday night before Charlotte went out, will be proved to have gone to Bruce's apartment and put the gun back. That's what will happen, Natalie, I promise you."

Jim had backed her up later, but Natalie's response to him had been cold. She had always been fond of Jim but she turned from him now, as she did from the others, sensing the opinion he didn't express. Her instinct was right. To Eve, Jim had said musingly, "It's all very well to try and keep Natalie's spirits up—but it may be a mistake. It's damned awkward about that gun, you know."

The acid of pain had eaten through Eve's armor at

that, and she had rounded on him furiously. Now they didn't talk about Bruce or his chances. They didn't talk about Charlotte Foy's murder either. In fact, Charlotte hadn't been murdered; she had simply died. That was Hugh. He had set the tone. His late sister-in-law, companion, and close friend had been taken from them by the grim reaper. Sooner or later it happened to everyone. Those near and dear passed on. Well, that was life and there was nothing you could do but submit.

He was really amazing. For a man who could make a most ghastly fuss about a burned muffin or a hard hotel bed, he accepted major wounds with astonishing stoicism. He did it so well, perhaps because he could make himself believe practically anything he wanted to. Had he gone out for his accustomed walk in the park on the night Charlotte died? Eve wondered. Was her father the one who had left that dreadful stain at the foot of the stairs in the lovely old house on the Square?

Let it not, she thought, be Hugh, or Gerald, or anyone connected with her by ties of blood. How would you ever get the poison out of your veins? It was, it had to be, the man waiting so queerly in the darkness and the fog at the foot of the steps the night Charlotte died. Why should anyone wait like that, without a purpose?

A hand touched her arm and she stiffened. It was only Jim, leaning across the aisle. "Don't look now, Eve," he said with a faint grin, "but isn't that gentleman up there near the water-cooler, the one behind the two sailors, a detective? Wasn't he with the Inspector at the shop that first day?"

Eve glanced at a big man in profile beyond two blue jackets at the front of the car who was gazing abstractedly at a baggage rack. It was Captain Pierson; she recognized him at once. "Yes, I think so, Jim," she said calmly, but her heart leaped. Bruce was under arrest, but if the New York police were certain he was guilty why were they having *them* followed and watched? It meant, surely it must mean, that they weren't sure about Bruce.

When they left the train at Eastport she whispered the news to Natalie and Natalie drew the same conclusion. Her face grew bright in the shadow of her hat. Her brightness didn't last. Hugh took her arm and detached her from Eve, as Charlotte had always tried to detach her. "Watch the step, dear." He led her to a long black limousine, and they all got in and drove to the big white house where Charlotte lay waiting.

The undertaker, Mr. Cable, received them at the top of the steps. Inside an organ was playing Handel softly. The big twilit spaces were thickly carpeted and full of the heavy perfume of too many flowers. Men and women were standing in groups or sitting on little gilt chairs. Eve knew some of them. She shook hands with the Smiths and the Bensons, with Miss Judd and the Reverend Doctor Harris, and with Cicely Thwaight, her blooming muted, her sixty-five-year-old skin rosy, her eyes bright with malicious curiosity under her white hair.

There were candles at the head and foot of the casket in which Charlotte lay, dressed in familiar black, her hands folded quietly on her breast. Eve knelt on a gray velvet priedieu and looked down at the woman who had been her aunt and was frightened. She felt nothing, absolutely nothing. With Bruce's arrest, with the terrible accusation against him, her capacity for feeling seemed to have stopped as though her nerve ends had been branded with a red-hot iron and permanently cauterized. She could see and hear, listen and reply, but people and things were an indeterminable distance away on the other side of a glass wall.

Jim knelt beside her. He was crying. Eve was childishly surprised. Then she remembered that he had been fond of Charlotte and that she had been good to him as a boy; she had sent him pocket money when he was at college and loaves of the raisin bread she used to bake. Jim took out a handkerchief and wiped his eyes surreptitiously, and they both rose.

Gerald was talking to Cicely Thwaight near a clump of palms. How he had—dwindled, Eve thought dispassionately. He had been gay and fearless and forthright as a boy, but now he looked beaten. He was only twenty-nine but already there was the foreshadowing of age in his set features, in his receding hair line. Even the shape of his head appeared to have changed. It was smaller and set differently on his shoulders. How crazy Charlotte had been about him as a child and when he was growing up. But he had disappointed her by marrying, and leaving the house and making a home of his own. Poor Charlotte, all her plans had gone awry. She had been so set on a marriage between Natalie and that Boston cousin of the Coreys. Instead, Natalie had engaged herself to Bruce.

What a battle there had been! Strong as Charlotte's will was, Natalie's was stronger. Eve had sometimes thought that if Charlotte had handled the situation differently, Natalie wouldn't have persisted with the engagement. Say no to her sharply and she became determined to have her own way whether she really wanted it or not. It was a natural human instinct. It was highly developed in Natalie. Eve could remember her at seven, screaming herself black in the face because she wasn't permitted to go to the circus with Gerald and a boy from school, and becoming ill, and doctors and nurses being sent for and the house on tiptoe. She had told Eve afterward, her eyes round in an innocent little face, "I can make myself sick. I can have a fever if I want to." If only Charlotte had used tact and judgment, Natalie might have given Bruce up. If she had, Bruce wouldn't— *Stop it,* she whispered to herself and forced her attention back to the dimly lit rooms.

Alicia was wonderful, circulating about, receiving murmured condolences and asking and answering questions. She was at her best at funerals and weddings, Eve decided. She ought to be able to make a fortune with a little handbook on what to do when the undertaker comes. Her black dress was just right, smart without being too extreme; so was her manner. She was competent, sustained and sustaining, sad with the restraint of good taste and full of solicitude for Hugh and Natalie. She glanced at them constantly to see how they were, whether they needed anything.

"Eve," Jim halted beside her. "Are you all right? Wouldn't you like to go outside and get a breath of air?"

He looked thoroughly miserable. Poor Jim, he took things hard, she thought with a pang of mingled affection and remorse. Natalie was like him in that; they were both too easily upset. Eve glanced at her sister. She was standing stiffly between Hugh and Susan, who were talking to the Bensons. Natalie wasn't talking. She was staring straight in front of her, tall and wide-shouldered, and too thin in her black coat and hat, and with no more expression on her face than if she were asleep.

"I don't think we ought to leave Nat," Eve told Jim, and he said compassionately, "Poor kid—no; we'd better not," and they went across to her. The minister appeared in his white surplice then, and everyone sat down, and the buzzing voices stopped. Mercifully the service was short. Ten minutes later they were all in cars driving along Queens Highway under leafless elms and past dead gardens to the cemetery on the eastern slope of a hill that overlooked the town and the river.

The Flavell plot, a big square enclosed in low iron railings, wasn't far from the gate. Eve's mother and Natalie's were both buried there. Eve got out of the car first and started across shorn turf which was hard and dry with frost. A crowd was assembled near the grave. It was made up of old acquaintances and the town's leading trades-men who had supplied the Flavells with the best of everything for years, and with the usual gathering of the merely curious.

She pulled up short, her heart leaping treacherously. Bruce was standing less than 20 feet away, leaning in-dolently against a headstone, looking at her. The brown of his big Army overcoat melted into muted tones of privet behind him. His light eyes probed hers under down-drawn brows that were dark bands in the strong angularity of a face from which the tan of tropic suns was beginning to fade.

Eve stood still. She would have escaped him if she could. There was nothing now between Bruce and her-self, there could be nothing—ever—and these casual con-tacts were incredibly hard to bear. The grave was beyond Bruce. He blocked her path to it. Outside the gates, the others were getting out of the cars. Eve hugged soft gray kidskin tighter to her, smiled briefly at Bruce and said, fumbling for lightness. "Hello, what are you doing here? Aren't you out of bounds or breaking training or something?"

Bruce continued to stare at her. The lights in his hazel eyes were bright, burning. He said, "Natalie wanted me to come and McKee arranged things so that I could leave the jurisdiction. I have no doubt that there's a gentleman in a purple derby hiding behind the bushes somewhere."

The voices and the footsteps were coming nearer. Bruce glanced past Eve and then straight into her eyes. "Are you going to marry Jim Holland? Are you going through with it?" He didn't move. His tone sent the blood flying into her cheeks.

She listened to winter birds chirping. The bars on his shoulder weren't silver, she thought, they were steel gray. There was a faded wreath lying crookedly on a long nar-row mound between them. The roses in the wreath were withered, colorless. She raised her head. The tailored collar of her coat brushed her hair in back. Her scarlet mouth steadied. She said, "I don't think I understand you. Am I going through with what—?" and gathered herself together and went on lying slowly and carefully and deliberately. "Of course I'm going to marry Jim. What has happened has taught me a good deal. I realize now that I can make Jim happy and that he can make me happy. Even if there was no question of Natalie it wouldn't make any difference. I loved Jim all the time."

Bruce kept on staring at her. She couldn't tell whether the light in his narrowed eyes was derision or not. A pulse in her throat fluttered. "So that's that," he murmured and took himself away from the headstone and walked past her as though she were a stranger, as though he had no further interest in her.

Natalie was coming through the gates. Bruce went to her and took her arm. She was beginning to shake. Gerald said, "Steady, old girl," and the three of them walked forward. Jim had already gone on with Hugh and Susan and Alicia.

Eve didn't follow. Her heart was full. She turned into a gravel path that ran gently down between headstone and an occasional weathered mausoleum. Fifty feet from the silent crowd on the hill above she paused beside a marble angel, stepped off the path, put her shoulders against the pediment, felt in her pocket for a cigarette and let the pain come. After a few moments it began to dull.

A crow cawed harshly somewhere and the wind blew. Beyond and below, to the east, hills and fields rolled to the Sound visible at only one point, a gray triangle threaded with white under the pressed-down lowering sky. The wind was icy but Eve didn't mind its searching chill. It was good to be alone for a moment, not to have to school her eyes and lips, not even to have to think. She looked absently at gravestones. Some of them were old. Lichen-stained writing on one said: *Jeremiah Couch, aged fourteen, lost at sea 1812, in latitude 44, longitude 36.* Her eye was caught by the name *De Sange* on a stone that wasn't old. Of course, Susan's husband was buried here; Eve read the inscription. It was short and unrevealing: *Lucien De Sange, born February 11, 1882; died June 17, 1921.* Near it, in the same plot, there was a tiny marble shaft. On that was lettered *Lucy, daughter of Susan and Lucien De Sange, aged 2 months and 4 days,* and the date *June 4, 1921.*

Poor Susan, Eve thought, she had lost her husband and her only child within a few days of each other in the same year. That was the year Natalie's mother died, making Hugh a widower for the second time. With his propensity for marrying, it was a wonder he hadn't cast an eye on Susan—or perhaps he had, and that explained Charlotte's dislike of her. Why had she never married again, Eve wondered. She was extremely attractive and there must have been men since Lucien De Sange. Was Susan like the woman in some book or other who said, "I will have no more husbands"?

Snowflakes were twisting down lazily. Eve lit a cigarette and drew smoke deeply into her lungs. The minister was praying. The prayer, sonorous and unintelligible, came faintly through the bitter air. There was no other sound. Then, close to Eve somewhere, a man spoke. He was on the far side of the marble angel, and invisible to her, but his voice was vaguely familiar. She recorded his words idly at first, without consciously listening:

"—surprised?" the man on the other side of the monument was saying. "But surely you knew I'd be—interested." It was a cultured voice, smooth and almost caressing, yet with an undertone of irony in it. His companion, whoever it was, made no reply and he continued, "We'll have to have a talk, my friend, a really serious talk. Yes? . . . Good. Suppose I call you later this afternoon."

It was then that Eve came wide awake, suddenly. She had recognized the voice. Her throat was tight and there was coldness all through her. The man on the other side of the marble angel was the man with whom she had collided outside the house on Henderson Square on the night Charlotte died.

For a moment she was too stunned to move. In spite of her own theories about the loiterer at the foot of the steps that night, she hadn't really believed that he had had an imporant part in Charlotte's fate. Now it was different. Now there was a connection—or why was he here, in this cemetery, miles from New York, at Charlotte's funeral? She had to find out who he was. The angel blocked her path. She turned quickly, started round yews banking the outspread marble wings, tripped over a sunken headstone and fell heavily to her knees. Her ankle hurt. She didn't pay any attention. She got to her feet somehow and ran on. The man was there, 30 feet from her, walking rapidly up the path. His back was turned. She stared at it, at the hat he had on and the coat, an expensive light tan polo coat, and caught her breath. This man had not only been watching the house the night Charlotte was killed, he had been in the Square the following afternoon, standing on the pavement across the street, and he had followed her to Bruce's apartment, because when she hailed a cab a block above Eldon Place after her escape with the rifle, he had been standing on the opposite corner.

The services were over and people were beginning to go. The man in the polo coat had reached the fringe of the crowd, was in it. All she could see was his hat. Sheer astonishment had brought her to a momentary halt. She mustn't lose him. She had to find out who he was. She was starting on again when there was a sound behind her, in the direction from which she had come. She looked back—and froze. Susan De Sange was there. She **was** coming toward her up the hill. It was to Susan that the man in the polo coat had been talking and *Susan wasn't going to acknowledge the meeting that had just taken place until she was sure Eve knew about it.*

Her handsome face was calm under a small black hat tilted over the shining waves of her hair. There was a white bird on the hat. She smiled at Eve. She said, lightly and too casually, "My dear, where did you spring from?"

Eve looked at her and then away. She brushed grass and a barberry twig from her skirt and stood erect and straightened her shoulders. She had interrupted a talk between the man in the polo coat and Susan De Sange. The conversation was going to be resumed; he had said so. When it was, she meant to be there to hear and see.

She said aloud, marveling at her own mendacity, "I— Where did *you* spring from? I was wandering around, looking at headstones. You should have come with me, Sue dear, some of them are really quaint. . . ."

Her glance shifted and she stiffened in dismay. Bruce was standing beyond Susan. He wasn't looking at Susan. He was looking at her. Had he heard Susan and the man in the polo coat talking? Eve wasn't sure. She was sure of only one thing. He distrusted her. She might have deceived Susan, she hadn't deceived him. He knew there was something wrong.

She turned a shoulder on him. They rejoined the others then. When they got into cars at the gate there was no sign of the man in the polo coat. They started across to the house on Red Fox Road, where, Alicia said, tea was waiting.

Bruce didn't go with them.

That was at a quarter of 4:00.

Chapter Fifteen

VIGIL IN BLACKNESS

"BUT I *can't* stay, Jim dear, I've *got* to get back to the shop tonight," Eve said. "There isn't another train until ten, and that would bring me in much too late."

Jim frowned down at her. He didn't like it. Now that the funeral was over, he was much more cheerful, more himself. They were in the hall of the Flavell house at the end of Red Fox Road in which Eve had been born and to which she had returned every year for uncounted summers. Originally it had been small, a white colonial house on a knoll among trees in a curve of the river. Now with the wings Virginia had added at the time of her marriage, and the nursery and playroom that had been built on for Natalie when she was a child, it was big and rambling. The front of the house was fairly close to the road, while in back and at the sides orchards and gardens ran down to the wide bay of the river and across the brook to the east. The place belonged to Hugh, but he would never have been able to keep it up without Natalie's help, Eve realized, looking in a beautiful old mirror, at the reflected vista of a section of the long lovely drawing-room where they had had tea when they arrived at 4 o'clock.

Alicia had seen to everything. The rooms had been opened and aired and the oil furnace turned on. She had even had Mrs. Eddey, who lived in the house in winter, make the scones Hugh liked. Lights and fires and warmth after coldness, drawn curtains shutting out the gray December afternoon, should have produced a brighter atmosphere. They didn't for Eve. Afterward she was always to remember that interval as a species of nightmare with a horror all its own.

The original plan had been that they were to take the 5:37 train back to New York. But when Susan announced, stretching shapely hands toward the flaming logs, that she was going to spend the week-end at her little cottage at the foot of the lawn, the others decided that they would stay on.

Hugh was beside Susan on the couch, firelight modeling his handsome high-nosed face against shadows. He said he thought it an excellent idea. Then Alicia spoke. It hadn't escaped Eve that if she was watching Susan closely herself, Alicia was doing so too. The latter had been upset when she found that Susan was returning to the house with them. At the cemetery gates she had said, holding out her hand, "Nice of you, darling, to take so much trouble for Aunt Charlotte, particularly when you weren't exactly fond of each other. . . . You're coming with us? Oh—*splendid!*"

That was part of the nightmare, Alicia's sub-acid sweetness, her narrow-eyed vigilance, the significant glances she exchanged with Gerald at their father's little attentions to Susan. Why should either of them care if Hugh and Susan were to marry? How would it affect their interests? It evidently did. Alicia wasn't going to leave Hugh and Susan alone together. She said abruptly, "You're right, Dad, it does seem stupid to go back to town and those dreadful policemen, when we can have a little peace and quiet here."

Bruce wasn't there then. He had come in for a few minutes, had walked with Natalie in the grounds and then into the village, alone. Gerald was standing on the hearth cleaning his pipe. He blew through the stem and grinned mockingly. "You don't mean to say you didn't spot the gent in the iron derby at the funeral, my pet? He came up with us in the train. I'll bet you anything you like that he's parked outside the gates right now."

Alicia looked at him and her color faded. She said

sharply, "What?" Susan dropped the sugar tongs and they hit the tray with a little crack. She didn't seem to notice. Hugh flushed angrily and sat up. The retort that although Bruce was out on bail on a technicality he was really under arrest for murder and that there was no need to look further was on his lips. It didn't come out in quite that shape, but the implication was there. He said, controlling himself with an effort, "Under the circumstances this—watch on *us* is an outrage."

It was impossible to mistake his meaning. Natalie got it. She was sitting on a hassock near Eve's chair, her tea untouched on a table beside her, her elbows on her knees, her chin on her clasped hands. She was in one of the dark brooding moods that used to make Pussy, their old nurse, so nervous. Her shoulder was toward the room, but she seemed far away, in a world of her own with no pleasure in it. Their father should have known better, Eve thought as she turned and looked at him. Her narrow face went stone white inside the frame of her pale softly shining hair. She sat like that for a moment and then leaped to her feet. She stood there, tall and straight and formidable, her eyes no longer opaque brown disks, but black and brilliant with anger.

"I won't *stand* this," she said in a hard dry voice, her hands clenched at her sides, her head thrown back, "I *won't.* . . . You think Bruce killed Charlotte, Papa. Don't try to deny it. I know you do. You *all* think so— all of you except Eve. Oh—how can you be so stupid, so cruel?" She swept the circle of appalled faces accusingly. "I'm not going to stay here any more. I'm going away. I'm going to—going to—"

She had been a young Valkyrie riding the dark wind of outrage and revolt. The weight of her emotion was too much for her. Her voice broke and her chin quivered. Tears began to stream down her cheeks, and she buried her face in her hands with a quick movement and started to cry as though she would never stop.

The others were up and out of their chairs. Gerald got to her first. They put their arms around her. They said she was wrong, that they didn't think Bruce was guilty, that she was exhausted because of what she had been through. They said that she must rest and get some sleep and stop worrying, that Bruce was going to be all right, everything was going to be all right.

Susan was the only one who didn't stir. She remained where she was, in a corner of the needle-point sofa, staring at the floor vacantly, almost stupidly—and she wasn't stupid.

Alicia and Gerald and Hugh and Jim made their peace with Natalie. She sat down and drank the tea Alicia poured out for her, obediently. But she didn't retreat. She said quietly, "It's harder for you than it is for me, I realize that. But I know Bruce, you see, I know he could never kill anyone, like that, for any reason. I don't care *how* much proof there is."

Things calmed down after that. Natalie had telephoned to Bruce and he was going to stay at the inn in Eastport for the night. He said he'd be over later. Eve was glad she was going to miss him. She said good-bye to the others. Only Jim remained to be disposed of. Susan was still in the house, but she was going down to her cottage soon, and Eve was anxious to get away, alone, before she left.

Jim had protested her departure vigorously. He had to stay on because he was due in Bridgeport early the next morning to receive added instructions about the job he was to begin Monday. He said, leaning against a newel post and looking at her discontentedly, "I don't see why you can't wait until tomorrow—I won't be in Bridgeport long."

Eve used guile then, and hated herself for it, apathetically, as she did everything. "Don't be an idiot, Jim. If we're to be married early in the week there are millions of things I'll have to see to." It was true, she thought bitterly, she had to spy on Susan, had to crouch and creep and eavesdrop on the woman who had been her friend.

Jim evidently took her averted glance, with pain behind it, for shyness. His Victorianism was ridiculous and rather touching. He was naïve in lots of ways. The bride must blush, she must be hesitant and a little fearful, so that she could be reassured and comforted—and loved. Icy fingers ran up Eve's spine, touched the base of her neck. She shivered, and lifted her face resolutely, and after the necessary moment drew herself out of Jim's arms.

"At least I can go to the station with you?"

"No you can't," Eve said firmly. "I want you to keep an eye on Natalie—and, besides, that engineer is going to call you back." A horn honked beyond the front door. She picked up her gloves and purse. "There's my taxi now."

It was dark out and cold. Snow was spitting intermittently, but the body of the storm held off. Jim put Eve into the cab, kissed her tenderly, told her to take care of herself, the door slammed and the car went down the short driveway into the road. Just beyond the gates the car lamps picked up a man's big dark figure. Captain Pierson of the Manhattan Homicide Squad leaped back into shadow, but not before Eve had caught sight of him. Perhaps she would need a policeman soon, she thought, when she had found out more. All she knew now was that the man in the polo coat who had been hanging around the house on Henderson Square on the night Charlotte died was a friend, or an acquaintance, of Susan's. If she went to the police with that they'd say, "Uh-huh—so what?" The man himself would probably deny everything and declare that she was crazy. His word would be as good as hers and she had no proof. No, she would have to go through with what she had in mind.

The first part was simple enough. At the foot of the lane, when the car swung into Imperial Avenue, she got out, paid the man off, said she had changed her mind and gave him a generous tip. She refused his offer to drive her back to the house. "Thanks, but it's only a step and I'll be glad of some exercise."

As soon as the car was out of sight she turned and started back, not by the route she had come but by a longer and more roundabout way. She didn't intend to re-enter the grounds by the front gates but through the fields to the north and across a little bridge buried in trees than ran through the property on that side. The police would never think of posting anyone there. No one who wasn't familiar with the terrain would know of that way of getting in and out.

It was dark, but Eve had a torch. She kept it on until she had traversed what would be three sides of a huge city block except that it was filled with woods and hills and hollows instead of bricks and mortar. There was a gate in the high wall that hemmed in the estate. It was an inconspicuous little gate behind a clump of birches. Eve lifted the latch and pushed the gate open.

The hinges creaked loudly. Her heart hammered and she held her breath, but no sound broke the stillness, except the gurgle of water, louder now, just ahead. There was nothing around her but darkness and close-pressing bushes. The stream she was approaching was narrow and swift and affected by the tides. At low tide it emptied itself into the bay, at high it rose 10 feet between retaining walls stained with green slime. The tide was going out. Eve came on the bridge sooner than she had expected. The entrance to it was choked with shrubbery. She shone torchlight through a gap in black alders and down on narrow gray boards nailed crosswise to spindly uprights.

Never substantial, the bridge had been torn loose in the hurricane and knocked about, but you could still use it if you were careful. One of the rails was gone, but the other was there. Eve grasped it, felt it sway in her grasp, and switched off her torch. The darkness was intense, and the slightest gleam of light would be visible from the lawns and gardens on the far side, once she was out in the open. She handled the shaky rail gently and started across, glad that she didn't have to look down on the jagged black rocks that rose in sharp pinnacles, 20 feet below, foam swirling round their bases in pools and eddies. At high tide all you could do was fall into the water but at low— She felt her way forward, testing every step, and was at last on solid ground on the other side. She came to a halt a few yards farther on.

If Susan and the man in the polo coat were going to meet, it would be in Susan's cottage, she decided. Refusing an invitation from Hugh to stay for dinner Susan had said, "I won't, if you don't mind. I've got some letters to write and things to sort through and then I'm going to bed. It's been rather a tiring day."

The big house on the hill above was hidden by trees. Presently a torch appeared near the front, a bright eye in the blackness. Someone was coming down the long slope, over the cobbles that led to the stables and the garage, under the oaks, and onto the open lawn where it flattened out.

Eve stepped into the lee of a clump of lilacs. They passed within 10 yards of her. She could hear the murmur of their voices, but not what they said. It was her father, with Susan. No fence separated Susan's place from theirs. Flat stones led to the brick terrace at the side of the cottage fronting on the brook. Susan unlocked the door and went in. Hugh followed, and lights sprang up in the windows.

Eve looked through one of them, into the portion of

the living-room that was visible. Susan had taken off her coat and was pulling off her hat. She tossed it to a table and turned to Hugh. He took both her hands in his and said something. Shame and distaste flooded Eve and she removed her gaze. When she looked again Susan was pulling down the living-room shades and her father's torch was a bobbing circle of brightness receding up the hill. Eve went round the lilac bushes on careful feet. Her father vanished from sight in the darkness, and she settled down to wait. The cottage wasn't too well constructed, the rooms were all on one floor, and by listening at a window she was sure that she could hear whatever was said.

She had been prepared for a long vigil; she had had no idea of how tedious waiting could be. In the first place, she was bitterly cold. In the second, as time went on and nothing happened, doubts began to assail her. It was true that Susan had talked to the man in the polo coat in the cemetery, true that she had tried to conceal her meeting with him—but suppose it was an innocent meeting, that Susan didn't know he was the man lingering outside the house the night Charlotte died? He might even have no connection with the various things that had happened since: the unlatched window in the shop, the morphine that had been dropped into her cocktail. She gave her head a little shake. No. Just as before the scene in the cemetery she hadn't believed implicitly in the possible guilt of the man lingering at the foot of the steps in the Square that night, now she couldn't bring herself to believe in his innocence.

Silence and blackness and the growing tinkle of snowflakes on dry leaves, the purr of water. She had no watch and no really accurate notion of the passage of time.

Over and over again she analyzed the few words she had heard. "Surprise? You must have known I'd be interested." Interested in what? In the burial of a woman who had been murdered? "I think we'd better have a talk, my friend—"

There had been intimacy and a sort of silky threat in his tone, as though he and Susan understood each other without the necessity for many words. It occurred to Eve suddenly how little she knew of Susan, nothing, really—except that she had lived abroad with a cousin for years and had traveled a good deal, and that the outbreak of hostilities had forced her back to the United States. "I'll call you," the man in the polo coat had said. Eve hadn't heard him call—but it was obvious that Susan had come down here to her cottage so that she could see him alone.

Pain and disillusionment mingled with Eve's cold reflections. She had been very fond of Susan, had liked her better than any woman she had ever known, and she had thought that Susan was her friend. *Well, think again,* she told herself.

What was that? Her heart hammered and she stood erect. Surely there had been a sound somewhere close to her in the darkness, a whisper of cloth or a footstep—or perhaps a coat brushing against branches. She stared into the blackness, trying to pierce it. She might just as well have been in a thick sack with the drawstrings tied. Except for a chink of light here and there inside the cottage off to her left, the darkness was absolute. She listened, turning her head from side to side. Sleet tinkled thinly and water ran—there was nothing else. But her nerves quivered and for the first time it occurred to her to be physically afraid. She was alone out here in the darkness and no one knew where she was. She had an almost overwhelming impulse to turn and run, up the slope and into the big white house, with its lights and people. Jim would be there, and Natalie—and Gerald. *Don't be a fool,* she told herself furiously—and stiffened.

She was on a stretch of turf perhaps a dozen yards back from the brook and facing it. The bridge was directly below and in front of her. Someone was coming toward it from the lane she had traversed earlier. The hinges of the gate creaked and a tiny circle of light spotted the gray planking. It was a man. He was whistling softly through his teeth. It was the man in the camel's-hair coat; there was a shimmer of pale cloth behind the light. Susan's visitor had arrived.

His torch swept the bridge experimentally, danced back. He stepped from between the alder bushes and out onto the planking, and came to a halt. He had stopped whistling. Eve stared fascinated. A funny thing happened. The torch he was carrying stood still too. Then it flew into the air in a wide arc and went out. At the same instant or perhaps the fraction of a second before, the sound came, very distinct and clear this time. It was a dull *smack*—exactly like the clean hit of a midiron lofting the ball in a 200-yard drive over the fairway. But it wasn't that. . . .

Weight crushed itself in under Eve's ribs. She tried to breathe and couldn't. Because there were other sounds. The man in the polo coat had fallen from the bridge down onto those jagged black rocks lining the channel. She heard him land, heard a muffled groan, then nothing —and then the footsteps.

Someone was running up the slope toward her, from the bridge, running straight at her, straight for the spot on which she stood. Horror locked Eve's muscles, her throat. It came unlocked. She opened her mouth to scream. The scream didn't emerge. The blow stopped it, and the night and the darkness and her terror were blanked out as she fell headlong.

Chapter Sixteen

THE MAN IN THE POLO COAT

EVE DIDN'T COMPLETELY LOSE CONSCIOUSNESS. But the blow and the fall had stunned her, and it was three or four minutes before she came back to full awareness, to find herself sprawled on her side on the ground, in blackness. It was cold. Her knees and the palms of her hands were on fire, and her head was ringing and a painful weight. She found her torch by accident and staggered to her feet.

Her recollections of what immediately followed were always blurred. Someone had struck her and run away. She had a confused impression that she ought to try and find out who it was, that this was important. And there was the man in the polo coat. He was almost certainly hurt and she would have to get help. "Susan!" she shrieked, "Susan!" and was going herself across the lawn and was out on the bridge with her torch lit. She held it, shaking, on the blackness below and sobbed futilely. The man in the polo coat was there, lying face down in water and foam. His arms were thrown out above his head. There was blood on one of them. He didn't move.

"What is it? . . . Who? . . .Where?" Captain Pierson had heard Eve scream. He was beside her on the bridge after a thundering dash down the hill. He looked where she was looking. He said "God," and gaped, and swung round in the nick of time. Eve was swaying drunkenly. Her torch joined another one in the channel below the bridge and she collapsed against him in a dead faint.

"I tell you we were lucky we didn't both go over. It was nip and tuck. Yep. For a minute there I thought we were both goners." Pierson was indignant and outraged at the ordeal he had been through. He wiped his forehead at the memory and looked at the Inspector.

The two men were in the spacious lamp-lit hall of the Flavell house at the end of Red Fox Road. It was a little after 8 o'clock. Eve was upstairs in bed in the room to which she had been carried. The local doctor was with her. The others were in the living-room with the door closed. The man who had fallen into the rock-strewn channel below the bridge was Edgar Bently, Susan De Sange's cousin by marriage. Bently wasn't dead. But his head had been injured, and in addition to a broken leg, a smashed elbow, three cracked ribs and possible internal damage, he had concussion. The ambulance had been summoned and he had been taken to the Norwalk Hospital. The surgeon who examined him had just phoned. He wasn't prepared to say yet how bad the concussion was or what Bently's chances of recovery were. It would take time to find out.

McKee had arrived in Eastport an hour earlier. He was pacing the floor prowlingly, his hands in his pockets. When he didn't answer, Pierson continued defensively, "It wasn't *my* fault. How was I to keep an eye on all these people? Why, you'd need an army for that, a regular army."

The Scotsman nodded. "It's all right, Captain. You're not to blame. If anyone is, it's Dwyer. He's going to try for an indictment of Bruce Cunningham early next week. I should have come up here as soon as I found out Bently was in the neighborhood—but no, our estimable District Attorney had to have a detailed statement from me *viva voce* that consumed at least three hours. Exactly what happened after Miss Flavell fainted?"

"Well, they all came running. Mrs. De Sange was first. She ran up here to this house, and pretty soon they were all over the place."

"Did they seem surprised to see Eve Flavell?"

"Surprise ain't in it. They were dumfounded. Particularly the big fellow, Jim Holland, and Natalie Flavell. She kept saying, 'But Eve was going back to *New York*,' and wringing her hands like she was half crazy. Holland went nuts, too. You going to talk to them some more?"

"Not now," McKee said. "Perhaps after I've seen Eve Flavell." He turned.

Doctor Newbold was coming down the stairs. Newbold was a thin, middle-aged man with glasses and a shock of untidy gray hair. He knew the Flavells, had taken care of them when they were in Eastport during the summer, as his father had done before him. He said that Eve was better. She was a bit bunged up but there was nothing the matter with her that a couple of days wouldn't cure. What she was suffering from principally was shock. "She's anxious to see you, Inspector. I said I'd take you up."

Pierson remained at the door of the living-room, and McKee and the doctor mounted the stairs. Eve wasn't in bed. She was on a chaise longue in front of the wide windows in a big shadowy room with lemon-colored walls and chinoiserie hangings. The gay French chintz curtains were drawn across the windows and the lamps were lit. Pillows banked Eve's head and shoulders. She turned toward her visitors as they came in, and flinched a little. Doctor Newbold said, "Easy does it. Don't move around too much, Eve," and to the Scotsman, "Don't tire her any more than you have to. I'll give her a sedative later." He went out.

Natalie and Alicia between them had undressed Eve and put her into white silk pajamas and a white negligée. A blue satin quilt was thrown over her knees. Her bandaged hands were linked loosely in front of her and there was a scratch down one pale cheek where it had come into contact with the ground. She told him quietly, looking into the depths of a mirror at shapes that weren't there, everything that happened from the time of their arrival in Eastport until the man in the camel's-hair coat fell from the bridge at the foot of the hill.

McKee listened intently, a hand shading his eyes. At the end Eve said, shivering, "I'll never forgive myself, never. I should have told someone, that detective, about him, that he was coming here to see Susan."

"Yes," McKee agreed, getting up and beginning to walk around the room. "It might have been better. On the other side of the ledger, your being down at the brook probably saved Bently from dying then and there. As it is, he has a chance."

Eve began to feel better. She had only grieved with the top of her mind for the man who had been smashed up on those terrible rocks. The real thing, the important thing, was that the attack on him cleared Bruce. Bruce had been at the inn when Bently was attacked. He hadn't come over to the house until afterward. He had come in to see her for a minute with Natalie. The doctor wouldn't let them stay, wouldn't let her answer questions. Bruce had given her one long smoldering glance, with derision in it, and bitterness and anger and a glint of mocking humor. He had been unusually tender and loverlike with Natalie. That was the way it should be, Eve told herself, and twisted away from flames and got back on safe ground and said aloud, "It means, doesn't it, Inspector, that Bruce isn't guilty, that he didn't kill Charlotte?"

The Scotsman paused and looked down at her lovely luminous face. Cunningham's whereabouts at the time of the Bently attack was the first thing he had checked. "Unless Bently's fall was an accident," he answered. "No, wait a minute, I don't think it was. I think it was meant to look that way."

Much of what had happened, factually, was clear to him from Eve's story. The telephone in the cottage was disconnected. Edgar Bently had called Susan De Sange, here in this house, at around a quarter of 6:00. He had talked to her and she had repeated the brief interchange between herself and Bently with the blank irresponsiveness of complete nervous exhaustion. "Edgar said he wanted to see me. I said all right. He said there was someone watching the main gate and I told him to come by the bridge across the brook."

"Why did he want to avoid being seen, Mrs. De Sange?"

A shrug. "Edgar was—devious."

"Was a time for his visit mentioned?"

"Yes. It was a quarter of six then. He said he'd be along in about three quarters of an hour."

"Did he tell you what he wanted to see you about—or did you know in advance?"

"I—didn't know."

Bently had been punctual. Someone had been waiting for him in the shelter of the bushes that masked the entrance to the footbridge, armed with a weapon, a golf club, a length of pipe, or a club of some sort. He was silhouetted against torchlight, made an excellent target. The question was not *how* the attack had been made, but by whom and why.

The why was the easier. Bently had been outside the Flavell house on the night Charlotte was killed, he had been in the restaurant on 52nd Street when the box of morphine tablets was thrown to the floor under the table; he had obviously seen something that made him a danger. But there was more to his activities than that. McKee told Eve that on Wednesday morning, the morning of the day Charlotte died, Bently had taken a room in a hotel on the south side of the Square. "He was in the park that afternoon, he was watching the house, he was also watching Mrs. De Sange."

Eve's hands gripped folds of blue satin and she closed her eyes. "Then you think it was Susan who—?"

"I don't know, I'm sure. There's—this." There was a

little ping as the Scotsman's thumb nail flicked the edge
of the telephone on a small table near the chaise longue.
"Mrs. De Sange took Bently's call in the library downstairs, but there are three extensions in the house—this
one here in Miss Flavell's bedroom, one in your father's
room, and one at the end of the hall. Any number of
people could have listened in on Bently's call to Mrs.
De Sange."

The clock ticked and the fire purred. Outside snow fell.
Eve lay very still. It was Bruce's life or her father's or
Natalie's or Gerald's or Jim's, she thought desperately.
It mustn't be Bruce, it mustn't be Natalie or Gerald, or
her father. It wasn't of course. They hadn't touched that
man. But the thought of the others, of Jim or Susan or
Alicia in such a connection, was equally absurd. . . .
"Can't you find out," she said in a low voice, "where
they all were when that man was hit?"

McKee's smile was thin. "This is a big house. Bently
was attacked at around half-past six. The people here,
your father and your half-sister, your brother, his wife
and Mr. Holland, were in their rooms, getting ready for
dinner, which was to be at seven. Mrs. De Sange was, she
says, inside her cottage at the foot of the hill."

Eve's face went blank. "Did you talk to Susan, Inspector?"

"Yes. Oh, yes."

"What did she say? Why did she try to conceal from
me that she knew Mr. Bently? Why did she pretend,
like that, in the cemetery?"

McKee didn't answer at once. He was seeing Susan De
Sange looking at him with her brilliant eyes curiously
dulled, her creamy skin blue white, her mouth compressed, and saying, "Edgar knows nothing, nothing. It
was just bluff. He was trying to put pressure on. . . . He
lives by his wits and he thought there might be money
to be made out of this. Oh, he's shrewd and clever. . . .

I didn't touch him. I didn't leave the cottage. I was waiting for him there when I heard Eve scream. I meant to tell Edgar that he would have to stop it, stop spying on me and on the Flavells."

Perhaps; McKee sat down in a slipper chair. He picked up a fold of the satin quilt and drew it absently through his fingers. "Do you get the apparent contradiction, Miss Flavell? Edgar Bently was apparently struck down because he was a danger to someone and that danger would appear to lie in his presence outside the house on the Square the night your aunt was killed or in his presence in the Cedars on the following night when the box of morphine capsules was disposed of. But—and here's the point—if what Mrs. De Sange says is true and Mr. Bently was after profit, why was he watching Mrs. De Sange and the house on the Square *before* Charlotte Foy died? There's a good deal we don't know. There's one important thing we do, and that is that your Aunt Charlotte had important knowledge in her possession that threatened your half-sister, Natalie. She said so to Natalie's lawyer, Spencer Gorham, over the phone. She said to him that afternoon, 'I've got to see you, got to tell you something—it's very terrible,' and when the lawyer asked her whether it affected Natalie she answered, 'Yes,' and added that she was frightened."

He settled back in the chair and lit a cigarette. Well, her fear was justified, he reflected. The proof of whatever Charlotte knew, or had learned, was in the small wooden chest that was in the suitcase she had intended to take to Boston with her. The contents of the chest had been removed after her death. If they could find out what it had contained. . . . He explained to Eve that Charlotte had taken the little wooden chest out of her bank the day before she died. "Did you ever see it, Miss Flavell?"

Eve nodded, her eyes suddenly bright. "Yes. I remember it very well. It was on account of the little box that

Charlotte slapped me for the first and only time in her life. It was long ago," she said in a thoughtful voice. "I couldn't have been more than five or six at the time. The box had always fascinated me. It was in Charlotte's desk here in this house. One day I tried to open it and Charlotte found me with it in my hands and boxed my ears roundly. I can still recall her face, how furious she was." She looked anxiously at McKee. "Does that help any, Inspector?"

McKee said slowly, "It means that even then the contents of the box were important to her." Then, 18 or 19 years ago, Hugh Flavell was a newly made widower and Susan De Sange a widow. Natalie's mother and Susan's husband had died within two months of each other in the same year. Their ghosts stirred faintly. The Scotsman contemplated them and fingered possibilities. Suppose, and it was the purest supposition, that there was something wrong about the death of Virginia, Hugh's second wife, for instance? Suppose, for the sake of argument, that she had been—removed? Well, what then? So then the assumption might have been that Flavell would inherit his wife's money, in which case he would have been a rich man and free to marry again. It hadn't turned out that way, but Flavell, or Susan, needn't have known that in advance. If Charlotte had found out that there *was* something wrong, she might have held her tongue for the sake of the children, contenting herself with a warning to Susan De Sange to keep off. Certainly Susan had left Eastport immediately following her husband's death and also certainly nothing had happened to the Flavell clan for more than 20 years and then Susan De Sange had reappeared. Shortly thereafter Charlotte had ceased to exist.

Try and find out more about those two deaths, McKee decided, and returned his attention to Eve. He took her back to the bank above the brook in darkness, and to the footsteps that had rushed at her, but she couldn't help him. They had been just footsteps, and then she was struck.

McKee nodded somberly. "Somebody was trying to cross the plate before the ball could be fielded and an alarm raised. You got in the way." He went to a table on which Eve's hat and coat lay. He picked up her little tricorne, spun it around on a forefinger. Blades of grass stuck to the soft black felt and it was out of shape. "This saved you from a serious, perhaps a fatal, head wound. But—" He put the hat down gently and went back to the chaise longue and held Eve's lovely eyes, wide and dark with strain, with his own intent gaze. "You might not be so lucky again. No. Look, my dear, if you discover anything, and it's quite possible you will —you're on the inside where you can see and hear—let me know, let me handle it. Is it a promise?"

Eve stared at her clasped hands. On the inside, with her father and Gerald and Jim. But Bruce was in danger. His innocence had to be established, no matter what happened. . . . Her breath failing at the thought of what might lie ahead, she pressed shaking lips together and nodded.

Pierson knocked at the door then, and McKee left Eve. There was news.

Standing in the wide graceful hall at the foot of the stairs the Scotsman looked at a pair of men's hand-sewn brown cordovan oxfords. They were practically new. The leather was water soaked. They had been found in the channel of the brook a hundred feet from the bridge. They hadn't been there long. They belonged to Gerald Flavell.

Chapter Seventeen

DELIBERATE AND COLD-BLOODED

"I DIDN'T KILL HER, INSPECTOR. I didn't. I tell you you're wrong." Gerald Flavell wiped his face with a handkerchief and did another fast turn up and down the rug. He ran a finger inside his collar, shook his head as though he were shaking off a weight. His eyes were cold—and wary.

"But you admit the shoes are yours," McKee said. "All right, suppose you tell me why you got rid of them and exactly what happened."

The two men were in a breakfast room at the back of the hall. Hugh Flavell and Alicia, Susan De Sange, Natalie and Jim Holland were still in the living-room with Pierson stolidly at the door. Alicia had given a little gasp when Gerald was summoned, but that was all.

"I'll tell you," Gerald said, throwing himself into a fragile chair that creaked protestingly at his impact. "God knows I'll be glad to get it off my chest. It was a terrible thing to do. I don't believe I'll ever forget it. I haven't been able to sleep, thinking of her lying there, untended, in the dark and the cold." He shuddered violently and swallowed a groan. "But I had other people to worry about—I had Alicia and the boy." He drew a long breath, got a cigarette lighted with a third match, and began to talk more or less coherently.

The trouble started, he said, when Charlotte came back from Vermont in November. He wasn't altogether surprised, not as surprised as he would have been if he hadn't seen her on the farm outside Bennington in the middle of October. He, Alicia, Natalie, and Hugh were on their way down from Quebec. Natalie wanted to see

Charlotte, so they stopped off. Charlotte hadn't seemed a bit glad to see them; she had hardly a word to say and she had looked frightful. He had laid it to illness; she hadn't been well for almost a year—but the change in her was mental as well as physical. She had a $10,000 mortgage on his place in Long Island. It was a good investment. The interest was paid regularly and he had never expected her to call it in. Yet that was exactly what she did. She wasn't back in New York two days before she sent for him and told him that she wanted her $10,000 in cash, at once.

Gerald said bitterly, "She had no head for business. I tried to explain to her that it was impossible for me to raise the money, that to go chasing around for it would hurt my credit, and that at the best it would take time to arrange another mortgage. But she wouldn't listen. She said she'd give me to the first of December, and that if I didn't produce by then she'd have old Gorham, that damn lawyer of the precious Coreys, start foreclosure proceedings. I didn't really believe she meant it, not until that afternoon we were all there in the house and she came back from the telephone and said she was going to Boston the next day. I don't mind telling you that it knocked me for a loop. I went home. I'd had plenty to drink and I fell asleep on the sofa. When I woke up Holland was gone and Alicia was out with the pup. I decided then to have a last try at Aunt Charlotte. I thought if I appealed to her for the boy's sake, that if I told her that a public foreclosure would just ruin me, she might change her mind. So I started across to the house on the other side of the Square.

"What time?" Gerald wrenched at his tie. "I think it was around half-past seven, but I'm not sure. There was a fog out and my head wasn't any too clear, so I went through the park where I wouldn't be knocked down by a car. The east gate is across from the apartment. I unlocked it with my key and walked along. I had a torch. I was past the fountain and rounding the bulge near the north gate when I saw a woman's purse lying on the ground. I picked it up. It was Aunt Charlotte's. I looked around—and saw her."

He paused and covered his face with his hands.

"Go on, please."

Gerald said in a muffled voice, his eyes covered, "She was lying there, down in among bushes. I didn't know at first that she was dead. Then I found out and I—" He broke down completely.

McKee filled the gap. "You wiped your shoes on the grass, left the park, went across to the Flavell house and let yourself in. In the hall, at the foot of the stairs, you slipped and deposited a smear of the blood you hadn't quite removed from your shoes, on the carpet. What made you slip, Mr. Flavell?"

"I was startled. There was someone moving around in the corridor on the floor above."

"Who was it?" Gerald didn't know. The Scotsman did. The cook and Hugh Flavell were the only two other people in the house and it wasn't the cook. . . . Leaving that for the moment, he extracted the rest of the story bit by bit. Charlotte Foy had loaned the nephew she had indulged and spoiled, various sums over a period of years, nothing big, a hundred now, two hundred again, and Gerald had given her receipts for these loans. He wanted the receipts back. Her keys were where she always kept them, in her top bureau drawer under a pile of handkerchiefs. The receipts weren't in the desk. He unlocked the suitcase. They were there, with a rubber band around them. He took them away with him and destroyed them.

"You also," McKee said pleasantly, "removed $9,000 in war bonds that you intended to cash in on later, when the furor over your aunt's death had died down. You were the beneficiary. You knew that your sister Eve wasn't likely to ask embarrassing questions."

Gerald turned sullen. "Charlotte wasn't fond of Eve. She meant me to have them."

"Where were the bonds?"

"In a brown envelope with the receipts."

"Not in the box?"

"In—oh, that wooden thing of Charlotte's. No."

"What did you do with the contents of that?"

"Nothing. I didn't touch it."

McKee looked steadily at Gerald from under frowning brows. He could be speaking the truth; he could be lying. Whatever the little wooden chest had held was of tremendous importance. In every case when you blew the froth away there was a small nucleus of important fact, a few drops of the real McCoy, the vital principle, the essence at the heart of murder, from which it derived. In this case it was the missing contents of the little wooden chest. Hugh Flavell's fingerprints, and Hugh's alone, were on the box. McKee had already taxed him with it. Flavell was a clever man. He didn't deny touching the box. He did deny opening it. He had said, "That little wooden chest of Charlotte's—it was a nice piece of craftsmanship. I believe I commented on it when I was talking to her in her room Tuesday night. I may even have picked it up—but it was locked and I certainly didn't open it." If what Gerald said was true, Hugh Flavell certainly had lied. According to his first statement, on the night Charlotte was killed, Flavell had gone upstairs to his study on the third floor at around 6 o'clock and had remained there until he went to bed in the adjoining bedroom at 10:30, yet Gerald had heard his father in the second-floor corridor at around 20 minutes of 8:00, as soon as Natalie was safely out of the house.

There had been fear in Hugh Flavell, rigidly controlled, at the mention of the wooden chest; there was fear in Gerald Flavell now. The catharsis of open confession, which Gerald had declared would be a relief, didn't appear to have done him much good. It wasn't open confession. There were, definitely, things he wasn't telling. He had been in the bedroom when Eve tapped at Charlotte's door; he had mixed the cocktail into which the morphine had been inserted; he could have gotten rid of the capsules in the restaurant on 52nd Street; he could have bashed Bently over the head earlier that night. He was guarded, watchful and afraid. He was also letter-perfect in his story. McKee took him back and forth over it a half dozen times, and let him go, with a warning.

"Stick around, Flavell. In case Joe Buchanan springs Bruce Cunningham for good, we may want to talk to you in more detail."

Gerald wheeled on him sharply. "How could Buchanan do anything for Bruce?"

McKee said quietly, "He could do a lot for him, negatively by saying that he himself went out last Wednesday night—in which case, with the apartment empty, someone could have replaced the murder rifle by using the key your sister Natalie—lost. He could do the same thing positively, by naming a visitor to the apartment who could have put the rifle back without using a key."

Something had happened to Gerald Flavell's handsome gray eyes—and they were too ingenuously open, too steady after the first quick flash. But he had himself well in hand. "I hope Buchanan does clear Bruce. I didn't kill Charlotte. I'm sure Bruce didn't either." McKee had nothing to say to that. He indicated that the interview was over, momentarily.

At the door Gerald hesitated and then made his request. He had already declared that Alicia knew nothing about his coming on Charlotte's body in the park, about his visit to the house or the war bonds. "Do you have to tell her, Inspector? Will the others, my father and Natalie, have to know? Tonight, I mean? If I could sort of break it to them gently they mightn't feel so bad."

Flavell's relations with his wife or his family were no concern of McKee's except insofar as they affected the investigation. He said indifferently, "Your statement will have to be checked—but not necessarily tonight," and watched the young investment broker take heart of grace and register a gratitude and satisfaction out of all proportion to the boon of temporary silence that had been granted to him. Gerald was mounting the stairs, his vigor almost completely restored. His resilience was amazing. The Scotsman turned away.

There was a call from the office for him. He went to the telephone at the end of the long hall and dialed Operator. Before he left New York, as soon as he received word that Hugh Flavell's fingerprints were on the little wooden chest, he had sent Detective Rumboldt to the house on Henderson Square to·talk to the servants. Rumboldt came on. His quest had been partially successful. Gloria Fox, the upstairs girl, had caught a glimpse, no more, of the things the chest contained. Charlotte's secrecy, the care with which she handled the box, had aroused the girl's curiosity. On Tuesday evening, while the family was at dinner, she had gone up to Charlotte's bedroom, had taken her keys from under the handkerchiefs in the bureau drawer, and had unlocked the suit-case and the chest. She had expected jewels, or money at the very least, gold pieces maybe, she said. Not that she meant to steal; she just wanted to look. She had looked and had been disappointed. All that was in the box was a flat package wrapped in white tissue paper. It wasn't very big. She had peeked through the folds as well as she could without leaving traces. There was some sort of yellow cloth in it and a string of pink stones.

Yellow—cloth and a string of pink stones, coral, tourmalines? McKee dropped the instrument into its cradle and stared blankly at wide polished floorboards.

Bend an ear as he would, the news he had so eagerly
awaited said nothing to him—yet it was there, behind
that enigmatic and unreadable presentation, the crux,
the core, of the dark riddle of crime and violence that
had erupted into murder. Charlotte certainly wasn't taking the chest and contents to Boston for the ride. They
were getting closer and closer; they weren't close enough.
He roused himself from motionless brooding. Gerald
Flavell was coming down the stairs. McKee spoke briefly
to Pierson, joined Gerald and they entered the living-
room together.

Jim Holland was reading a book in a big chair in a
corner under a lamp; Natalie was beside Alicia on a love
seat near the fire, her eyes big in a face that had thinned
and sharpened. Susan De Sange and Hugh Flavell were
at opposite ends of a sofa in front of the second fireplace.

They all looked up quickly, apprehensively as the door
opened. Alicia jumped to her feet. She stared from
McKee to her husband. Gerald's bearing reassured her.
She touched her lips delicately with her handkerchief,
and a diamond flashed on one of her well-cared-for hands
with the greedy fingers. Perhaps the jewel was one of the
reasons why Gerald's creditors were hounding him "like
wolves." Alicia said brightly, "Well, darling, you're alive,
I see—which of us is for the torture chamber next?"

No one echoed her lightness, her smile. Hugh Flavell
was rising from the couch. His movements were stiff.
Instead of a young fifty, he looked sixty and arthritic.
He walked toward McKee, pulled up a few feet from
him. "Inspector?" His voice was curt.

"Yes, Mr. Flavell?"

"I want an explanation."

The boot, McKee thought ironically, was on the other
foot. Hugh Flavell had lied round the clock, about remaining in his study on the third floor of the house on
Henderson Park on the night Charlotte was killed, and

about the little wooden chest and his casual handling of it. "An explanation of what, Mr. Flavell?"

"Of what my daughter, Eve, was doing down there by the brook when Bently fell from the bridge, instead of being on her way to New York on the train."

Susan De Sange, who had had time to pull herself together, broke in. "I think," she said calmly, "that the poor child suspected me. She was right, in a way. I'm not proud of Edgar. He came up to me in the cemetery when I was going to look at my own graves. Eve heard us talking. I didn't realize it or I'd have explained to her then who Edgar was. If I had, she would have told me about his being the man with whom she collided outside the house on the Square on Wednesday night, and we could have gone to the police together."

It was very smooth. It was altogether untrue. Susan De Sange's earlier agitation denied it.

She had addressed the room as a whole. It was Hugh Flavell who answered. He turned toward her. He said, "Eve suspected *you*, Susan? Oh, she's a fool, a fool!" He was very angry. He was in love with Susan De Sange. Alicia Flavell and Gerald were emphatically not in love with her. Alicia's prominent eyes resting on Susan were icily hostile and she said in an insinuating tone, "If Mr. Bently recovers, it will be nice to hear the explanation of his—attentions to us, shall we call them?"

The remark could be a feeler as to Edgar Bently's condition. As far as these people knew he was dying when he was put into the ambulance. McKee had already arranged a little experiment with Pierson. He laughed lightly, and the Captain tapped and opened the door.

"Telephone call from the Norwalk Hospital for you, Inspector," he said, and looked around uncertainly. "Do you want me to—?"

"Yes, go on."

"Mr. Bently's conscious and able to talk."

Susan De Sange was staring at Pierson. Something went inside for her, some stay, some support, so that although she didn't move it was there, in her still face, her tightly clasped hands, the impression of a side-slip, a cave-in. . . . McKee's attention was abruptly diverted.

Hugh Flavell did a retake. He too was staring at Pierson. Without the slightest preliminary warning he was falling forward in a slow-motion curve, his face cyanotic, swollen, his eyes half-closed.

"Papa!" Natalie screamed, and jumped up and ran toward him. Gerald and Jim Holland both leaped. They caught the stricken man before he reached the floor.

"You're *sure* Bruce Cunningham was in his room here in the village when Bently was slugged?" New York's District Attorney went on pacing the floor of the big old-fashioned bedroom in the Eastport inn with a slow step.

It was 10 o'clock on the morning following the scene in the dark gardens of the Flavell house on Red Fox Road. McKee had just finished telling Dwyer, who at his insistence had come up from the city on an early train, of the events of the previous night.

The Scotsman said patiently, "Hold it for a minute, counselor. You're not figuring on two killers in this case, are you? No? Good. Then, we're agreed that the person who killed Charlotte Foy and tried to poison Eve Flavell was the person who struck Bently and sent him down on those rocks under that foot bridge."

Dwyer's nod was reluctant and gloomy. "I'm afraid you're right, Inspector."

"I know I'm right," McKee answered. "I can assure you on my word as an officer and not as a gentleman that Cunningham was a mile and a half from that bridge when Bently was laid low. We had a man watching him, and he was here in his room down the corridor. No, Cunningham didn't attack Bently. Cunningham didn't poison Eve; ergo, Cunningham did not kill Charlotte Foy."

Dwyer ruffled butter-colored hair with a moody and irritable hand. His case had been cut from under his feet and he was all abroad. He turned on McKee sharply. He said in a sour tone, "Couldn't you have told me this in New York? Did you have to bring me all the way up here?"

McKee exhaled smoke in a long stream. "I brought you up here because Buchanan has been located, and I thought you'd want to talk to him yourself."

Dwyer came to an abrupt halt. "Oh. He has? I see." His china-blue eyes were bright again. "That'll do it, McKee," he said with rising vigor. "That'll do it. This case is going to crack now. If Cunningham isn't guilty, someone took that gun of his, shot the Foy woman with it, and put it back in the Eldon Place apartment last Wednesday night after Charlotte Foy was dead. Buchanan was there all evening. He'll know who it was. . . . When will he be here?"

"He's on his way over now in a car from his aunt's farm in Dutchess County," McKee told Dwyer. "He ought to have arrived a good half hour ago, but the roads are bad."

The District Attorney was all eagerness again. The Scotsman wanted to ask Eve a few more questions for the record, so in order to save time he left Dwyer to wait for Buchanan and drove across town to the house on Red Fox Road.

The big living-room with the two fireplaces was bright with crisp winter sunlight and fragrant with sheaves of flowers Natalie had ordered from a neighboring green-house. Eve and Natalie and Bruce Cunningham were there, Bruce and Natalie talking before one of the fires, Eve, in a monks-cloth robe of soft yellow with a blanket over her knees, was on a sofa some distance away, reading a paper. All three greeted the Inspector cheerfully.

Eve said, smiling up at him, that she felt much better, and Natalie and Cunningham came toward the sofa. Natalie looked happy. She had regained her smartly groomed air. Her coat and skirt were beautifully cut and her hair and eyes and skin glowed. She gave Cunningham's sleeve a small pat and said eagerly, "Bruce won't have to go back to jail now, ever, will he, Inspector? As soon as that Mr. Bently can talk, he'll tell who hit him and then—" She pushed at a spray of orange chrysanthemums in a big blue vase. A shadow crossed her bright face but she continued steadily, "We'll know who killed Charlotte."

Cunningham said drily, "It can't be too soon for me. I hope Bently won't pass out on us."

McKee took out his little red-leather notebook and began clearing up minor details. His ink gave out. "May I—?" "Over there," Natalie said, and he crossed to a desk at the far end of the long room and filled his fountain pen. A nurse poked a head in the door. Hugh Flavell wanted to see Natalie. She left the room and went upstairs.

McKee was putting the cover back on the inkwell when the door at the south end of the room opened again. Alicia Flavell stood in the opening. She didn't see him. She appeared to have had an uncomfortable night. Her oval face was swollen. Her eyes were fastened on Eve and on Cunningham standing beside the couch, his hands in his pockets. They both turned. There was a curious air of tension about all three. The room was still for a clock tick. Then Alicia began to talk.

"You're at it again, aren't you?" she said in a low voice, with venom in it. "The moment Natalie's back is turned, you begin. You've succeeded in fooling her, but you haven't fooled me—and you didn't fool Charlotte, either. Charlotte saw you that afternoon—the afternoon of the

day she died. She was in the dining-room and she opened
the door and looked in and saw you two whispering
together in front of the hearth."

Eve sat up suddenly on the couch. The blanket fell to
the floor. She swayed a little as she got to her feet. She
faced Alicia, her eyes dark pools of shock and horror.
Alicia had to be stopped, she thought; she couldn't wreck
Natalie's life like this, couldn't smash everything with
one blow.

Bruce began to speak. He said in a slow level voice,
eyeing Alicia steadily, "Are you out of your mind?"

Alicia took a step toward him. Her eyes were blazing.
"No, I'm not out of my mind," she said furiously. "Gerald's been questioned by the police. I think that what
you people have been up to has been the cause of all that
has happened. I think Charlotte intended to tell you,
Lieutenant Bruce Cunningham, what she thought of you
and that after that she meant to go to Spencer Gorham in
Boston and lay the whole thing before him, so that your
marriage to Natalie could be stopped."

In the background, unseen and unnoticed in the whirl-
pool of clashing interests and emotions, the Scotsman
turned to a window and looked out across maize-colored
fields. He didn't want to believe Alicia, but he knew she
was right, knew also that he should have been aware of
the truth, from the beginning. It had been there in Eve
last night, in the face she lifted to his when she spoke of
Bruce Cunningham, her lovely eyes wide with renewed
hope.

It had been in Bruce Cunningham, too, that day in his
rooms on Eldon Place. McKee looked, without seeing it,
at an old summer house with a cap like a mushroom
above gray water. The whole thing added up damningly.
Natalie had made a will leaving the bulk of her fortune
to Bruce Cunningham in the event of her death. Suppose
the Lieutenant had been planning to have his cake and

eat it. He could have intended to marry Natalie and
then, later on—

McKee stood erect. His eyes began to shine between
narrow lids. All at once he knew his reasoning was completely and absolutely false. Granting that Bruce Cunningham loved Eve Flavell, he would never have given
her that lethal dose of morphine. It was a contradiction
in terms. The conclusion was inevitable. Cunningham
had been shopped by someone who had wanted the .351
Winchester to be found because, if anything happened to
Natalie, Cunningham would inherit—but a man accused
of a crime couldn't benefit by it, particularly if he was on
his way to the electric chair. All of which meant that the
rifle with which murder had been done had been removed from the Eldon Place rooms before Charlotte was
killed and returned there after her death on Wednesday
night by *someone else.*

The Scotsman wheeled. The door was closed and Alicia
was gone. She had become aware of him, too late. Flight
was her only recourse. A coward had killed Charlotte
Foy—and Alicia was a coward. Bruce Cunningham and
Eve were both staring at him mutely. McKee started to
speak, and stopped. There were footsteps and voices in
the hall outside. The door was flung open and District
Attorney Dwyer came stamping in.

He pulled up just over the threshold. He had been cast
down at the inn, a half hour earlier. He was triumphant
now, his face a pink moon, his round eyes blue. He
glanced at McKee and then away from him at Cunningham.

"Lieutenant," he said, "you agreed you would come
back to New York whenever we wanted you?"

Cunningham's brows rose. "Of course."

"All right," Dwyer snapped with a flourish. "You're
coming *now.*" He swung on the Scotsman. "Buchanan's
over there at the inn. He talked, plenty. This is what he

told me. He says that Cunningham's rifle, the .351, that killed Charlotte Foy, was in the Eldon Place living-room at a little after seven-thirty on the night she was shot to death, that he saw the gun and handled it, and that there were no visitors whatever to the apartment that night and that *he was in the living room continuously all evening long.* Cunningham is the only person in the world who could have put that gun back after it blew Charlotte Foy to Kingdom Come."

He rounded on the flier. "I'm taking you back to New York with me on the first train, Lieutenant. This time you're not going to get out on bail. You're under arrest, Cunningham, not as a material witness, but for the deliberate, cold-blooded, premeditated murder on last Wednesday night of the late Charlotte Foy."

At the door, beyond Dwyer's burly figure, there was a flash of pale gold. It was Natalie's head. She had come downstairs in the middle of Dwyer's peroration. Her head went up and up. It sagged; she gave a strangled cry and crumpled.

Chapter Eighteen

A Tiny Green Shred

COMMISSIONER CAREY LOST HIS TEMPER. "McKee, if you can show me how anyone *but* Bruce Cunningham could have fired the shot that killed the Foy woman, I'll give you all the help you want. Bruce Cunningham, and nobody but Cunningham, could have had possession of that .351 between seven and eight o'clock on Wednesday night when Charlotte Foy was shot—Right?"

"Yes."

It was 9 o'clock on Sunday night. At noon that day Dwyer had returned to New York with Lieutenant Cunningham and had lodged him in jail to await formal indictment within 48 hours. The Scotsman took a turn up and down the carpet in the Commissioner's big office on the second floor of the long gray building on Centre Street.

"How can Cunningham be innocent?" Carey demanded.

"I don't know," the Scotsman murmured abstractedly. He was thinking of other things. "I want to know what the little wooden chest contained, the chest Charlotte Foy was taking with her to Boston to show to Natalie's lawyer."

"Pshaw! A bit of yellow cloth and an ornament of pink stones. Some old keepsakes."

"Then why were they removed? Why have they disappeared? Why can't we find a trace of them anywhere? And what about Bently?"

The Commissioner swept Bently aside. "Dwyer thinks that the fellow may have fallen off that bridge by accident, or that Eve Flavell may have been up to some hocus-pocus in an attempt to clear Cunningham. No, for once you're off the track. Cunningham's as guilty as hell."

He told McKee plainly that only his long and brilliant record kept the case open and kept him on it. The scope he was permitted was meager. He could have two men and a couple of days.

McKee picked up his hat, said, "Thanks," dryly, and walked out of the office and went in search of Sergeant Cutts. But the head of the Ballistics Bureau was in Detroit. "We don't know when he'll be back, Inspector, maybe in a week."

It was a blow. McKee had been relying on the Sergeant. He spoke to the telegraph bureau and said he was anxious to get in touch with Cutts, that it was urgent, and then went to see Bruce Cunningham, partly to retest his own faith and partly to find out more about the history of the .351.

The interview between the two men was short and inconclusive. It uncovered no new evidence of consequence. It was to have a far-reaching effect at which neither of them could guess.

Outside, stars sparkled in a frosty sky; inside those walls the gloom of night was not dissipated by the glare of an unshaded electric bulb at the far end of a long narrow cubicle in front of the cell block. A key grated and the door of Cunningham's cell opened clankingly and the flier came walking out of the shadows, tall and erect and with a stride, as though he was glad to stretch his long legs. McKee waited for him beside a deal table below a barred window.

The Lieutenant's lean, definitely planed face was tired, but his glance was steady and direct. The turn of events hadn't broken his morale, or even put a dent in it. He knew that McKee had overheard Alicia's charge. He didn't discuss the situation except to damn her out. "Nice little hell-cat, isn't she?" He struck the table with the palm of a muscular brown hand, and the identification tag on his wrist tinkled thinly in the stillness.

McKee made no comment. It wasn't basically his affair. That Bruce Cunningham should have engaged himself to one sister and then fallen in love with the other was regrettable, for all their sakes, but it had happened before and it was a private problem that they would have to work out for themselves. Its only interest for him lay in the effect it had had on the murder of Charlotte Foy.

He asked Cunningham questions. The flier said he had overheard part of the conversation between Susan De Sange and Bently in the cemetery in Eastport, and that he had followed Bently to the village and had lost him.

Of the rifle he said that it had been given to him more than a year ago by a friend in Eastport who was joining the Canadian Air Force. The Flavells were familiar with it. Gerald had tried it out on the rifle range in the meadow across the brook and had been enthusiastic about its performance. All the time he himself had been away the .351 had been in the Eldon Place apartment, as far as he knew.

So much for the gun. As to the gathering in the Flavell house on the afternoon of Charlotte's death, his recollection was poor. If he loved Eve Flavell, he was extremely fond of the girl he had mistakenly engaged himself to. The thought of her made him miserable. He said curtly, "I went to the Henderson Square house last Wednesday determined to tell Natalie the truth. She has a right to know, for her own sake. She wouldn't want what I have to give her. It isn't enough." His voice shook a little. It hardened. "Eve stopped me from telling her that day. Eve was wrong. She's doing exactly what she accused Charlotte of doing, interfering with Natalie, babying her, not letting her alone. Natalie's got what it takes. There are plenty of men in the world—and God knows I'm no bargain. Six months from now she'll be engaged to someone else and as happy as a lark. I tried to tell Eve that but she wouldn't listen—perhaps she didn't want to. Well, what I didn't do then I'm doing now. I've written to Nat." He took a sealed envelope from his pocket.

McKee looked at it thoughtfully. If Cunningham was determined to break off the engagement, he agreed that Natalie ought to know as soon as possible. It would be a shock at first, but she was young and volatile and she would get over it. The only question was one of timing. He was anxious above all things to keep the Flavell household on an even keel, and the slightest disturbance might upset the emotional balance and provoke the dis-aster they had so far managed to avoid. Eve had been poisoned and Edgar Bently had been sent hurtling from the footbridge down onto those rocks, but so far Char-lotte's was the only life that had been taken. He said slowly, "I'm not sure that it would be wise to send that letter at this point, Lieutenant."

"Why not?"

"Because Natalie isn't the only one involved," McKee answered. "Because—" He picked his way through tor-tuous ice that was beginning to form a faint pattern on the surface of a black stream flowing sluggishly but in-exorably toward an unknown goal. "You're here where someone wanted you, out of the running. With the situ-ation stabilized no further attempt of any kind will be made until—"

"I've been permanently disposed of, by the state?" Cunningham's smile was wry. "But I don't understand what you're getting at, Inspector. Say I am eliminated, wiped off the slate. . . Good God—" he sat up sharply, his jaw a white ridge, "you don't mean that those girls—that Eve—that there's any real danger?"

"I'm afraid there is, Lieutenant, as far as Eve Flavell is concerned. She's been in on a good many angles of this case, has interfered more than once."

If there had been the shadow of a doubt in McKee's mind as to the genuineness, the depth or the permanence of Cunningham's feeling for Eve Flavell, it would have been dissipated by the flier's reaction. No one could have simulated the emotion that turned his sun-browned skin livid, made blazing disks of his light eyes and sent him stumbling to his feet, his head twisting from side to side, his composure smashed. His chair went to the floor with a thump that woke the echoes, and the warder appeared running. McKee motioned him back. Cunningham was oblivious. He was saying in a loud voice, "Not Eve—*no*. I can stand anything but that—anything."

"Sit down, Lieutenant. Miss Flavell is all right at the moment. I've got men up there watching the house. She's in no immediate danger."

McKee spoke with a confidence he was far from feeling. He did manage to reassure Bruce Cunningham, and the flier pulled himself together and asked questions in his turn.

"Why was Charlotte killed, Inspector? That's what I want to know."

The Scotsman's brown gaze was opaque, hooded. "She was killed to prevent her from going to see Natalie's lawyer in Boston. That's all that's certain. We've established that whatever Charlotte had to communicate to Gorham was a threat to Natalie. The proof of that threat boils down to a handful of yellow cloth and a string of pink stones wrapped in tissue paper and enclosed in the little wooden chest she took from the bank the day before she died. Hugh Flavell's fingerprints, and only Hugh Flavell's, are on the wood of the chest. He denies having removed the contents. His denial isn't worth the paper it's written on."

"Yellow cloth—and a string of pink stones." Like the Commissioner, Bruce Cunningham was completely at sea.

McKee couldn't enlighten him. "Yes," he said, "and

until we know the meaning of those things we'll go on drifting." His cigarette tasted foul. He threw it on the cement floor. The simile was too close to fact for comfort. That was exactly what they were doing—drifting, drifting around in fog and blackness, rudderless and without oars, while far off, the distant crash of surf sounded the warning of impending shipwreck. It hadn't yet come but how long would this state of affairs last? The answer was simple. It would last as long as the situation remained static and Bruce Cunningham was the goat.

Cunningham understood. He said, "The police have to have a culprit. I've been selected. As long as I'm it, whoever killed Charlotte won't make another move?"

"That's the general idea," McKee said dryly. He pushed back his chair and rose. "It's not going to happen like that."

"How are you going to prevent it?"

"By finding out which one of those people disposed of the box of morphine tablets under the table in the restaurant on 52nd Street. Whoever eliminated Charlotte Foy poisoned Eve."

"It has to be one of them?"

"It has to be."

"A bullet from my .351 did kill Charlotte?"

"Yes."

"But—" Bruce Cunningham ran bemused fingers through his short dark hair. "The rifle *was* in the Eldon Place apartment on Wednesday night from seven-thirty on—unless Buchanan is lying?"

"Buchanan isn't lying."

"Then how—?"

McKee gave the lieutenant the same answer he had given the Commissioner. "I don't know, now. But if you didn't put that bullet in Charlotte Foy—"

"I most certainly did not."

"Then one of those people did."

That was all the Scotsman could be prevailed on to say. It was getting late and he had work to do. He summoned the warder, saw Cunningham returned to his cell, and drove back to the office and to a desk piled high with reports.

There was nothing yet from Cutts.

In Eastport, Hugh Flavell was better. So was Eve. The others were all in the house on Red Fox Road, kept there, ostensibly at least, by their solicitude for Hugh. In the Norwalk Hospital Edgar Bently's physical condition had improved, but his mind was still clouded, so that there was no immediate prospect of his being able to talk.

The photograph that had been torn during Susan De Sange's interview with Charlotte Foy less than two hours before the latter's death had almost certainly been destroyed; the relationship between the two women and the bitter quarrel they had had 21 years earlier, continued to engage McKee's attention. On one day all had been sweetness and light between the big house on the hill and the little one at the foot of the lawn; on the next all intercourse between them had come to a sharp end. This had been verified by Gerald, who, although he was only eight at the time, remembered it quite clearly and by Jim Holland, who was seventeen. The quarrel between the Flavell house and the cottage had further been corroborated by neighbors and acquaintances—but not its cause.

When Charlotte Foy first returned to the house of her brother-in-law, Hugh Flavell, after his second wife's death, Susan had been with her constantly, helping with the children and with Hugh. When Susan had been going through her own trouble, when she lost her baby and, shortly afterward, her husband, Charlotte had been more than kind. McKee lingered over the history of that husband, Lucien De Sange. Not much was known of him in the country town except that he was considerably older than his young wife and that he drank heavily. He was an absentee husband for the most part. Then, on one of his infrequent trips to the cottage, he had come down with an attack of delirium tremens, which appeared to have been a habit with him. Susan was ill herself at the time, and Charlotte had nursed De Sange during the final bout from which he fortunately failed to recover.

The interesting point, for the Scotsman, was that it was directly after Lucien De Sange joined Hugh Flavell's second wife in the cemetery on the other side of the river that the chasm between Charlotte and Susan opened. Within the month the younger woman closed the cottage abruptly and left Eastport. Twenty years passed before she and the Flavells re-encountered each other, through Eve, in New York. With Susan's reappearance death had come to the Flavells again, suddenly and violently.

Was this coincidence, or was it something more sinister? McKee looked at shadowy pictures of Charlotte Foy alone with Lucien De Sange during his last hours, listened to the stricken man's babbling tongue—and told himself that he was being a fool. Both De Sange and Virginia Flavell, *née* Corey, had been dust for a long while —and there was nothing to go on now.

He was mistaken. Pierson called him from the police station in Eastport at 12:05. Less than a half hour earlier, when everyone else was in bed in the house on Red Fox Road, Susan De Sange had gone down to the library and had removed a photograph of her defunct husband from an old album in a closet there.

Todhunter had watched her through a window. Before he could intervene she had torn the photograph up and had put a match to the pieces. She hadn't been able to complete her work. Pierson's entrance had evidently scared her off. But the record of her activity was contained in the caption on the mutilated page, in Charlotte Foy's handwriting. It said: *Lucien and Gerald, with Gerald's first trout, March, 1921.*

Pierson added that Mrs. De Sange didn't actually know she had been overseen. McKee said, "I don't want her to know," and put the instrument gently into its cradle. March of 1921 was the month Virginia died. . . . Lucien De Sange had been there. . . . Undoubtedly it was another and larger photograph of him that had been destroyed by Susan De Sange, except for the one corner, during her visit to Charlotte on the previous Wednesday afternoon. Both women's fingerprints were on the scrap that had escaped unnoticed during what must have been a struggle between them.

Where a good deal was still unclear, one thing was obvious. The attractive widow of whom Hugh Flavell was enamored didn't want her dead husband to walk again—as far as the police were concerned. There was a story there. Talk to her about it tomorrow, he decided grimly. Meanwhile the door to the case was opening little by little. The phone rang again while he was testing theories. It was Sergeant Cutts in Detroit, and Cutts gave the door another push.

McKee put the problem of the Winchester repeating rifle that had to be in two places at once squarely in the ballistics expert's lap.

At the other end of the wire Cutts said musingly, "You're *sure* Cunningham didn't kill her, are you? Well, now, Inspector, that's a pretty tough nut to crack. Let me see. . . ." He went on talking in a phone booth in Detroit and in the narrow room bright with light and empty with silence in New York McKee went on listening and jotting down instructions he didn't understand.

It was 20 minutes of one when he put the receiver back on the hook. It was 25 minutes past two when Fernandez, who had heard that he was in town, came in and found him crouched over his desk staring at nothing, his eyes bright in an exhausted face.

On the desk in front of him there was an array of weapons that had been brought up from Centre Street. Jim Holland's Army Colt was there, and Eve's little revolver, and the revolutionary blunderbuss belonging to the Gerald Flavells and the walking-stick shotgun of European manufacture that was Hugh Flavell's, all of which had been collected and sent to Headquarters on the morning after Charlotte Foy died.

Fernandez read the tags. He stared. He said, "What the devil are you *up* to?"

"Oh, looking for something Cutts told me to look for."

"But, good God, Chris, why?" Fernandez demanded. "Charlotte Foy wasn't killed with a revolver or a flintlock or a shotgun, she was killed with a bullet from Bruce Cunningham's .351—or was she?"

"Yes, she was killed with a bullet from Cunningham's Winchester."

The Chief Medical examiner was exasperated. "Then what in hell are you doing with those things?"

McKee didn't answer. He went on sweeping a magnifying glass right and left up and down over weapon after weapon. It was just short of three o'clock on the morning of Monday, December 9th, when he found what he had been instructed to search for, a tiny brownish-green shred of some fragile substance barely visible to the naked eye. It was in the firing mechanism of the walking-stick shotgun.

The Scotsman transferred it to an envelope with a tweezers and the most exquisite care. Every atom of it was precious. Five minutes later he was on his way to the C.P. Laboratory with the envelope in his pocket.

Chapter Nineteen

An Extremely Agile Mind

"WELL, I MEAN, McKEE—after all, twenty years is a long time, and if there *was* any hocus-pocus, anything wrong with the details of the deaths of either Lucien De Sange or Virginia Corey, and it would have to have been poison from the circumstances, you wouldn't have a hope. Even arsenic in the soil would be hard to be sure about, after twenty years."

"I realize it." McKee stared moodily at wet cement sliding away in front of them. Rain slanted down grayly. The two men were in a cab leaving the Norwalk station. It was a little after one o'clock on Tuesday afternoon.

Fernandez had come up from New York to have a look at Edgar Bently, to see whether anything could be done to put him into shape so that he could be made to talk. The Medical Examiner looked with approval at a woman with pretty legs struggling with a bundle in front of a supermarket. "All right," he conceded, "say for the sake of argument that there was something wrong and that Susan De Sange or Hugh Flavell or both are involved. Are you centering on them exclusively?"

"By no means. Jim Holland was seventeen at the time. If there was anything going on he could easily have known about it."

"Holland? Oh, the big fellow who's going to marry Eve. By George, I envy him. She's lovely. Those eyes. . . . But what about Gerald and Alicia?"

"Skeletons have an annoying way of not staying in the cupboards where they belong and, whatever Charlotte Foy knew, someone else could have found out."

"Hold up a minute, McKee, I want to get this straight.

Charlotte Foy was killed because she was taking proof of some sort of dirty work at the crossroads to Natalie's lawyer in Boston—but she didn't meet Susan De Sange until she came down from Vermont in late November—and as early as the middle of October she was trying to contact Spencer Gorham, who was West."

"True," McKee said, "but she could have heard from Natalie, by letter, that Susan De Sange had turned up and was back within the citadel or she could have heard it from one of the others, Hugh or Alicia or Gerald, when they stopped in at the farm on the way down from Canada, at the beginning of October."

"Whatever Charlotte knew or found out, threatened Natalie—but how, McKee?"

"I seem to recall that Hamlet had rather a bad time of it with his father's ghost," McKee said dryly. "If Charlotte had been permitted to talk, in Natalie's case it might have been her mother's. A woman with red hands could scarcely be a desirable stepmother—but that's all water over the dam. Charlotte didn't talk."

"That being so," Fernandez remarked dispassionately, "I don't see how you're going to get at the truth."

"The little wooden chest," McKee said with a snap to his voice. "When I know who, besides Gerald Flavell and Hugh, could have been in the Henderson Square house on Wednesday night after Natalie left it with Bruce Cunningham, I'll know who killed Charlotte. We won't know why until we establish what the contents of the chest meant."

"Yellow cloth," Fernandez murmured ruminatively, "perhaps a scarf—remember how Isadora Duncan was killed?"

McKee's nod was curt. "And lots of others, and not by accident but by seizing the two ends firmly and drawing them tight around a throat."

"Your idea is that Edgar Bently knows something?"

"Oh, yes,—decidedly yes. Susan De Sange returned from Europe early in the spring. She didn't come up here into Connecticut until last Tuesday, the day before Charlotte died. On that day Bently, who is often in Eastport, ran into his dead cousin Lucien's attractive widow near the entrance to Red Fox Road. It appears to have been a chance meeting and they were only together a few minutes—but I think Bently followed Susan De Sange to the cottage at the foot of the Flavell grounds and then to New York. He didn't do that without a reason. It must have been a pretty good reason from the lengths to which he went. In New York he not only took a room in a hotel on the south side of Henderson Square that was handy to the Flavells and Susan De Sange, he was actually watching the Flavell house, with Susan in it, before— keep that in mind—and very shortly before, the bullet that killed Charlotte Foy was fired."

"That's the one thing I don't get—" Fernandez shook his head discontentedly— "how Charlotte Foy could have been killed with a bullet from Cunningham's .351, if Cunningham didn't do it."

"Well, he didn't, and she was," McKee said. "The bullet's in Dwyer's possession, and you can have a look at it any time you want to."

"Then, if the .351 killed her, why were you so damned interested in that walking-stick shotgun last night and this morning?"

"Cutts," McKee answered, "and he's by no means sure. All he has is a theory. He didn't explain it to me in detail; he simply told me what to look for. What's more, even if he does succeed in solving a riddle that seems insoluble, it will simply throw the whole mess on the table. *How* Charlotte could have been killed by someone other than Bruce Cunningham won't tell us *who* killed her, or why. That's what I want more than anything else—motive. That's why Mr. Edgar Bently has got to talk."

"Well, I'll do the best I can for you," Fernandez promised. "I'll give you a ring at the Eastport police station as soon as I've examined him."

He got out at the foot of the hospital hill a few blocks along, saying that he wanted a walk, and McKee drove the remaining 10 miles alone.

A half hour later he was walking with Pierson in the lea of a hill crowned with a tall stand of oaks, through whose black leafless branches the roofs and gables and chimneys of the Flavell house made a somber pattern against the wet, gray sky. Rain fell steadily, and although it wasn't two o'clock, the light was narrow, down drawn, and distances were blurred. Below them the sullen water was rising steadily, whipped into whitecaps by the wind. Ducks, heads low, were swimming in a formation of five on the push of the incoming tide near the rickety footbridge from which Bently had been thrust.

McKee walked with his eyes on the ground and listened to Pierson report nothing new. Occasionally he stooped to examine a low-growing shrub, then straightened and moved on.

Pierson kept staring at him curiously. "Looking for something, Inspector?"

The Scotsman reached back into the 13th century. " 'That no man myghte se hym for muche mos and leues. Mos, also musch, moss, moul. . . .' *Pyxidanthera barbulatam*, Captain, a prostrate and creeping evergreen plant having small leaves and numerous white or colored flowers, and generally found in the pine barrens of New Jersey."

Pierson restrained his irritation with difficulty. The Inspector was in one of his moods. He was often like this toward the end of a case, irrational, a little nuts. "If it grows in New Jersey, what would it be doing here?"

"Transplanted perhaps," McKee said, "or carried on the wind. It needs sheltered places. . . . Ah." He paused at the edge of a semicircular grouping of white birches shivering in the wind. The ground in among them was carpeted with a great shawl of the moss for which he was searching.

The C.P. lab had identified the tiny shred he had delivered to them at on toward four o'clock that morning as a stem of *Pyxidanthera barbulatam*. He looked down at the soft gray-green rug. That this particular type of moss should be here didn't prove anything decisive, but it was suggestive and interesting. He knelt and gathered a few tufts of the soft fronds for form's sake—and for Cutts. After that, leaving Pierson at the footbridge, he went to see Mrs. De Sange in the rain-drenched cottage she had entered alone, an hour earlier.

She opened the door to him in a well-cut black dress that displayed her excellent figure to advantage. "Oh— come in, Inspector." She hadn't expected to see him, and there was terror in her, under surface composure. Dust smeared her fine hands; the nail of her left forefinger was broken and there were wide runs in the expensive stockings covering her handsome legs; she had been giving them rough treatment. The runs began at the knees and laddered down.

"A vile day, isn't it?"

"Very nasty, indeed. If it freezes, the roads will be in bad shape."

A door on the left was partially open on a room that wasn't a woman's. There were only two bedrooms in the cottage. It was probably the one Lucien De Sange had died in. Furniture had been moved about in it, recently. There were tracks of castors on the grimy floor, and the footboard of a bed was pushed out from a wall.

McKee had entered the house with the intention of confronting Susan De Sange with her destruction of her late husband's picture the night before, and of asking her a number of questions. He had been depending on the element of surprise as a weapon with which to make a break-through and establish a bridgehead within the almost impregnable fortifications of this woman's aplomb, her deviousness and her impenetrable *savoir faire.* He threw the intention away. Susan De Sange was in the middle of a campaign of some sort; let her go on with it, by all means, and then move in on her.

He said pleasantly that his visit was routine, that there were statements to be signed in triplicate. "It's just a formality, Mrs. De Sange. You'll be here tomorrow? Good. It can be done then. I'm starting in on another case and I want to get everything in order."

She stood facing him, at the end of the wide hearth, scrubbing at her fingers with a scrap of rose-colored linen. Her hands stopped moving.

"This one is—finished, Inspector? There's—no hope for—Bruce?"

Logs flamed in the stone fireplace, in which things could be burned. The room was warm. Susan De Sange looked as though she were bitterly cold. The edges of her lips were blue.

"Unless new evidence turns up, I'm afraid not."

She was staring beyond him at shadows. She gave a low cry and buried her face in her hands. McKee waited a moment, and, when she neither moved nor spoke, he left the forlorn little cottage whose meritorious prettiness was so inappropriate to the woman who owned it and who, before he interrupted her, had been searching it inch by inch for something she hadn't yet found.

Pierson was waiting for him outside with a message. There was a long-distance telephone call for him at the police station. Five minutes later, in a dark little room at the back of a hideous red brick building on Main Street, McKee was talking to the man he had been trying to get hold of for almost 24 hours—the stout middle-aged Doctor Hendricks, who had attended the Flavells in New

York for more than 15 years.

McKee hadn't seen Hendricks since Thursday morning, when Hugh Flavell had fainted on being informed of his sister-in-law's death; he had been convinced then that the Flavell physician had more on his mind than he was giving forth. Going over the case himself from the beginning the night before, he had been struck (1) by Natalie's indisposition when the maid had summoned Charlotte to the girl's bedroom early on Wednesday evening and (2) by Charlotte's remark that she wasn't satisfied with Hendrick's treatment of Natalie and wanted Natalie to see her own doctor in Boston.

A terrible suspicion had begun to form itself in the Scotsman's mind. It was only a suspicion. He didn't lead Hendricks; he simply asked questions.

Hendricks said that, yes, Natalie hadn't been up to snuff for a month or six weeks preceding her aunt's death, but that he hadn't been able to find anything organically wrong. He said it defensively, in his best pontifical manner.

"What were her symptoms, Doctor?"

"Oh, headache, some abdominal distress, a general lack of tone—nervous indigestion I should say, brought on by fatigue and too much work on committees and flying here and there at all hours. Natalie had never been very robust."

The Scotsman moved an ash tray an inch on the battered desk in the hot little room, moved it back again. "What about her pupils, the salivary glands, the heart rate?"

"The heart? The salivary—" McKee couldn't see Hendricks start and stare and wipe his forehead and fall back in his chair, his lips sagging, his face green. He felt these things over the phone.

In his office on the first floor in an apartment off Henderson Square, Hendricks put his finger on the buzzer.

He knew what the Inspector was driving at, and what was worse, knew that he had been uneasy at the time—but the thing had seemed utterly impossible. . . . The nurse came.

"Miss Natalie Flavell's folder."

It was brought. Hendricks looked at it. He spoke into the receiver, woodenly. He said, "Digitalis?" and McKee said, "I think so, yes," and Hendricks went sedately mad.

"My God, Inspector, the stuff was there, in the house, I prescribed it for Hugh Flavell—what are we going to *do?*"

McKee didn't know. He got rid of Hendricks. He said, "Natalie isn't getting any digitalis now, and I'll call you tomorrow," and hung up. Although the necessity for action clamored at him, he sat on, staring through a cracked window at rain falling, his thoughts as dark as the landscape outside: the black trees, the gray river, buildings huddled along its bank veiled in the approach of dusk. Poison for two and a bludgeon for one. The poison had varied as opportunity provided. First Hugh Flavell's digitalis was used, and then Charlotte's morphine pills, when they offered themselves.

An extremely agile mind was behind this clever murder, and one of the greatest police departments in the world had been outgunned, outflown, and outmaneuvered, at every turn. A slow anger built itself up in him. He reviewed the testimony, holding it in restraint. Natalie's money, the money that had increased so enormously with the war, was at the bottom of the whole black business. Charlotte had been afraid of it all along. When she returned to the Henderson Square house her fear had crystallized. She might not have known that Natalie was getting the digitalis; she did know that there was something wrong with her and that the threat, the danger, was real. It was significant that she hadn't confided in the people closest to Natalie, in Hugh Flavell or Gerald or Alicia. Instead she had redoubled her efforts to get to Spencer Gorham, who was Natalie's lawyer. She hadn't succeeded. She was dead, and the household that would have been disrupted and blown apart by her disclosures was still a united whole. All those people were together, here in Eastport, under one roof: the collapsing Hugh, Gerald and Alicia, Susan De Sange, Jim Holland and Natalie and Eve.

Digitalis; he put out a nervous hand and called the local man who was attending Hugh Flavell.

There was digitalis in the house on Red Fox Road.

McKee put the receiver back on the hook and metaphorically felt his way across a mine field in darkness. Bruce Cunningham was in custody for the murder of Charlotte Foy. Until he had been offered up as the human sacrifice the law demanded, it was probable that nothing more would be attempted. Probability wasn't enough. Yet—what could they, the police, do to hold the line? Nothing—

The Scotsman sat up sharply. There *was* a way, he thought. . . . It might not come off, but if it did—he went on exploring and fingering and arranging; if it did— then they would have the proof they needed. He got up like a man walking a tightrope, got into his raincoat, pulled on his hat, and walked out into the bitter, rainswept dusk.

Chapter Twenty

A SMALL PINK BEAD

". . . AND I DO WISH you'd make that slatternly girl wear an apron, Stella. I know that help is hard to get and that it's only for a few days. . . . Oh—you startled me, Inspector." Alicia whirled round in the middle of the big hall in the house at the end of Red Fox Road. "Come in."

McKee was already in. He had opened one of the double front doors without knocking. Alicia dismissed the elderly housekeeper she had been berating, and extended a gracious hand. She had on black satin slacks and a mandarin coat. Jade earrings swung from her ears, and her hair was brushed back from a smooth olive-skinned face expertly made up, but she was badly worried inside her handsome decorative shell; her movements were sharp and her artificial voice was half an octave too high.

She showed him her worry openly, with a conspiratorial glance around the big hall and up the stairs. "I haven't said a word, Inspector, not a word, although sometimes it's been rather hard. . . . Poor Nat. You've come to talk to her, to tell her?"

The eager brightness in Alicia Flavell's full brown eyes didn't match the compassionate shake of her head or the compression of her thin-lipped red mouth. After the scene with the District Attorney on Sunday morning she had evidently expected the police and a show-down. The delay, the inaction, were getting on her nerves.

She went on confidentially, moving closer to him, "It isn't only Nat; it's Jim Holland, too—poor fellow, he's been begging Eve to marry him this week, to go with him and see some houses in Lordship. It's frightfully trying to watch, when all the time you know he and poor darling Nat are living in a fool's paradise."

McKee looked at her thoughtfully. If anything happened to Natalie, Hugh Flavell would be a very rich man. But he had a heart condition and his life wasn't a good risk; a shock, for instance, might polish him off. Gerald and Eve were his natural heirs. Should Eve be disqualified in advance, put out of the running, Gerald would be the sole beneficiary of Natalie's entire estate.

He said aloud, patting Alicia's hand, "Don't worry, Mrs. Flavell, something will be done, as soon as we get the necessary evidence. I'd like to talk to Miss Eve Flavell now, about another matter. If you wouldn't mind getting her for me?"

"Of course not, Inspector." Alicia turned. But Eve was coming down the stairs; she had seen the Scotsman arrive, from her bedroom window. There was white at the throat of the dark dress that followed the lines of her slender erect figure, and her head was high, but her lovely black-fringed eyes under the dark delicately marked brows were luminous in pools of shadow, and the curve of her red mouth was tight with strain.

She went with McKee into the big empty living-room and the door closed. Five minutes later he was gone and Eve was alone. She sat on where he had left her, huddled in a wing chair beside the leaping fire, the words he had said repeating themselves over and over in her brain: "When you and your sister go to bed tonight lock your doors and see that they're locked."

Fear was one thing, she thought dully, certainty was another; there was no appeal from it. She and Natalie were to lock their doors against—someone in the house. She began to shake. *Stop,* her mind warned her, *don't think, just obey orders.* "Don't leave your rooms, either of you, no matter what happens. There will be a detective under your windows all night. If anything alarms

you, you have only to open the window and call Captain
Pierson."

He had told her more. Edgar Bently had been struck
with a length of iron pipe—there were specks of rust
in the wound in his head—and there was a lot of iron
piping in the stables, left there by plumbers.

Outside, rain beat drummingly against the windows;
inside, the room was warm, bright. The wide dark floorboards, the shimmer of the rug, the pattern of the gray-
blue chintz chair on the other side of the hearth, the fat
yellow sofa against the wall, the dull glow of a cherry-
wood desk taking gleams from the fire and doing things
to them, were a shifting kaleidoscope that wouldn't stay
in place.

Someone spoke in the hall; someone answered. Eve
drew a long breath, took a compact from her pocket and
did her lips shakily. They smeared and she wiped redness
away and did them again. Danger to Natalie, she thought,
to her young sister whose shoulder blades were too sharp,
whose chin was too pointed, who was painfully wasted
under clothes that were growing too big for her. It wasn't
fair. Natalie had suffered too much already, and for all
her courage and fortitude she was in such a state that the
slighest added blow might tip the scales. . . .

"Hello there, build a new plane today, my bucco?"
That was Gerald. The front door was closing. A stick
clattered. Jim was back from Bridgeport. "Where's Eve?"

The room took one mad swirl and settled into place
before the determined push of her will. Jim was coming
toward her, big and solid and giving a little to his bad
leg, his face ruddy from the wind and the rain. "What
a night!" He stooped and kissed her lips lightly and
straightened, and gave her a long look.

He knew there was something wrong. She had an almost
overwhelming impulse to confide in him, to lay down her
burden, let him help her with it toward the impossible

goal of tomorrow. The Inspector had said, "Bently was operated on in the Norwalk Hospital at five o'clock. When he comes out of the ether he'll be able to talk. It may take time, but I can promise you that by tomorrow it will be all over."

Leaning against the mantel Jim said quietly, "What's the matter, Eve? Anything happen while I was away?"

Eve shook her head. Then, to her horror, she began to cry. It was an involuntary reaction she couldn't control. It was her last break in technique. Jim knelt in front of her and wiped her eyes with his handkerchief. "There, now I've ruined your powder. Come on, give me your compact and I'll fix your face." He took her chin in his palm. "What is it, Eve? Tell me."

She smiled unsteadily and drew on the lighted cigarette he put between her lips. "Nothing happened, nothting whatever—that's the point, Jim. I'm tired, and the day has been so long."

He nodded his understanding. "Let's get out of this and get married, darling. We would have been married almost a week ago if Charlotte hadn't been killed. What do you say? We can go to New York tomorrow. I can get the day off—" His fingers smoothed hair back from her hot forehead.

"Not tomorrow, Jim. I can't leave Natalie now."

"Oh, but Eve, look here."

Alicia and Gerald, and then Natalie, came in and saved her from another argument for which she hadn't the strength. Natalie's face was pale and tired in the frame of her long, soft, fair bob. She looked at Eve hopefully. "I got down as soon as I could. What did the Inspector want? Did he say anything about Bruce?"

Eve said cheerfully, "Yes, he saw him, and Bruce told him to tell you that he's getting the first decent sleep he's had in a year and that you're to pay him a visit on Thursday. It's all arranged."

Alicia toed a log into place with her slipper and looked sideways at Eve. "Dear me, you seem to be a favorite. You'd think the Inspector would have told that to Natalie. Was that all he wanted?"

"No," Eve said, her dislike for Alicia accelerating sharply, "he asked me more questions about Edgar Bently, whether he was alone that night, whether there mightn't have been someone with him."

It did as well as anything else. Alicia was watching her. Gerald said with an utter lack of logic, "You mark my words, that fellow's at the bottom of the whole business. Wait and see if I'm not right."

Wait and see added itself to the dreadful inner singsong that never stopped ringing in Eve's ears. *Lock your doors tonight and wait and see.*

"Edgar? What about Edgar?" a cool contralto voice asked. It was Susan. She came up to the hearth and looked at Eve inquiringly. There were no runs in her stockings, no dust was on her hands. She was her usual calm self, so sure of the road she was traveling that she didn't have to bother much about other people.

Eve said as she had been instructed to say, "They don't know whether he's going to get better or not, Sue. He never recovered enough to be able to talk," and could have sworn that the flash in Susan's brilliant eyes was relief in spite of her slow, "Poor Edgar, he was always as crooked as a dog's hind leg, but I feel sorry about him."

Then Hugh was there, downstairs for the first time since his attack, pallidly handsome in a smoking jacket that gave him a cavalierish air, and Alicia was hovering around him solicitously. Gerald mixed cocktails and, shortly after, they went in to dinner.

Natalie was beside Eve. She was very quiet, but she ate her soup obediently when Gerald got after her. "Come on, young one, how about a little of the old life, the old pep?" Mrs. Eddey changed plates, and the candles mirrored themselves in the rubbed-pine paneling. Everything was perfectly normal and agreeable to the outward eye, but not to Eve. Her father regarded her with animosity and suspicion every time she spoke, although she had long since made her peace with the others for the deception she had practiced the night Edgar Bently was hurt. Alicia continued to jab at Susan and Susan continued to disregard her, although she was a very proud and independent person. Gerald was too determinedly light-hearted and devil-may-care, and Jim stared too long at nothing, his face heavy in repose. But there wasn't anything which pointed at any one person.

It was the same in the living-room afterward. Eve sipped her coffee and listened to Jim and Gerald argue helicopters, and inside of her the ceaseless mental combat between what was and what seemed to be, produced a permanent twilight with shadows converging from every direction. Only the person she looked at was clear, and the others, offside, were slipping and sliding and changing shape monstrously, until she looked again with quick frightened glances and they were themselves.

Her father played cribbage with Susan before the fire. Later she and Natalie and Gerald and Alicia played bridge, and Jim read a book on turning lathes and smoked his pipe, and the evening went on and on. The only thing that sustained Eve was the thought of Bruce, of his release, of his vindication. Even that was stained and darkened by the perpetual question mark that danced before her eyes.

Just before they broke up at ten o'clock there was a telephone call for Natalie. She went out listlessly; she came back, after quite awhile, a different person. Her narrow sensitive face was irradiated, as though a light had been turned on behind it. A stir went through the room.

The call was from Anthony Burchall, Bruce's lawyer.

Natalie didn't say very much there, in answer to questions from Hugh and Gerald and Alicia, except that Burchall was encouraging and hopeful, but as soon as Eve and she were upstairs alone, she threw her arms around Eve impetuously and hugged her, words pouring out of her joyfully.

Bruce hadn't told Anthony Burchall much about Inspector McKee's visit, but Burchall thought there was something in the wind, very definitely. "Wouldn't it be wonderful—oh, Eve, think how wonderful it would be—if, on Thursday, I wouldn't have to go to that jail to see Bruce, but that he'd be free?"

The thought of Bruce's freedom was an overwhelming wave Eve had to fight. That he should be out of danger, soon, was a release from the intolerable grip of her ever-present fear. It increased and brought home to her the pain of her separation from him, a separation that, no matter what happened, nothing could bridge.

Natalie went on talking and making plans, strewing her things around and getting into white silk pajamas that made her look like a tall child. It didn't seem to occur to her to wonder who was going to take Bruce's place in a cell, behind bars. Eve was glad. That would come soon enough—and she had a right to a little happiness. The Inspector had left it up to her as to whether or not she should tell Natalie of the orders he had given. She decided not to. She would be within call, with only the bathroom between them, its doors open—besides she couldn't bring herself to destroy Natalie's bright mood.

Joy could be as exhausting as grief. Natalie was very tired. Eve made sure the door was locked, made her get into bed, and switched off the lights and went into her own room. Ten minutes later she was in bed herself, with the big window less than three feet away up as high as it would go. Down below it, in the rain and the darkness, there was a detective, if she should need him, and both bedroom doors were locked. Nothing, no one could get at them. The thought was reassuring. She had intended to stay awake as long as she could, but the strain of the evening had exhausted her and almost immediately she fell deeply asleep.

Two hours later she woke suddenly, completely and without apparent reason. There was a tremendous knocking in her ears and her whole body was shaking. Yet there was no one in the room and no sound except the ticking of the clock and the drip of the rain. She lay still, fighting for control, and listened. Then she heard it, between one drop of water falling and the next. Somewhere near her, someone was turning a door knob softly to and fro.

Eve didn't have to orient herself. She was out of bed in an instant, grabbing up a robe and throwing it around her and going into Natalie's room. Her sister first and then the detective. . . . She moved in blackness toward Natalie's bed, her hands out, so as not to bump into anything and make a racket. Her fingers touched wood, touched the satin of the quilt. She explored its softness, her palms flat, and her heart took a sick leap and stood still. The bed was empty. Natalie wasn't there. She wasn't anywhere in the room; her door was unlocked.

Careless now of noise Eve flew across the bathroom to the window in her own room. She put her hands on the sill and leaned out into the fog she couldn't pierce. The rain had almost stopped. "Captain," she called in a quick voice, "Captain Pierson," and waited—and began to shake. There was no answer; there was nothing but darkness and fog and the slow drip of water from the eaves and farther off the whisper of the rising wind.

At that moment the man Eve sought was in a police booth a quarter of a mile away, talking over the telephone to Inspector McKee in the Norwalk Hospital. It was 20 minutes of two.

Pierson said, "I thought you'd like to know," and made his report. It was brief. Susan De Sange was supposed to be sleeping in the Flavell house. At 12:45 she left it and went down to the cottage. She locked the door behind her when she went in, but the Captain had made use of the cellar door, whose lock had been picked in advance. Pierson said, "She went on with her search, Inspector, and she sure gave that room her husband died in a good comb over. Well, she found what she was looking for about twenty past one. About time, too—she's been at it for three days."

"Did you see what it was, Captain?" McKee scarcely dared to hope for an affirmative, but astonishingly Pierson said, "Yop, I saw it, Inspector. It was a bit of luck. She walked into the living-room and put something down on a table near the fireplace and went back into the bedroom to straighten up and I took a look. It was a pink bead."

"A pink—"

"Yah. A small pink bead with holes in it like for stringing and a kind of a design in black on one flattish side, a kind of a little horseshoe. It was pretty dirty, but it was pink all right."

So they were getting to it at last; McKee thought of the string of pink beads in the little wooden chest in Charlotte Foy's bedroom that had vanished out of existence. . . . No, not quite. "Where is it now, Pierson?"

"She has it, Inspector. She finished with the bedroom and I had plenty of time to duck. I didn't brace her; I didn't know what you wanted me to do."

McKee said instantly, "Go back to the house and wait. Todhunter may need you. I'll be along in an hour or so." He left the telephone booth and went down the wide dim corridor to the solarium near Edgar Bently's room, where Fernandez was dozing over a magazine. The hospital was jammed and Bently had been put, of all places, in one of the emergency rooms in the maternity section.

Fernandez sat up with a yawn. He came sharply to attention when McKee told him what he had just heard over the phone. "By George," he whistled softly, "you were right, after all. She must have taken the stuff out of the little chest."

"Yes. How soon will Bently be ready for me?"

"Maybe in another half hour."

It wasn't soon enough. "All right," Fernandez said, "we'll try him now."

The two men started down the corridor. It was no longer empty. Nurses, their skirts rustling, were carrying wrapped bundles to the mothers for the two-o'clock feeding. A baby wailed thinly. One of the nurses said something to another and they both stared at the two men. McKee looked past them at the door of Bently's room. A male attendant was coming through it with a feeding cup on a tray. He got hastily out of their way and the cup did a little dance and landed on its base jinglingly.

McKee came to an abrupt halt. He stared at the tray without seeing it. Instead he was seeing Bruce Cunningham's thin dark face when he heard of Alicia's disclosure to the District Attorney, his sharp movement—and in that instant the tiny missing cog slid into place and it was all there, the whole picture of Charlotte Foy's murder, full and clear down to the smallest detail.

Fernandez was staring at him. He said impatiently, "Well?"

McKee said fumblingly, "I've got to go. . . . Bently's got to be placed under arrest. . . . I've got to get back to Eastport," and without another word or so much as a glance through the half-opened door at the stricken man in the high white bed he had waited so long to see, he turned and, conquering an impulse to run, walked rapidly toward the distant elevators.

Chapter Twenty-One

BLINDING, BURNING HORROR

IN THE BEDROOM on the second floor of the big dark house on Red Fox Road, Eve didn't remain long beside the open window with the fog drifting through it—and silence, and no voice, no help.

Anger flared in her briefly, died away. She had no time for anything but Natalie. Fear was a fever all through her. She pushed it aside. How Natalie had been induced to leave her room didn't matter; nothing mattered except to find her, as quickly as possible. Eve refused to think beyond that.

Her own door was still locked. She opened it and ran out into the corridor. It was long and empty and dim, except for a pool of light around a shaded lamp near the head of the main staircase. Her father's room and Gerald's and Alicia's were in the left wing; Susan De Sange and Jim Holland were in the wing to the right. Which way? Eve paused to listen. But there was nothing to guide her. There was no sound whatever, except the rain outside and the moan of the wind.

Her back was to the room she had just left. She couldn't see the closet door beyond the bed open, or the man who emerged from it, and who stood in concealing darkness, watching her.

She was seeing something else. Her bedroom was opposite the staircase at the front of the house. The flight going down was to the right, the flight going up, to the left. The only way to turn was right. She half turned, and saw it. Her heart hammered, and for the moment sight left her eyes. She brushed a hand across them and put it to her throat. A white satin mule, Natalie's mule,

was lying on the fifth step of the stairs going up in a long
flight to the third floor.

Eve didn't waste any time. She was around the newel
post in a flash and was running up the wide shallow
treads. She found the switch at the top and pressed the
button. It was lonely up here and cold, and the long narrow hall, like the one on the floor below, was empty. Only
the emptiness here was deeper, the silence more unstirring. This was the old part of the house, seldom visited
nowadays; the strip of carpet down the middle of the
hall was faded and dusty, and the plaster needed a coat
of paint and the air had a queer stuffy smell. Natalie
wasn't in the huge game room that took up the whole
right side of the top floor. She wasn't in the first two half-
dismantled bedrooms opposite. Eve tugged at a stiff
latch of a third door and confronted a cluster of de-
crepit mops, and barely repressed a shriek as a mouse
scuttled between her bare feet. She went on, moving
farther and farther away from the head of the main staircase and deeper into the faint green gloom toward the
back of the house, in a nightmare of doors with nothing
behind them but cobwebs and blankness and rolled mat-
tresses and bedsteads in corners. Servants slept here in
summer. Now there was no one.

No one—yet Natalie *had* to be up here, or why was her
mule lying on the stairs, empty and unbearably pathetic,
a little satin trifle that had fallen or dropped from a long
slim foot? The fear Eve had so far managed to keep
down was rising in her like a tide. In a minute it would
be panic. She didn't like this place. She didn't like it at
all. Tears she wasn't conscious of dribbled unheeded
down her cheeks.

She was at the last door. Beyond it there was only the
dark mouth of the little narrow twisting rear staircase,
cork-screwing down into the depths of the silent house.
The door was high and very wide. The lower half was

made of heavy planking, like the others, but the upper half was slatted, like a venetian blind. Eve looked at it and the coldness between her shoulder blades spread all through her. Pictures were coming dimly, of Gerald being spanked by Charlotte for opening this door, of Charlotte saying to him angrily, "Do you want to be killed?"

She knew what it was then. Behind it was all that was left of the old plumbing system that back in the seventies and eighties had provided the house with water. There was some sort of big beam and tanks. To a child it had been queerly frightening and unpleasant, like something out of Dante's Inferno.

She wrenched at the knob and the door came toward her smoothly and easily, almost of its own volition, as though it were inviting her in. It opened out, blocking the hall and cutting off most of the light.

Standing on the threshold, Eve peered in, her throat stiff. The beam was there, running into darkness, with emptiness on either side of it instead of a floor. She tried to pierce the blackness where the floor should have been, but could see nothing and hear nothing except rain on the roof overhead and somewhere in front of her the faint chuckle and drip of more water. If only she had brought a torch, she thought despairingly, and put her hand in her pocket instinctively, and found a flap of paper matches. She took it out and struck one. The little flame burned up brightly. Its brief glow was banked with heavy shadows. But it was better than nothing.

There was a drop of about five feet into what seemed a small sunken square room but what was really a tank. It was lined with lead. Natalie wasn't anywhere in sight. Eve struck another match, and stared. Directly below where she stood there was a kitchen chair with a curved back. It hadn't been there long. There was no dust on it. It had evidently been used as a ladder. Eve stepped down on the seat and then to the floor. Wet metal was cold and slimy under her bare feet and the shadows kept banking up so that she couldn't get a clear view all at once.

The water, trickles of it, was coming from the rusty mouths of intake pipes leading in from the gutters. She swung a little with a new match, and her heart took a great sickening leap.

In one corner, the right hand corner farthest from the door, there was a rectangle cut out of the floor. It was five feet long by three wide. There had once been a cover on it. There was no cover on it now. Natalie's other mule was lying close to the edge of the black oblong.

Eve got down on her hands and knees at the edge of the gaping hole. She leaned far over it, a match held high. Below, far below, wet bricks went round and round and down and down, and at the bottom of what she realized was an old cistern that must have acted as a storage tank, a tiny flame shone back at her from a circle of black stagnant water a million miles away.

Natalie wasn't down there; she couldn't be.

There was a sound behind Eve. It was very slight. She swiveled and staggered to her feet and swayed dizzily. The big door above her head that she had left wide open was almost closed. But another door was beginning to open. It was a small door she hadn't seen before, a mere slit in the leaden shell. There was someone behind it, someone who was coming out.

Eve gasped and sobbed aloud and tried to get air into her lungs and couldn't. A blinding, burning horror that shriveled her senses wound her in a sheet of flame. "No," she whispered stiffly, and took a step backward and then another and another. She couldn't take her eyes off the little moving door, and the figure she knew was there.

It was coming out from behind the door now, was coming toward her—and she was alone up here at the top of the house—at the edge of that black pit. . . .

Water dripped somewhere. "No," she screamed again, "no."

She knew who was behind the door.

The sickness of death filled her. She stepped back. Her heel went out over emptiness. She teetered and was falling into a night that exploded into broken flashes of sight and sound.

Chapter Twenty-Two

HITTING THE BOTTOM

EVE PUT THE RECEIVER BACK on the hook in the gay little room at the rear of the shop on 19th Street. It was three o'clock on the afternoon of January 14th. Outside, snow was falling. Fat white flakes churned and twisted beyond the barrier of the dotted-swiss curtains at the front. The lights along the green walls were on. There were pools of shadow between them.

Eve sat in an armchair beside the desk and looked dully at the distant door. It would open presently and the past would come in, in the shape of the head of the Manhattan Homicide Squad, the past she wanted to forget and knew she never could. More than a month had elapsed since that last terrible scene in the house in Eastport. She knew very little of the details of what had happened, except that an indictment for first-degree murder had already been returned. Eve had come down to New York as soon as she was able to travel. She had wanted to get away from everything, in space, at least. She couldn't get away from the horror. That would be with her always.

Bruce had been released from the Tombs weeks before. She knew that much. There was a numb void inside of her where the thought of him had once existed.

She was sitting there, looking at the falling snow beyond the curtains, when the door opened and a great drift of flakes followed Inspector McKee into the shop. He wasn't alone. The elegant Medical Examiner was with him. The two officials greeted Eve quietly, and she forced herself into the mechanical surface response that had become second nature to her and that had no connection with reality. The tank at the top of the house on Red Fox Road and the horror that had filled her were the only real things in the world. They had killed everything else.

McKee said he had come to check on a few final details. Eve answered him dutifully. She said "yes" and "no" and "I think that's right." He gave her papers to sign and she wrote her name and put down the pen and waited, but the Scotsman didn't immediately depart.

Instead he settled himself more comfortably in his chair and lit a cigarette. "I suppose, Miss Flavell," he said, "that there are some things that are not quite clear to you."

Eve looked at the backs of the books in the bookcases opposite. The ones on the top shelf were a little crooked. She couldn't speak. Her silence didn't seem to deter the Inspector. He began to talk, half to Fernandez and half to her. He said, "Todhunter, one of my detectives, was in the closet in your bedroom on the night the arrest was made. He followed you out into the corridor and up the stairs to the third floor where he was joined by Captain Pierson. They didn't move sooner; they waited outside that little room until the attack on you came—because we had to have proof."

Eve folded her hands tightly and thought of the black depths into which she had so nearly been flung, of the shadows, and the sound of water dripping. . . . She pushed soft hair from her forehead. "There's one thing I do want to know, Inspector," she said slowly, "one thing that isn't clear. How was the crime committed? How was Charlotte killed with Bruce's gun when Bruce didn't kill her?"

McKee gave Eve, then, the explanation that with the help of Sergeant Cutts of the Ballistics Bureau, he had given earlier to the Commissioner and to the District Attorney and that, with supporting evidence, had procured Bruce Cunningham's instant release.

"A chapter on firearms in a volume of Gross in your father's extensive library in the house on Henderson Square is the answer to that," he said. "Late in October Bruce Cunningham's rifle was removed from his rooms in the Eldon Place apartment. It was taken up to Eastport and several bullets were fired from it in the meadow across the brook. One of the bullets was recovered."

McKee took from his pocket the red shotgun shell with which he had come provided. He drew out an envelope. There was moss in it, some of the moss he had gathered in the Flavell grounds in the hollow beside the brook. From another pocket he took a spent rifle bullet.

"Look," he said, and his fingers moved, wrapping a thin covering of moss around the leaden slug. "The bullet discharged from Bruce Cunningham's rifle that later killed Charlotte Foy was treated like this. The moss served as a protective covering for the markings on it, kept intact the six lands left by the rifling of the Lieutenant's .351 when the bullet went through the barrel for the first time up there in Eastport."

He dropped the moss-covered bullet into the empty cartridge shell. He added more moss and stuffed it tightly and held the treated cartridge shell out to Eve on the palm of his hand.

"A shell like this, loaded with the bullet from Bruce Cunningham's rifle, was placed in the breech of the walking-stick shotgun that was in the umbrella stand in the hall of the house on Henderson Square. It was now ready for murder when the opportunity should present itself. Meanwhile Lieutenant Cunningham's rifle had been returned to the Eldon Place apartment. On the night Charlotte Foy was killed, her appointment with the Lieutenant on the telephone was overheard. She went to keep the appointment and was shot from outside the railings by Cunningham's doctored bullet, propelled, not from the rifle, which was safely in the Eldon Place apartment, but from the firing mechanism of the walking-stick shotgun. When the moss-protected bullet struck Charlotte it still bore the six lands of the Lieutenant's .351, although the gun was never anywhere near the scene. That was why you were given the morphine here in the shop. That rifle had to be found by the police."

Eve didn't say anything.

Outside, snow fell and the fire whispered busily. "An extremely clever piece of work, McKee," Fernandez said, and looked at the girl's lovely still face with a troubled glance. There was something frightening in her composure.

It affected McKee, too. He got up and began to walk to and fro. Eve hadn't been present at that final scene up there in the house on Red Fox Road. When Pierson and Todhunter jumped down into the tank she was mercifully unconscious. McKee shared Fernandez's opinion that they had to break through the wall of ice Eve had built around herself. Sorrow, revolt, tears—anything was better than this white immobility. The sooner she hit bottom, the sooner she would come up. He began to talk again, giving her the background for murder, succinctly.

"In the spring of 1921, your father, Charlotte Foy, Gerald, you and little Natalie were living in the house in Eastport. Virginia Flavell, your father's second wife, had been dead some six weeks. Immediately following Virginia's death, Charlotte had returned to take care of you all. The Corey fortune, left in trust for Virginia's infant daughter Natalie, had put the household on a new footing, and there was no longer any lack of money. There was plenty for everything."

McKee put an elbow on the mantel and looked down into the glowing coals. "In the cottage at the foot of the lawn at that time, Susan De Sange lived alone with her baby, visited at rare intervals by her husband, Lucien De Sange. Susan had been a close friend of Virginia's and of Mr. Flavell's. When Charlotte took over, she and Susan hit it off equally well and the situation remained the same. That spring there was an epidemic of whooping cough."

He lit a fresh cigarette and tossed the match into the flames. "The Flavell children caught it first, you and Gerald and the six-weeks-old Natalie. But no particular anxiety was aroused. The attack was light and you all had the best of medical care. Then Susan De Sange came down with it and Charlotte had her hands full. She nursed not only you three children, but also Susan, devotedly. The only one who escaped the infection was Mrs. De Sange's baby, largely due to Charlotte's care.

"That was the situation up until the night of June 4, 1921. On that night, after she had returned from the cottage where she had made Susan comfortable, and had attended to Susan's baby, Lucy, Charlotte went up the hill and into the big house. You and Gerald were in bed. Hugh was in the library working on his books and Jim Holland, a guest in the house, was studying in his bedroom for his entrance exams to Yale. It was the nurse's night off. Charlotte went into the nursery for a final look at the six-weeks-old Natalie.

McKee paused and turned toward Eve. "That was when it happened. Little Natalie Flavell, in a paroxysm of coughing, had rolled over on her face, and when Charlotte snatched up the child, her worst fears were realized. Natalie Flavell was dead."

The words *Natalie Flavell was dead* crashed in a deafening cadence against the barrier of Eve's numb withdrawal. She raised her head and looked at the Scotsman. He nodded.

"Standing there beside the crib in the big luxurious nursery that had been especially built for the dead child she held in her arms, Charlotte was appalled. She thought sickeningly of what the death of the little Natalie would mean, of penury instead of opulence, of your father's return to financial worry, of Gerald of whom she was very fond and who needed an expensive operation, because the money, settled on Virginia's baby, would return to the Coreys and vanish forever from the Flavell orbit. Virginia's fortune had been settled on her infant daughter and her daughter was dead.

"It was then that the idea occurred to Charlotte," McKee said. "Keep in mind," he continued musingly, "that she had had a terrible shock, that she was wrapped up in Gerald and in her brother-in-law Hugh, and that the inhibitions that ordinarily governed her were in abeyance. She wasn't an imaginative woman, but she had a clear logical mind. Holding the dead baby in her arms, she thought of the live one in the cottage at the foot of the hill, thought of it first with anger and revolt and then with a question. The children were both girls and they were both of approximately the same age. She and the nurse were the only ones who handled the infant Natalie. Charlotte also took care of Susan De Sange's child. Susan hadn't seen her baby in almost a month for fear of giving it her whooping cough. If she put one child in place of the other, and got rid of the nurse, no one would ever know. The more she considered the idea, the more feasible it sounded. She put it into action.

"There were no particular difficulties. Mrs. De Sange was ill in a bedroom on the far side of the cottage. Charlotte went down there with the dead Natalie. The actual transfer was simple. The only thing that differentiated the two children were the pink bead bracelets around their wrists, bracelets that had been put on in the Norwalk hospital where they were both born. One bracelet spelled Natalie, the other Lucy. But in taking Lucy's bracelet off to make the change, the elastic broke and one of the beads dropped to the floor, and in her haste and confusion Charlotte was unable to find it."

McKee took out the pink bead that Susan De Sange had dug from between the floor boards in the cottage on that night more than a month ago. Light shone on what Pierson had called a design in black. It was the letter U.

He looked beyond Fernandez and Eve at the storm sweeping past the windows and thought of Alicia's furious revolt in the house on Red Fox Road when she saw the Corey money going over the hill, of her charge that the whole story was false and that Charlotte was dead and he had no witnesses.

He had produced his witness. It was Natalie herself. After they removed her from the little control closet in the tank room where they found her unconscious, crushed down into a corner, her eyes closed, the marks of bruises on her throat, and as soon as she recovered she told him everything. She had said, "The money isn't mine. I've got to tell the truth in spite of what it will mean to—to Papa, and to—Bruce. The money will have to go back to the Coreys, in Boston."

He went on clarifying aloud, for Eve. "Charlotte sent for Natalie in Vermont in the middle of October. When Natalie stopped to see your aunt on her way down from Montreal, Charlotte revealed the entire story. She said that if the original fortune hadn't increased so enormously, if Natalie had been going to marry one of the Coreys instead of Bruce Cunningham, it might have been different. Things hadn't arranged themselves that way and her mind was made up. She was going to get in touch with Spencer Gorham and right the wrong she had done twenty-one years earlier."

Eve said in a low voice, a hand shading her eyes, "Natalie wasn't the only one who knew?"

"No," McKee agreed. "Susan De Sange knew when she returned to New York last spring and first saw Natalie and, in her, the image of Lucien De Sange as he had been as a young man. Bently knew or suspected through Susan. Mrs. De Sange confronted Charlotte with the portrait of Lucien that day in the house on Henderson Square. Charlotte tore the photograph from her. She said, 'You found it up there in the cottage,' referring to the pink bead. She was wrong. Mrs. De Sange didn't find it until later."

He rolled the bead in a cupped palm and went back in memory to that December night and to the stricken group of people in the living-room of the house on Red Fox Road, with Eve unconscious on the floor above. He looked at one person who was the nucleus, the center of a sudden disturbance, at the quick surge of a strong young body, the uplifting of a fair head. . . .

Natalie Flavell had stood like that for a moment, her hands plunged into the pockets of her dark-blue housecoat, her narrow white face twisted out of shape, the violence and rage and hatred she had held in check cunningly for so long blazing in the wide staring brown eyes that gazed through the dark windows at the prospect of escape in vain. . . .

It was over, done with. He gave himself a shake and returned to the present. Eve's head was bent, her shoulders huddled. She had to have it, he decided, had to have all of it in one clean blow, so that the healing process might begin. He went on inexorably. "When she couldn't dissuade your aunt, Natalie killed her. She gave you the morphine, discarding it later at the Cedars. She knew how you and Bruce Cunningham felt. She wanted to destroy you both. She attacked Bently at the footbridge up in Eastport, because she was afraid he might have been outside the Henderson Square house when she followed Charlotte and because he was in the Cedars when she got rid of the morphine.

"I had Anthony Burchall telephone to her that final

night. When she was told, on my instructions, that Lieutenant Cunningham was going to be cleared, she determined to get rid of you, at least.

"She was feigning unconsciousness when we found her on the floor of that little closet in the tank room. She put the marks of those bruises on her own throat, just as she took the digitalis earlier in an attempt to gain time and keep Charlotte from going to Gorham. Fortunately for us Pierson saw her enter the tank and wait for you to follow the clever trail of her dropped mules."

Eve buried her face in her hands. Outside, it was growing dark and the snow was coming down harder.

Fernandez cleared his throat and began to talk, quickly, to McKee. "I still don't see, Chris, how you were able to say a couple of days before the wind-up that you knew who it was."

The Scotsman shrugged. "It was the little wooden chest that told me. The tiny yellow woolen shirt and the bracelet of pink beads in it that had been the real Natalie's meant nothing except to Charlotte. But they would have inspired curiosity and questions that might have aroused suspicions if they were found. Whoever killed Charlotte removed them. Hugh Flavell entered her room after she was dead to investigate the chest's contents. His were the only prints on it. Obviously he hadn't polished the box in order to give us his prints as a gift. Charlotte handled the box before she went out that night. The polishing of it, therefore, took place after she left the house and before Hugh Flavell entered the bedroom. The person who had done the polishing was the perpetrator. And the only one who could have done it was Natalie."

Eve's face was still hidden. *Give her time,* Fernandez thought. "While we're on the subject, McKee, why pull that quick-change act in the corridor in the Norwalk Hospital? Why did you stand there gaping at those nurses, and at the orderly coming out of Bently's room?"

"I wasn't seeing either of them," McKee said, watching Eve, "or, rather, I did see the nurses with the babies. It was the old association of ideas. I had just been told about the pink bead. Looking at the nurses with their bundles my mind registered the word *baby*. The feeding cup the orderly was carrying jingled at the same moment. The jingle reminded me of Bruce Cunningham's identification tag. You see? Baby, identification bracelet, bead. I guessed then what Charlotte had done."

Eve sat up. She took a wisp of linen from her sweater pocket and wiped wetness from her lashes. Her face was in shadow. "For me," she said in a blurred voice, "the worst is that I'm responsible for everything that happened. Natalie was driven to what she did because—of myself and Bruce."

It was what McKee had been waiting for. "Not at all, Miss Flavell." He drove at her brusquely. "You're wrong, completely and absolutely wrong. If Lieutenant Cunningham had never existed, Charlotte Foy would have been killed just the same. From the moment Charlotte told Natalie the truth she was doomed. Natalie has boasted that she would have killed Charlotte then and there, in Vermont, only that she was afraid of discovery."

"Boasted!" Eve cried with sick horror.

Fernandez intervened then. He said quietly, "In my opinion, your sister—the girl you thought was your sister—will never be given the extreme penalty, Miss Flavell. She isn't insane but she's definitely a border-line case. I gather that she was always volatile and none too stable. Charlotte's revelation sent her over the edge and off the normal beam. She couldn't bend, so she broke."

Eve stared at him. Light flickered in her gray eyes. She opened them wider. *Not the extreme penalty*. Life was beginning to come back to her, death to go away. Doctor Fernandez was right, she thought, recalling Natalie's sudden sharp outbursts of temper as a child, outbursts that seldom came to the surface in later years, because she wasn't thwarted or checked. Yes, given that temperament and the blow Charlotte's revelation had dealt her, it was all logical enough, logical and terrible. But as she forced hersef to look at it, directly and without flinching, for the first time, her own sense of personal responsibility grew less heavy, and she could breathe again, and feel.

She sat up with a little sigh. "Does Bruce know it all?" Her voice was low but steady.

McKee was getting to his feet. Eve was seeing straight now; their work here was over. "Yes," he said, "the Lieutenant knows," and didn't say anything more. He shook hands with Eve, so did Fernandez, and then the two men were gone and she was alone.

She got up stiffly and went to the hearth and stood there looking down into the fire. Bruce knew she was not to blame. The pain in her accelerated. Bruce knew —and he had never come near her. Jim had been kinder, Jim whom she had wronged and who had said good-bye to her without a word of condemnation or reproach. A cold wind struck between her shoulders. She half turned, and remained motionless.

Bruce was coming into the shop. He was coming toward her, snow on his cap, on the wide shoulders of his heavy coat with the silver insignia on it.

She watched him come, in silence, her heart pounding. His face was dark and still and intent, and his eyes were fastened steadily on hers.

"Eve," he said, and was beside her, with her two cold hands in his. "I came as soon as I could," he said. "I've been to Washington ever since I was released—a special job. . . . I couldn't get here sooner or send you word—I wasn't supposed to communicate with anyone."

Eve held herself very straight. She was still numb, but the pain was gone. She could bear it now—she could bear anything. "Bruce," she said in a small whisper. "Bruce."

He gathered her hands closer. He said huskily, "Jump in a cab and ride with me over to Mitchell Field. I'm flying west at five-fifteen. I may be away a long while—but when I come back—"

He didn't kiss her. Yet standing there, their hands linked and with that imminent parting looming between them, a curious sense of peace took possession of Eve and of the tall man in uniform looking down at her. Without words they both knew that, when the personal horror they had gone through had been dulled by time, they would be together again for good.

"Wait until I get my coat," Eve said, with a lilt to her smile. She snatched it from a hanger and Bruce put her into it and they moved to the door and out into the storm side by side.